LANSHOUD

··
ROSEMARY SHOWELL
··

Copyright © 2012 Rosemary Showell

All rights reserved.

ISBN: 147752066X

ISBN 13:   9781477520666

Library of Congress Control Number: 2012909449

CreateSpace, North Charleston, South Carolina

My first attempt at writing is dedicated to my longsuffering husband, Arthur, whose faith in me seems to know no bounds, and to the lights in my life, our children,

PHILIP, NICOLA, AND ANDREA.

Acknowledgements

I give my unending thanks to my cousin Mary McNamee, who kept asking for the next chapter, and especially to my friend Elaine Britton, who not only collected but then tirelessly poured over the manuscript, time and time again, for giving me their unwavering support and encouragement. I would also like to offer my grateful thanks to my friends Mary McFeely Jeanette Bennet and Lindsay Simpson who made me believe the story was worth writing. To my editor Ray I offer many thanks for his expert guidance and encouraging comments that gave me the confidence to believe I could write.

Preface

The Wild Hunt

Throughout European literature, myths and legends abound of The Wild Hunt, a group of phantom riders who race through the countryside at night terrorising local communities. The tales vary depending on the area from which they originate, but the details are mostly the same. There is a phantom rider on a huge black steed with glowing eyes, leading a troop of ghostly horsemen, accompanied by baying hounds, who tear through the countryside, often amid a violent storm. The leader of the pack is thought to be anyone from a Norse god to a local hero back from the dead. It is said to be a bad omen and a harbinger of death to see the hunt.

Chapters

1. The Letter 1
2. James 9
3. Katie and Gill 15
4. The House 21
5. Banchory 29
6. Tapping 39
7. Molly and Alice 45
8. Jack 51
9. The Camerons 59
10. The Hunt 63
11. Rotterdam 73
12. Lizzie McIntosh 81
13. Jonah 91
14. The Team 101
15. Tosh 107
16. Emilio 117
17. Bella and Bun 127
18. The Riders 131
19. The Cellar 137
20. Paddy 145
21. Caleb 153
22. Luke 165

23	Abigor	173
24	Rafe and Uri	183
25	Waiting	195
26	The Healer	205
27	The Messengers	215
28	The Cellar	229
29	The Angels	235
30	Memory	243

CHAPTER ONE

The Letter

The day the letter arrived was much like any other. I was tired, having woken several times during the night, never knowing what had woken me, and as usual, I found it difficult to get back to sleep again. That deep, dark hole that my psyche sank into on wakening, in the weeks after Paul died, that crushing, terrifying pain in the chest that made me realise for the first time the true meaning of heartache, that made me want to lose consciousness by sinking back into the oblivion of sleep, had gone now. In its place I was left with the inability to rest, for sleep came only after trying to read or watching TV, both of which required a degree of concentration of which I was totally incapable.

A double bed is more than just a piece of furniture. It has, you see, a special sort of emptiness when you have been used to having someone else beside you and that person is missing. For months afterwards, I tossed and turned around the large bed, and when I eventually managed to fall asleep, I would awaken again, startled by every creak and groan of timber or pipe as the house settled. I tried covering a pillow in one of Paul's T-shirts and put my arms round the pillow, the texture and his smell still clinging to the fabric, helping me to fall asleep, but never for long. I grew into the habit of leaving the curtains open a little to allow the streetlight to take away some of the darkness, and I would lie watching the lights from passing cars make patterns on the ceiling, dozing on and off, never reaching a deep sleep. As a result I woke early every morning, exhausted, as though I had never slept at all.

It was a warm, sunny morning in early July. As I came down the stairs, the letterbox rattled as the postman, early that day, pushed the mail through. I ignored it and padded through to the kitchen in bare feet. Everything shone because I had attacked the house with a frenzy the night before; something I did in the hope I would be physically tired enough to sleep. I made tea and took it through to sit on the stairs in the hall. I sat watching the sun filter though the stained glass on the front door, with my head against the wall, looking forward to another long day of nothingness. I wasn't living anymore, just surviving. I had taken to sitting on the stairs because I felt secure there. It was a small space, and I felt safe, sheltered, protected; like being in a little cave, I was enclosed there between the house and the banister, and it never felt as though there should be someone else there.

Katie dragged me to my GP, who prescribed Diazepam, but I had never taken it. Though it may seem perverse, the pain of losing Paul was preferable to the numbness of forgetting he had ever existed. It was meant to be a temporary coping mechanism to help me deal with the panic attacks—the ones that made me freeze in the middle of supermarkets, my chest so tight I was unable to breathe or that left me bewildered, lost, not knowing which way to turn, gripped by an unreasonable fear that would strike out of the blue, in the middle of a crowded street. The doctor was very sympathetic and gave me a pep talk; she wanted to refer me to a bereavement counselor. I, on the other hand, wanted to scream at her that nothing, nothing would help me, that there was a black pit where my life used to be, but my throat held a lump that wouldn't move and my tongue had stopped working. I just nodded and managed to smile as she handed me the prescription; if I had spoken, the tears would come in floods. I had to get out of her room. I walked out into the corridor, and there was Katie watching for me in the waiting room. Katie knew; she stood up and walked to meet me, saying nothing. Her arm around me, she led me out of the Health Centre, into the car park and into her car. She stopped me collapsing as the grief overwhelmed me again. She drove me home.

I was not a weakling, someone who needed to be led through life. I was a successful career girl working in the acquisitions department of a financial institution, esteemed by my colleagues, recognised for innovation in a firm totally dominated by men, but I had become a wreck because Paul Michael Cameron had died, washed overboard in a storm while he was out sailing. His precious little boat, the other love in his life, had been in for repairs, and he went out alone to test it; for the first time in his life, Paul, who was an expert sailor had broken the rule, had failed to check the weather, and the unforgiving sea does not give second chances. It claimed his life.

I spent months torn between anger and grief, but now six had passed and I was just beginning to believe I could survive. The panic attacks had stopped, and with all the goodness in their hearts, Katie and Gill tried to fill my days and nights as much as they could. They cleaned my house, they cooked, they made me eat, and they even made me laugh. They both practically moved in, and then, when their own lives caught up with them, they took it in turns to babysit me. Either I continued with my downward spiral or I pulled myself together; the hardest thing was to stay alone in the house without Paul, but I owed it to Katie and Gill to get myself sorted and so began the reliving of my life one day at a time.

The hall stairs had become my place, the only place in the house that didn't seem empty, the only place where I didn't feel so alone. The sun shone through the stained glass panel on the front door and the myriad of colors spilled onto the mail lying on the mat; the trees lining the driveway shivered in the breeze and filtered the sunlight, making the colors dance. It was some ten minutes before I saw it, the envelope among the others, and cream against the brown and white envelopes. I picked the mail up and opened everything but the cream envelope. It was expensive paper with a faint pattern or watermark running through it, the type designed for important correspondence. My name was printed as it would be on a business letter, and the envelope was not franked but had a postage stamp and no postmark to give a clue where it had come from. The thing was, it was probably just another piece of junk mail, cleverly disguised to make it stand out, but because I had a strange feeling about it and as long as I didn't open it, it could be anything I wanted it to be. Into the kitchen, some bread into the toaster, water for the plants on the window ledge, jam from the fridge, knife from the drawer, plate from the cupboard, tea refill, and game over, it was probably junk mail and I might as well open it.

As I unfolded the letter the word solicitor jumped out at me. I thought, oh God, what now? I had put so many things off, too apathetic to deal with them. Although I had always paid the bills, they were in Paul's name, as he had, in a very chauvinist way, insisted it was his job to manage most of our finances. Everything had now to be in my name, and I couldn't bear it, just couldn't bear saying, please change the account into my name because my husband is dead, while my mind was screaming, *He's dead, Paul is dead, Do you understand? I will never ever see him again.* Domestic accounts, car insurance, life insurance, maintenance contracts, every time I thought I had covered them all, something else would turn up—little things like magazine subscriptions, loyalty cards; so what now? I gazed at the letter through unfocused eyes, trying not to think, the usual well of tears blurring my vision.

I read it and I read it again. It said quite simply that I was a beneficiary in a will and was required to call by appointment at the offices of Messer's Galbraith and Anderson in St. Vincent St. Glasgow. A telephone number was included. That was all, short and sweet.

I could not imagine any reason why I would be a beneficiary in anyone's will. I had no relatives, no children: my elderly parents had died in a road accident only a few months before I met Paul. My mother was forty-three when she had me, and I was her first and only child. Paul's parents were dead, though it turned out he had an aunt and uncle in Inverness whom he had never mentioned; they turned up the night he died. For people I had never met in my life before, they were extraordinarily kind. They took over all the funeral arrangements and did all the running about to deal with the undertaker and to register the death. Unlikely as it seemed, I supposed there might be an outside chance that one of them had died and they might have left something to Paul's widow, though it was only a few weeks since I had last spoken to them. At the time of the funeral, I was too distraught to think, but since then I wondered why Paul had never mentioned them. One of the things he and I had in common was that we were both alone in the world, or so I thought. I had touched on it when I last spoke to Gwen, Paul's aunt, but she told me they hadn't seen Paul for years, not since the funeral of his own parents. They had heard on the news that Paul was missing and then turned up at the house on the actual night his body was found. They were both retired and lived quite a simple life in Inverness, and since the funeral, they had telephoned a couple of times to see if I was all right. I imagine someone would have contacted me if something had happened to one or both of them. Failing that, there was absolutely no one who would leave me anything. Money wasn't a problem. I wasn't struggling financially; I was making ends meet, but I had been on indefinite unpaid leave since Paul died, so anything left to me in a will would be welcome. I supposed there was of course always the chance it was a hoax. But there was only one way to find out, and since my social diary was very, very empty, I decided to call that day.

I showered and dressed in a smart cream linen dress. I had lost weight. My thick, auburn hair could do with a trim. I tied it in a bauble and pulled it into a shoulder-length ponytail. I decided if I was to inherit any money (chance would be a fine thing), then I would get some black bin bags and put everything I owned into the charity shop and start again. With nothing else to do but wait, I considered phoning Katie or Gill, but it would only confirm their view that I couldn't survive without their daily support. I didn't want to appear too anxious either, and so I waited until ten a.m., and then phoned the telephone number in the letter. A pleasant secretary with a young voice knew immediately who I was and gave me an appointment with Mr. Galbraith at two p.m. that day. And that is how on my first day of my new life, I came to be sitting at Croy Station waiting for a train to Glasgow. Nothing could have prepared me for what lay ahead.

I had left early, deciding to take the train rather than drive, just to make the day last a little longer and to have the company of other people, even though they might not actually speak to me. We didn't have a lot of friends, Paul and I; he had always said we didn't need anyone else, we had each other. So I lost friends along the way because Paul and I did everything together—except for Katie and Gill, that is. We had been students together, sharing a flat for five years, and they were like my sisters. There were Christmas nights out with my colleagues and other odd social occasions, but other than that, I never saw any friends. Even on those rare occasions, I found it hard to enjoy myself; it was difficult to relax knowing Paul was sitting outside waiting to pick me up. It didn't matter where I was going or how far he had to travel, Paul insisted on being my chauffer home. It became a standing joke in the office. I never told him how annoying it was, his going to so much trouble to look after me, and I didn't want to hurt his feelings. In hindsight I saw no one socially for the six years we were married, which may seem strange, but it happened so gradually, so insidiously, that I didn't notice that Paul became the whole of my life from the day I met him.

It wasn't long after my parents died. I was sitting in Buchanan galleries having some lunch when this gorgeous guy asked if the seat beside me was taken. Paul was the stuff of dreams—intelligent, sophisticated, and caring. We started chatting, and I found myself confiding in him in a way I had never done with anyone. The electricity between us was instant, and he had my phone number by the third cup of tea. I could go on forever about the man I fell in love with and the six wonderful years we spent together; now I was angry, angry at him for letting it happen, for not checking the weather, angry at the waste of his life and mine. It didn't seem right that the sun was still shining and the birds in the trees lining the station were singing their hearts out—it was just wrong, all wrong.

The train pulled into Queen Street Station in Glasgow, and all the passengers got out onto the busy platform. I took the exit onto George Square, and the usual *Big Issue* seller was there. I didn't want the magazine, but I handed him a ten-pound note. I wanted to share my luck, and the look on his face was worth it. Surely whatever I had inherited would be worth more than ten pounds. I knew that I might live to regret my hasty bout of generosity; it did occur to me that my inheritance was possibly no more than a Grecian urn or something equally decorative and maybe worthless.

It was only 12:18, plenty of time to have a wander around the shops or have some lunch before going to the solicitor. But I wasn't very hungry, so I had some juice and a muffin and opted for shopping. George Square was manic. Office workers sat on benches eating packed lunches, shoppers laden with bags rushed toward the station to catch their train, a very angry traffic warden argued with a motorist who hadn't got the hang of the one-way system. Two Japanese tourists with three cameras apiece snapped everything in sight. Sisters of Charity stood quietly at the corner of the street hoping for donations in their collection can, and a couple of policemen escorted a loudly singing drunk into a police van. Meanwhile the nose-to-tail traffic circled the square with hordes of people risking life and limb to dodge between them, everyone in too much of a hurry to wait for the green man. Children were laughing and crying, friends talking, a teenage boy and girl hand in hand stopping to kiss. An elderly couple, the old man perspiring in the heat but keeping his tweed jacket on and his tie respectably tied. It was a crowd, a crowd of people, and I felt so lonely. I suddenly and for the first time completely understood the old saying, *you can feel lonely in a crowd*.

The Letter

At exactly 1:55 p.m., I was standing outside the red sandstone building that housed the offices of Galbraith and Anderson. As I pushed open the heavy, old, wood-and-glass doors and stepped into a foyer with floor tiling dating back the early 1900s, I had an overwhelming feeling that my life was going to change forever.

CHAPTER TWO

James

The secretary opened the door, and a distinguished-looking elderly man in an immaculate pinstriped suit rose from behind a gleaming walnut desk and offered his hand. "Adam Galbraith, Mrs. Cameron. I am delighted to meet you. Please take a seat." He indicated the armchair opposite, and then spoke into the intercom on his desk. "Laura, tea please, or would you prefer coffee?"

"No thank you, I have just had lunch." I sat down, immediately sinking into the butter-soft leather of the armchair. The desktop was so polished I could see my face in it.

"I trust you found us without any difficulty?"

"Yes, thank you."

"This must seem very strange to you, Mrs. Cameron, receiving our letter out of the blue, so to speak." He had a deep, cultured voice with a trace of a Highland accent, and he spoke very slowly, enunciating every word. "It is normally our practice to include a little more information regarding the nature of a will, but the circumstances surrounding this bequest are unusual in the extreme. I will give you some details now, but my colleague, Mr. James Anderson, will be joining us shortly. He is presently engaged on a call. James will be at your service in the transfer of the estate and will offer his support to you over the next few weeks."

Estate! I thought. *Support!* What kind of support?

He cleared his throat. "Mrs. Cameron, there is no easy way to prepare you for what I suspect will be a great but not unpleasant shock, so I will come straight to the point. You have become the sole beneficiary of a very large estate valued at approximately..." He hesitated and looked down at the paper in his hands as if he was checking the details. "In the region of seventy-five million pounds."

He paused and looked up from the paper, studying my face, allowing me time to absorb the information. I wasn't sure I had heard right. We just looked at each other, and there was a prolonged, deafening silence.

"I'm sorry could...would you say that again?"

He did, and I stared at him, bewildered. To say I felt disorientated would be an understatement. So he watched me, and I stared at him, and neither of us spoke until it dawned on me that they must have the wrong person.

"That's not possible. There is no one who would want to leave me anything, let alone a fortune. You must have the wrong person." Then I thought I must have misheard. I almost whispered, "Seventy-five million?"

He pursed his lips, nodded, and said again very slowly, "Seventy-five million pounds."

My brain felt as though it was doing cartwheels. "There must be some mistake. Or is this a joke?" I looked around, wondering stupidly about hidden cameras for a TV program or something.

"There is no mistake, Mrs. Cameron."

He reached over to the intercom. "I think some tea now, yes? Or would you prefer coffee?"

"Tea," I whispered. "Thank you."

He spoke into the intercom. "Some tea please, Laura."

"Who?" My voice croaked, it was all so surreal. I cleared my throat. "I'm sorry. Who left this money?"

"Ah, there lies the rub." Again he spoke very slowly. I presume the shock had given me a vacant look, and he was anxious to make sure I understood. "I am afraid I cannot tell you that—literally cannot tell you—because I don't know." There was a knock on the door. "Come in," he said.

The secretary entered with a tray. "Thank you, Laura. That will be all." Laura left, closing the door behind her.

Adam Galbraith leaned back into his chair. "Let me try to explain. Twelve years ago a gentleman hired our firm to oversee the management of a house and grounds in the northeast of Scotland and also to invest a large sum of money, which was to be passed anonymously, on the death of his client, to the sole beneficiary named in his client's will. He stipulated that the beneficiary should remain ignorant of this bequest until the day of the client's death and should, forever, remain ignorant of the identity of the benefactor." He paused. "Mrs. Cameron, you are that beneficiary."

There was again silence for several moments, as I had been holding my breath and was still holding on to it. He watched me, waiting for a response. When I didn't speak—because right then I had no idea what to say—he placed his hands, palms together, fingertips at his mouth, elbows on his desk, and considered me carefully, as though he were choosing his words in a manner that would carry the message through to my now-overwrought brain.

Painfully slowly he said, "You have been bequeathed in the region of fifty million pounds in cash, the property, and the rest of the funds tied to the upkeep of that property."

My heart was pounding in my chest, palpitations, with the beat so loud I was sure he could hear it. I kind of laughed. "Mr. Galbraith, I am sorry, but you must have the wrong person. There is no one who would have left an estate to me; I have no family."

He rattled out, "Mrs. Cameron. You are Erica Cameron, formerly Erica Vansterdam, widow of the late Paul Cameron; you came to Glasgow from the Netherlands as a three-month-old baby with your father, Aalbert Willem Vansterdam, and your mother, Elaine McDonald."

He reached into his desk and took from an envelope an A4-size photograph, which he turned and slid across the desk for me to see. It was a photograph taken outside a church of a bride and groom, hand in hand and gloriously happy; it was Paul and I on our wedding day.

I picked up the photograph. Although it was our wedding, this particular photo I had never seen. "Where did you get this?"

He ignored the question. "I did say it was an unusual case, Mrs. Cameron, and it is indeed, for we who have overseen the maintenance of the estate have never met the deceased. We simply undertook through a third party to maintain the estate, after which we were instructed to hand over the entire bequest to you. A grant of representation has been issued, that is, an order of the High Court that confirms a grant of probate or a grant of letter of administration and that the personal representative is now free to administer and distribute the estate. As the deceased's personal representatives, we are therefore in a position to hand over the estate to you immediately."

I shook my head. "No, this can't be right." I felt quite faint.

"Are you all right, Mrs. Cameron? I suggest a little brandy may make you feel better. I appreciate this must be very difficult for you to comprehend." He took a small silver hip flask from his desk drawer and held it up for my approval.

I nodded yes.

"Please forgive me, but I anticipated your reaction." He poured a little into a glass; I took a sip and felt the brandy burn my throat and the warmth immediately spread through me.

"We established your whereabouts and your identity before we wrote to you." He cleared his throat. "Mrs. Cameron," he hesitated again, "today you have become a very wealthy woman."

At this point the door opened, and a man in his late thirties came in.

"Ah James," Adam Galbraith sighed. "Mrs. Cameron, I would like to introduce my associate, James Anderson."

James Anderson was fresh faced, with fair, tousled hair, the kind that curls if it's allowed to grow. He took my hand. "Very pleased to meet you, Mrs. Cameron." He then eased himself into the other chair and poured himself some tea.

"James is here to tell you a bit more about the estate and to take you through the paperwork. At your convenience he will also take you to the property. It is specifically requested by the deceased that a representative of the firm be at your disposal during the transition of ownership. James will be there to smooth over any problems with the management of the estate."

Adam Galbraith leaned heavily on his elbows on the desk, clasped his hands together, and considered me carefully. "There is, however, one very important detail that I feel we should make clear immediately. There is a codicil in the will that stipulates that you must be in residence in the house for a minimum of one year. You may leave the house, of course, but for no longer than a few days at a time. You must, however, sell the house you live in now, and we can arrange that for you, if you so desire. It is important, however, that you understand that if you choose not to comply with these conditions, you will lose not only the house but every penny of the bequest." There was another pregnant pause, and both he and James watched for my reaction. It was madness.

"But that's bizarre. You mean I have to live in this house, sell my home, move to Aberdeenhire?"

"It is precisely so. Those are the conditions of inheritance, but you do of course have time to consider."

I almost laughed. "Time to consider, there is no choice, realistically, is there?"

"No" he said. "Personally, I didn't think so."

James Anderson leaned forward. "We have never had to deal with anything quite like this before, and we are as mystified as you are. The conditions of this will have intrigued those of us who knew of it for many years, and we were rather hoping you would shed some light on it."

He smiled at me, and in the midst of this dream—for that is what I thought it must surely be—I saw he had a lovely smile. I shook my head. "I am stunned. I have absolutely no idea."

Mr. Galbraith rose rather stiffly from his chair. "If you will excuse me, I have some business to attend to, so I must leave you now with James, who will give you more information and discuss with you how you wish to proceed." He walked around to my side of the desk. "It has been a pleasure to finally meet you. I bid you good day, but I hope that you feel free to contact me at any time if you feel I may be of assistance."

As he took my hand, I asked him one more time, "You are sure it's me? Is there definitely no way there could be any mistake?"

"No." He smiled gently. "There is absolutely no doubt." He gathered papers from the desk.

"My kindest regards, Mrs. Cameron, and I hope we may continue to serve you in our capacity as legal advisors." He patted my hand and left the room.

James moved around to Mr. Galbraith's seat, and we spent the next half hour going over details and signing papers. Finally, he announced the money would be in my bank at close of business that day. I tried to imagine the reaction of the friendly girl who usually served me in the bank in Cumbernauld Town Centre the next time I had to make an over counter withdrawal.

"All done," James said, putting the last papers into a leather folder. "Mrs. Cameron, you are obviously shaken, as anyone would be under these circumstances. Did you come alone?"

"Yes."

"Did you drive?"

"No, I came by train." I was holding the cup, but my hand was trembling.

"I think it would be better if I drove you home."

"Thank you, but I don't want to put you to any trouble."

"It's no trouble. I just have to let my secretary know, and an early finish on Thursday is just what I need."

An hour later I stepped out of the offices of Messer's Galbraith and Anderson in a daze. The car crawled through the busy Glasgow afternoon traffic, and by the time we reached the motorway, I was beginning to feel better. I had been shivering, but a combination of James Anderson's kindness, the brandy, and the heated front seat in his car both warmed and calmed me, though I was as confused and numb as I had been on the day of Paul's funeral.

"Are you doing OK, Mrs. Cameron?"

"It's surreal. I feel as though I am in the middle of a deep sleep and this all just a dream."

"Understandable. A heck of dream though, eh?" He grinned.

He added bits of information on the way home. The house I had inherited was in rural Aberdeenshire between Stonehaven and Banchory, in beautiful woodlands called Fetteresso Forrest. He hadn't seen it himself but knew it was, as he put it, a substantial property, old, part of it dating back to the sixteenth century, possibly older. By the time we reached home, I had learned that there was a housekeeper called Mary Johnston and a gardener-cum-handyman, Caleb Peterson, who was her son-in-law.

James insisted on seeing me safely in my front door. He accepted tea, and seeking assurance that I would be all right, suggested I phone someone for company. I phoned Katie and Gill and asked them to come over that night for dinner; I told them I had the most amazing news. I refused to tell them any more except that it wasn't anything bad—at least that was what I thought then. James arranged to meet me in Stonehaven the following morning, and he left his mobile number.

CHAPTER THREE

....

Katie and Gill

After James left, I sat looking around at the home that Paul and I had built together. The hardest thing of all would be selling this house. I wondered why that was a condition of the will, then thought maybe it was to make sure I stayed in Aberdeenshire because I would not have a home here to come back to. Why did it matter so much to someone that I stay in that house? Well, full of memories my home might be, but they were painful ones. It was after all only bricks and mortar. Maybe it was time for me to stop living in the past; to do so was just self-inflicted misery. It was time to move on. I decided I would take the photos and pieces of furniture and ornaments that mattered to me and make the move. I could put up with anything for a year, for seventy-five million pounds. I thought about phoning Gwen and George Cameron, Paul's aunt and uncle, but what was I supposed to say? "Hi, I was just calling to see if one of you had died and left me some money?"

They arrived together, a whirlwind of coats and perfume. Gill, carrying a cake box from Peckam's flounced past me into the kitchen; she had collected Katie along the way. "My God, you are white as a sheet," Katie said, concern creasing her brow as with one hand she tossed her coat and with the other manoeuvred me into the kitchen. "I am starving; it was so busy

I had to skip lunch today. I have had nothing to eat but a Kit Kat since breakfast." She plonked a couple of wine bottles on the work surface.

"OK, spill the beans. What's this news? You have absolutely no idea the speculation on the way here." Gill was giggly, on a high, the kind that usually meant there was a new man in her life.

"So what's his name?" I asked, taking the Chinese food out of the oven. "You have so obviously got a new man."

"That smells so good. Oh, you bought a banquet," Katie said, lifting lids and helping to fill the plates. Together we spread the plates of Chinese food in the center of the table.

Gill answered, "He's not new. It's been six weeks, six fantastic weeks."

"Six weeks!" I said sarcastically. "Wow! You kept that quiet." Sometimes Gill's boyfriends didn't even last three.

"Right, come on, what's the big deal? What's so important you couldn't tell me on the phone?" Gill opened a drawer and searched around, looking for the bottle opener.

"I think you better both sit down."

Katie turned to look at me, sensing something in my tone. "You sound serious. Where's the bottle opener?"

"I don't know where the bottle opener is. Just listen for a minute." I took a deep breath. "I got a solicitor's letter this morning." I paused to get their attention. "Telling me I was a beneficiary in a will."

"Nice," Gill said. "Found it." She held up the bottle opener like a trophy.

"I went to see him today, and basically, someone has died and left me a fortune."

"A fortune? What do you mean? How much of a fortune?" Gill asked.

"You're kidding." Katie looked at my face. "No, you're not, are you? How much of a fortune?" She poured the wine into the glasses from the bottle Gill had opened.

"A very large one, plus land and a house in rural Aberdeenshire." Now at last I had their full attention, and they both looked at me blankly.

Katie sat down at the table. She studied my face. "This is not some kind of joke?"

I shook my head. "No."

"How come?" Katie asked. "Who left it to you? Is it something Paul had?"

"No, not Paul. Anyway, this is serious money." I told them the story.

The food lay untouched on the table. "Seventy-five million! My God! I don't believe it." Gill sat down with a thump, glass in hand. "You sure it's not some kind of hoax?"

"No, that's what I thought. It is absolutely true. I know it's incredible, but it's true. I have to meet the solicitor to view the house tomorrow morning."

It took some time to sink in. Katie and Gill were speechless, which had to be a first. Then with dawning realisation Gill broke the ice. "Oh my God, you are rich!" she screamed with delight. "A generous millionaire friend is just what I need!" We started laughing then, more and more hysterically, hugging one another.

Over dinner we discussed who my benefactor could have been. Katie asked, "Is there no one you can think of who might have been around when you were young? I don't know, a friend of your parents or something? I mean, you don't just hand over a fortune to someone you don't know."

"I suppose they had friends, but no one close. They were very private people. Anyway, what kind of person leaves that amount of money to a friend's child?"

"Someone who has a debt to pay, maybe. What about in Holland?" Gill asked, pouring more wine.

"My father lived in Rotterdam. He met and married my mother, who was a Scot working there, but she was homesick and couldn't settle, so they went back to Scotland. My Scottish grandparents died before I was born. My father had a brother, but they hadn't spoken to each other for years, so I didn't know him, and my Dutch grandparents were also dead. I mean, clutching at straws, I suppose it's a possibility, my uncle being my only relative, but why would he keep it a secret? Surely he would have contacted me. It is just completely baffling."

"Well, maybe," Gill said through a mouthful of chow mien, "it's because he had a falling-out with your father. Maybe he was sorry, or it was ill-gotten gains, drugs, or something. Do you know why they lost contact?"

"No. Anyway, a house in Aberdeenshire? I mean, why Aberdeen?"

"Why not? Maybe he was in the oil industry and intended to contact you but didn't get around to it," Katie suggested.

"No, that doesn't wash. The solicitor said they had been maintaining the house for years, and they had never met anyone. Everything was done through a third party."

"You were born in Holland, weren't you?" Katie asked.

"Yes, and I was only twelve weeks old when my parents came to live in Glasgow."

I thought for a moment. "The only other people I can think of are Gwen and George Cameron, Paul's aunt and uncle."

"Oh, yes," Gill said, "the couple who took over at the funeral."

I nodded. "They did take over, but in a nice way. No, I didn't get the impression they were wealthy people; I can't see them having anything to do with it at all. In fact, I didn't even know they existed before the accident. Even so, they were indispensable at the funeral, but apart from a couple of 'how are you doing' phone calls, I haven't heard from them since."

We spent the rest of the night like that, talking over endless possibilities. We lounged on chairs and the sofa, legs tucked underneath, wine in hand, and talked half the night away, exploring all the possibilities of who could have left me this money and what the house would be like and would I sell or keep it as a holiday home. Gradually the initial shock melted away and the excitement crept in, and suddenly I was relishing the prospect of seeing the house the next day. I told them about the arrangement to meet James Anderson in Stonehaven. "I don't suppose either of you fancies a weekend in Aberdeen?" I asked. "The solicitor said the house was ready to move into. I don't know what that means exactly, but we could book into a hotel if there is a problem."

"Sure, I'll come," Katie said. "I'm intrigued. I'd love to see it, and it's just what I need—a weekend away."

It was what Katie needed; she needed it probably as much as I did, a change, something different. She had been separated from her husband for almost a year, and he was now pressing for divorce; Katie would not contest it. She had met Ben when we were at university, and they were married a year later, with Gill and I as her bridesmaids. It quickly became clear that it was a horrible mistake. Pauline, Ben's mother, was a first-class bitch, a control freak who had tied the apron strings so tight that her weak, cowardly son was strangulated by them. His father, who had a permanently tired look, gave into his wife and her tantrums at every turn for the sake of peace, and Ben had learned to do the same. From the moment they returned from honeymoon, Pauline injected her insidious poison. Under the guise of giving help and advice, she criticised Katie's cooking, the style of their furnishings, the amount of time Katie spent at the shop, even the cleanliness of their flat. She had the nerve to clean the flat and rearrange cupboards and wardrobes while Katie worked; letting herself in with a spare key she had taken without asking. Pauline demanded all Christmas Days, Easter Sundays, family birthdays, etc. be spent with her. She thought nothing of arranging barbeques, family dinners, etc. on days when Katie's family had a celebration of some kind, with absolutely no consideration for what Katie or her family might want.

Initially Katie tried to stand up to her, but Pauline reacted by phoning Ben and telling him that the entire family were devastated that he didn't want to spend time with them anymore, and of course that started Katie and Ben arguing. Perhaps the most disagreeable thing of all was that she criticised Katie to other people. It fooled no one, for everyone who knew Pauline knew she had an inflated ego, probably caused by inflicted low self-esteem as a child. She needed to run Katie down in order to make herself look good. In spite of Pauline, the marriage might have survived because Katie, who loved Ben, was determined to make it work, and so she gritted her teeth through most of it. But unfortunately Katie came home exhausted from work one day to overhear Pauline confidentially telling her neighbors that Katie kept her son's home like a pigsty. She told her avid listeners that she was devastated because her son was used to better things, and she, Pauline, was devastated that marrying that woman had reduced her son to living like that. For Katie it was the last straw, and she gave Pauline her marching orders. Unfortunately Pauline cried crocodile tears on her son's shoulder, and the spineless wimp comforted his mother, leaving Katie's eyes wide open. For the first time, she saw what we had seen from the beginning. Gill and I agreed we would have booted her out the door long ago.

"I'll definitely come, though I do, however, have a dinner date tomorrow night." Gill groaned. "Oh, but he's really keen, so he'll keep, and I wouldn't miss this weekend for the world. He is so obsessed with me, and I just don't know why because he teaches history and is surrounded by leggy, nubile, teenage girls batting their eyelashes at him day in and day out."

"Maybe it's your intellect he's attracted to," Katie said with just a little contempt in her voice. Gill's false modesty was legendary. "My Gillian's a beauty," her mother used to say, and she was right. Gill, with her long, jet-black hair, sallow skin, high cheekbones, and almond-shaped brown eyes, coupled with an excellent figure, made her a magnet for anything in trousers. Gill had a different man every few months, and occasionally they overlapped. She was incorrigible, and when we were at university, her laissez-faire attitude to commitment led to countless times when Katie and I had to provide sympathetic shoulders for her rejected lovers to cry on. Gill, full of life, always animated and cheerful, was a constant source of entertainment, usually at some poor guy's expense. But she was great company. She could recount something very simple that had happened to her that day and leave you helpless with laughter. She was vivacious, colourful, and slightly eccentric, but she was always good to have along.

I was lucky to have such good friends, and because they had offered to come with me, the forthcoming trip to Aberdeenshire, I thought, would be less stressful and might even be fun, though I had almost forgotten what that was. Katie arranged to pick me up in the morning, and they left around midnight, with Gill adding that she hoped I appreciated the fact she was giving up a hot date with her "gorgeous history professor" and that she might have to help me spend some of my millions so that she wouldn't pine too much for him. I locked the door feeling better than I had in months.

CHAPTER FOUR

The House

Stonehaven, for those of you who have never been there, which incidentally included the three of us, is the most beautiful little seaside town, nestled in a bay fifteen miles south of the city of Aberdeen. The bay and the pretty little houses can be seen from the Aberdeen to Glasgow side of the motorway. That Friday morning we approached it via the A90 with Gill at the wheel. She had insisted on driving, which, as things turned out, proved to be useful since she was the only one with a four-wheel drive. I was in awe, as always, at the first sight of the powerful North Sea from the motorway; it was a bright, sunny day, and the vast expanse of water sparkled.

I had arranged to meet James Anderson at a hotel on the harbor. Enchanted, we followed the winding cobbled street down to the little beach area, where a line of brightly painted rowing boats were tethered and children played on the sand between them. We had tea at a table outside the hotel and sat basking in the incredibly hot sunshine, cooled by a sea breeze, watching the lifeboat crew going through a drill and then setting out to sea.

When James arrived, I introduced him to Gill and Katie. Katie gave me a raised eyebrow look, the "he's all right" look, and then when James turned to order some drinks, she looked at Gill with mock despair and mouthed, "Stop salivating; it's embarrassing."

James said the house was situated nine miles from Stonehaven in Fetteresso Forrest. "We take the Slug Road, which connects Stonehaven to the A93, leading into Banchory and Royal Deeside. The Slug Road is the boundary between the Fetteresso Forrest and the Durris woods. Are you heading home tonight, or do you intend to stay?" He asked.

"Actually, we intend to stay for the weekend," I said.

"OK, well, I checked it out this morning; the house is fully habitable and kept clean. Food might be a problem, but we can call in at the supermarket. Everything else has been kept in a ready-to-move-in condition; in fact I can honestly say the house has been waiting for you."

James suggested I travel with him so that he could give me some more details, and Gill and Katie followed behind. We stopped first in the square at the centre of Stonehaven and James stayed in the car making some calls on his mobile while we went grocery shopping. There was a small supermarket that yielded milk, butter, rolls, bread, biscuits, a couple of bottles of wine, tea and sugar, a couple of tins of salmon, potato crisps, and a few bars of chocolate. At the butcher-cum-delicatessen across the square, we bought bacon, eggs, Lorne sausage, some lovely cooked chickens, fresh farm potatoes, and some tall jars of carrots and peas; we made sure we weren't going to starve.

Forty minutes later James turned onto the Slug Road. We drove past rolling fields, scattered farmhouses, and a few isolated cottages. He pointed out the dry-stone wall bordering the right hand side of the road, right at the start of the Slug Road, and told me to look for a gap to maybe get a glimpse of the amazing but ruined Ury House. The scenery was quite spectacular, and we passed only two other cars, though James said at peak times it was a well-used road. Around fifteen minutes later, we turned onto a single rough track road that led to the house. It became quite dark, the giant conifers keeping out the summer sun as the track wound deep into the woods. Eventually the road widened, and James slowed the car to a halt at the edge of a clearing. He turned and looked at me.

"Well, Mrs. Cameron, are you ready?"

I nodded, a little bemused at the drama, and then, in a heart-stopping moment, he turned the car into the clearing. The car slowed to a halt, and

I stepped out, crunching the gravel underfoot. Katie and Gill pulled up alongside us.

Stepping out of the car, Katie said, "Oh my God."

Gill stepped out from behind the wheel and stood staring with her mouth open.

"This is my house?" I asked, stunned.

James was watching me, smiling. "Welcome to Lanshoud," he said.

We stood transfixed, in a sort of stunned silence, taking in the vision of what was more of a mansion than a house. James stood by, patiently waiting. I was lost for words.

"I don't know what to say. I never expected..." I faltered. "It's..." I faltered again.

"Yes, it's amazing. To be truthful, I never expected this either. Substantial was an underestimate, really," he said.

The unreality of it put me in me in mind of the old black-and-white movie of Daphne Du Mauriers's *Rebecca*, the bit where Maxim de Winter brings his new bride to see Manderlay for the first time. Well, that was exactly the effect it had on me; nothing James had told me had prepared me for the size of Lanshoud or the splendor. Even if this house had not been mine, I would have been awestruck by its presence, and I use the word *presence* unreservedly because that it what it had—a presence.

"Erica, did you know about this?" Katie asked as she wandered over and put her hand on my arm, still gazing up at the house.

I shook my head slowly, still gazing up the huge ground floor bay windows and solid granite walls. "No, I had no idea."

James consulted his papers. "Ten bedrooms, six public rooms, and the three acres of the forest around the house are part of the estate. The rest is Forestry Commission." The gravel in the clearing continued all the way to wide stone steps leading to the front entrance. At the bottom of the wide steps, he offered me a set of keys, holding out a large iron key. "This one opens the outer doors."

I took the key and walked up the steps. The name Lanshoud was carved into a block of stone above the huge solid oak doors. The key turned easily, but the doors were heavy. James leaned over me to help me push, and I stepped into a tiled entrance hall with another large, half-glass door that opened into a wood-paneled hall. The staircase in front of me was wide and led up to a galleried landing that circled the entire house. There were double paneled doors to the right, lying open, and I could see a large, open stone fireplace. We wandered from room to room opening doors, exclaiming in utter disbelief at the extent to which the rooms were beautifully and expensively furnished.

I turned to James. "Yes," he said before I could ask. "All yours—the furniture and furnishings, everything you see is now yours."

Behind the staircase, a few steps down led to a huge, semimodern kitchen with a stone floor, fitted units, a gas cooker, a central island, and an enormous antique pine table with enough chairs to sit sixteen. Another door to the right of the kitchen led to a larder.

"Well, we needn't have bothered with the shopping," Gill said. "Look at this." The shelves were stacked with tinned food and jars. Though the kitchen had a small fridge, a massive, American-style fridge was running in the larder, but it was empty apart from milk, bread, a large block of cheese, and butter. Beside it was a well-stocked chest freezer. We climbed the stairs to the wood-paneled landing, and James took a floor plan from his pocket and spread it out to see where we were.

"OK, let's see, there are ten bedrooms, some with smaller rooms off, looks like dressing rooms. There are six bathrooms, a nursery, and a linen cupboard, all on this floor; three bedrooms to the front and back of the house and two on each side. Downstairs there is a dining room and a drawing room to the left, a sitting room, a morning room, and a study with extensive library to the right. There is also a conservatory on that side that leads off the study. The three doors under the staircase are a cloakroom and a boot room. It has a door leading to the side of the house, and the last door leads down into the cellar. Oh and there are also two attic rooms; the stairs leading to them are behind the door at the far end there." He pointed to the far right of the landing. "And I think this must be the master bedroom here." At the end of the left-hand side of the landing, three steps led up to another small landing area, off which lay the master bedroom suite. It was larger than any bedroom I had ever seen.

"I just can't believe this," I said, stepping through the door.

A magnificent four-poster bed sat against the left wall facing a stone fireplace. Because it was at the corner of the house, it had two windows, one looking over a paved area and manicured lawns at the back, and one to the side, looking over the conservatory onto flower beds and what looked like apple trees. Two rooms led off to the left, a dressing room with fitted wardrobes and an ornate dressing table with a glass top and Queen Anne legs. The other was a large bathroom with a Victorian-style bath on curved legs and ornate gold fittings. A painting above the fireplace caught my eye, of a figure with a white crescent-moon-shaped hat, red-and-black-diamond-patterned all-in-one suit, and patterned tights, carrying a pole—a harlequin.

James followed my gaze. "A Paul Cezanne, though not an original, I'm afraid. I saw that last year in the National Gallery of Art in Washington."

We wandered though the house opening doors and checking out rooms, and ended up in the kitchen, where we made tea and sandwiches. We found a tray and carried it all though to one of the smaller rooms, which James, consulting the floor plan in his hand, said was the study.

"It's cold in here." It might just have been nervous excitement, but I felt a shiver. I wondered if there was a draught from the glass doors of the conservatory. James had a look but said they were double glazed and well sealed. He explained that Mrs. Johnstone had left the heating on for us. It was gas central heating and not mains gas, but it came from large tanks situated at the back of the building at the side of house, which was garaging for six cars. These tanks had to be refilled by tankers when empty, but he said I didn't have to concern myself with that, as Caleb Peterson took care of those things.

It was the middle of summer and the sun was shining, but I shivered again. I couldn't understand why it was so cold.

James explained, "These old granite houses are always cold. The walls are so thick that any heat from the sun doesn't penetrate, and the surrounding trees don't help. Coupled with large rooms and high ceilings, the house, well, it is always going to be cool if not cold. The fires have been laid in all the downstairs rooms though, so we can light a fire."

We settled in the study. James put a match to the fire, and within minutes it was roaring up the chimney. Though it took some time to actually produce heat, the flames were comforting. When it did heat up, we sat and basked in its warmth, talking about the house and the local area. James told us Fetteresso was a huge forest that stretched up into the Grampian Mountains and on the other side of the Slug Road lay the Durris woods reaching down to the Clune woods.

"So you are all staying for the weekend?" James asked, lifting a salmon sandwich and managing to drop some of the salmon down his tie. He wiped it with his napkin and looked in dismay at the stain left behind.

"Would you like a bib?" Gill asked "I sure there will be one somewhere; there is everything else in this house, or we could improvise with that napkin."

I rather liked the fact that he blushed and laughed when Gill teased him about needing a bib. "That's the plan," I answered. "At least the weekend, though I might stay longer."

"What then?"

"She sells up, of course, gathers up her fortune, and jet sets to a luxury hotel in the tropics with her faithful friends." Gill lay back, arms behind her head, stretching her feet towards the flames.

James looked at me meaningfully. I hadn't mentioned the codicil to Katie or Gill.

"There is something I haven't told you," I said. Both girls looked at me, and everyone waited.

"What?" Katie asked. "What haven't you told us?"

"I didn't tell you because I didn't know what I was going to do about it." I hesitated. "I can't leave here, at least not to go home permanently. The will stipulates that I have to live here for one year from the day I take possession of the keys, or I lose the house and every penny, and I have to sell the house in Cumbernauld."

"What?" Gill, who had been sprawled across a sofa, sat up straight. "Oh, for God's sake, this just gets crazier and crazier."

"And what have you decided?" Katie asked calmly.

"Oh, seriously, she can't rattle about in this place for a year on her own," Gill said.

Katie looked at Gill. "No of course not she has a choice. Hmm, let me think. I know! She can just say no to the seventy-five million." Katie turned back to me. "So what have you decided?"

"I will have to stay, of course. I wanted to see the place first, but I would be lying by omission if I didn't tell you I am worried about the enormity of it all. I am not sure I can do this alone." I wanted to say if only Paul were here, for yet again I was reminded of the tragedy of loss, of what our lives could have been together and of how much I needed him.

"Hey, you are not alone," Gill said, arm around my shoulder again. "Do you honestly think that Katie and I would abandon our very rich, and soon-to-be very generous friend? You've had enough change to deal with lately; you know we're not going to bail out on you now."

"You can't stay here; that's ridiculous. I can't ask you to put your lives on hold again for me. What about your job?" I asked Gill. "What about the shop, Katie?"

"Now you are being ridiculous. Even if the shop was a problem, which you know fine well it isn't, are you trying to tell me that you seriously imagine for one moment that we would leave you here alone?"

Dear, sweet, dependable Katie, she was adamant that she was not leaving me, that I would not be staying there alone, "in a house of this size in the middle of nowhere. It's not going to happen. I am staying."

James interrupted. "Ladies." He stood up. "Much as I am enjoying your company, I will need to leave you to sort things out. I have to be back in Glasgow before seven."

It was so comfortable, and we were getting on well together, that it was disappointing when James said he had to go. I saw him to the door.

"Anything at all, Erica, anytime, just call me. You will find it hard settling into a house of this size. This is the number for Caleb Peterson the gardener and Mrs. Johnston the housekeeper, who is his mother-in-law. Mrs. Johnstone will be here at nine o'clock on Monday, and I will give you a call on Monday morning. There will no doubt be teething problems."

He had no sooner closed the door when Gill said, "What a dish. Now I would have said it was your body he was after," she grimaced, "but now there is your fortune to consider." She sighed, looking around the room. "I've got no chance."

By dinnertime we had agreed that both Katie and Gill would take a year out from their jobs. For Katie it was no problem. She owned a gift shop, and her manageress was perfectly capable of running it. She would sort it out on Monday. Gill was a freelance graphic designer. She would have to wrap up a few projects, but she said it wouldn't take her that long. We would have to collect clothes and things from home, and there would be minor things it would take time to sort out, but I think by then we were all beginning to see that this vast amount of money was life changing, and change was something we all needed. Katie was separated from her husband, and Gill had no ties except for the new guy, but she had just met him, and though the wrench would be terrible *for him*, she said, she thought he would cope. Apart from him, there were no other people to consider.

"Anyway, maybe he will fancy a wee weekend in Aberdeen," she said, laughing.

"Yep, I think we could just about squeeze him in somewhere," I said.

"Eh, any squeezing to be done, it will be me doing it."

We made a meal of the chicken and vegetables and then settled in. We decided the master bedroom was mine, and I left the girls to choose from the rest. They chose, not surprisingly, the rooms beside mine. Katie jumped onto her king-sized bed and purred like a cat at the feel of the exquisite, hand-embroidered feather quilt.

"I think I've just died and gone to heaven," she said, luxuriating in its softness.

By nine o'clock the house was dark, and we had to go around switching on lights.

"Funny," Gill said, "not having to worry about the electricity bill."

There were beautiful, very expensive pieces of furniture in every room and soft, thick carpets, but the drawers and cupboards were mostly empty, as though no one had ever lived there. There were things like pens and stationary but no more than you would expect to find in a holiday home. I hung up the few clothes I had brought with me in the dressing room, and they looked ridiculous in the enormous wardrobes. There were, however, some personal ornaments around. On the dressing table in my room, a lovely, old-fashioned companion set lay on a matching tray, gold handles with silk inlaid behind glass on the back of the brush and mirror, and on the corner of the mantelpiece stood a little porcelain figure of a harlequin poised in the middle of a dance. There were basic toiletries in the bathrooms, but again no sign of anything to give a clue to the identity of the previous owner. I had brought a fleece with me, and chilled by the air in the room, I put it on. The radiators were on, but the air was still to cool to be comfortable. I felt exhausted. I sat on the bed and lay back, closing my eyes.

CHAPTER FIVE

Banchory

The next I knew, there was a knock at the door. My head fuzzy with sleep, I heard a voice call "Good morning." The door opened, and Katie and Gill were standing in the doorway with a tray of boiled eggs, toast, orange juice, and tea.

"What time is it?" I asked, stretching and rubbing my eyes.

"Ten o'clock," Katie said, putting the tray on the table beside my bed. "We found you sound asleep, lying horizontal across the bed last night, so we just threw the quilt over you. You must have migrated to the pillow during the night."

I looked down to see I was still wearing yesterday's jeans and fleece. "I am sorry. I just lay down and must have dropped off."

"Don't apologise" Gill said. "You needed it. We were all tired, but you were exhausted. You didn't even stir when we came to see where you had got to."

Katie sat down beside me on the bed. "Eat up before it gets cold."

"Thanks. Really, I appreciate that you have gone to all this trouble, but I'm not hungry. I'll just have the tea and get something later."

"Eat," Katie said. "It's not open to debate."

"OK, OK." I took a bite of toast, munching to keep her happy. "Did you both sleep well? I don't even remember lying on the bed."

Later I remembered that at the time, they looked pointedly at each other.

"Like logs," Katie said.

"I don't suppose you have made any plans for today?" Gill asked.

"No, not while I was sleeping."

"Look out the window." Katie nodded toward it. "Bet you thought it was summer just 'cause it's July. Well, it's a dull, grey, miserable day, and it's freezing. We haven't even brought the right clothes, and probably you haven't either. At least you have a fleece even though it's been slept in."

"We thought we might go into Banchory today. There should be somewhere there we can buy warm clothing," Gill said.

"Yes, OK, but I need a shower first." I yawned, getting up and heading for the bathroom.

"Right, but please eat, try to eat some more." Katie said, pointing to the tray.

Gill drove down the road through the woods and turned left onto the Slug Road. It was a bumpy ride. Though we were all on different networks, none of the three mobiles had a signal. We followed the road signs and took a fork in the road signposted Kirkton of Durris. We drove down past the huge, dark trees of the Durris woods, past farms and the little village of Woodlands of Durris. There we turned toward the South Deeside Road and went across the bridge past Crathes Castle and into Banchory. We parked the car in a grassed area outside the Medical Centre. It was meant to be summer, but in Banchory the sky was full of dark clouds, and there was a constant drizzle of fine rain. Though strangely it had been cool—cold even—at Lanshoud, in the town it was a muggy, damp day, and everyone was complaining about the humidity. Thin rain jackets covered shorts and T-shirts, and a rainbow of umbrellas protected summer shirts and dresses. Small children whined at their harassed mothers, wanting to be out from under the plastic cocoons of their prams and pushchairs. Boys played football on the grass, refusing to wear their jackets in the rain that was no more than a mist yet still soaked everything and dripped steadily off the leaves on the trees.

Banchory seemed to be just one main street of shops with a few down the side streets. The town held no surprises. There was the usual small supermarket, a newsagent, a furniture shop. A store sold expensive cookware and crockery mostly to tourists and locals made affluent by the oil industry and the well-heeled incomers who had sold their overpriced, cramped houses in London and bought larger detached properties in Aberdeenshire. A deli sold dried black pasta, beetroot crisps, organic wines, dried fruit, and organic chocolate. The proprietors kept three little tables in the large picture window to allow customers to have a drink and look out at the bustle of the beautiful little town. Here two immaculately groomed ladies, cool in their cream linen, sipped hot chocolate. There was the usual tourist trap selling tasteful but predictable souvenirs: hand-woven lace, kilts, tartan skirts, scarves, shawls, and sweaters from the woolen mill; wine glasses, bowls, and vases made of Edinburgh crystal; a thousand or so miniatures of different whiskies. China plates painted with pictures of the salmon leap at the local falls or of the castle just a mile away, or if all else failed to tempt the tourists, figurines of grouse, stags, or highland cows were always popular. Finally we found what we were looking for—a shop with camping gear in the window. It sold everything from warm and waterproof clothing, tents, and hiking boots to water bottles and torches.

The bell tinkled on the door of the old-fashioned shop front, and we were greeted by a friendly elderly man with a rich tan and snowy-white hair. We browsed for a few minutes, and then bought three waterproof jackets, fleece jackets, walking boots, and waterproof trousers. They were excellent quality and therefore not inexpensive—in fact, in about twenty minutes, we managed to spend what a few weeks ago I would have considered a fortune. I may have had millions in the bank, but my psyche hadn't registered it yet, and the customary and previously necessary habit of thrift held fast.

I turned to see Katie and Gill browsing through a stand with metal walking poles.

"Are we going to need those? Are you planning on hill climbing?"

They both looked a bit coy, and Gill had a large torch in her hand. "Oh you never know," Gill said. "The woods around the house will be lovely for walks."

The shopkeeper asked if he could help. He said he detected our West Coast accents, and so I told him I taken a house in the woods between here and Stonehaven.

"Very nice. Off the Netherlee is it, or the Slug Road?"

"The Slug Road. The house is off the Slug Road but quite far into the woods."

"Oh, well, you will definitely need your walking boots. The forest is huge, very deep and very dark and very easy to get lost in, there are lots of trails. It stretches for miles up into the mountains."

"You've walked there then?" Katie asked.

"Oh yes, many times. There are walking and cycling paths, but it's still very easy to get lost. The trails are narrow and get very overgrown. Because of the height of the trees, it's always dark, and that puts some walkers and tourists off."

"Do you know the house called Lanshoud? It's a big very old house. I was told it's sixteenth century or earlier even," I asked him.

"No I've not heard of that one, but you know there is a lot of interesting history and old houses around here. Fetteresso Castle is a fourteenth-century tower house. There's the Roman Camp of Raedykes. It's located several miles northwest. A full legion camped there, and there have been a lot of archaeologists interested in the area. There's an old grave that some say is the grave of Malcolm the First, but others say it's older than that, going back to prehistoric times, and of course we have the Knights Templar who have been here. There is a Templar tower just across the bridge at Drumoak. Aye, there's a lot of history around here."

Gill interrupted. "We'll take these too, please." She held out two of the largest torches in the shop, and I was even more puzzled when Katie held out three of the sturdiest walking poles in the stand. I opened my mouth but hesitated with a feeling that it might be better to ask outside.

"Well, very nice to meet you, and hope to see you again," the shopkeeper said as we left.

"I'll bet he does, after what we have just spent." Gill hefted shopping bags over her shoulder.

"What was all that about?" I asked.

"What? Was what about?" Gill replied.

"Oh, come on. I saw the looks. Unless we are going mountain climbing, what do we need those for?" I pointed at the heavy poles with metal snow grips hanging from them.

"Och, it's something and nothing." Katie shrugged her shoulders. "Call it security." She continued walking even though she must have realised I wasn't going to let that one pass. I stopped in the middle of the street.

"Security? What do you mean security? What have walking poles got to do with security?"

They both stopped and turned; again I didn't miss the furtive glances at each other.

"Think about it; it's not rocket science. Three women alone in a big house in the middle of nowhere, that's all," Gill said and started walking.

Instinctively I knew they were hiding something. "Wait a minute. Don't walk away from me. Are you suggesting you might have to hit somebody with them?" I almost laughed. "Why do you suddenly think we need some kind of weapon for security?" I had raised my voice by the looks coming from two women standing at the bus stop.

Katie looked at her feet. "Look, this isn't the place. Can we talk about it later?" She started walking again.

I caught her arm. "No, Katie. Now I know there's something wrong, and I want to talk about it now."

Katie bit her lip. "OK, I saw a tea shop down the side street. C'mon, we'll tell you about last night." Katie turned off the main street into the cobbled side street.

The teashop was quaint, with little, round oak tables, lace tablecloths, and tiny vases of highly perfumed garden roses in the centre of each table. We ordered one tea, two lattes, and some cake. The waitress came back with a large, vintage, wooden tiered cake stand, which she stood beside the table. Pink and white Madeline's of raspberry jam and coconut. Pineapple cakes with yellow icing covering cream and pineapple jam. Chelsea buns, their pinwheels of pastry and raisins covered in white icing sugar with a glace cherry in the middle. Currant cakes, squares of flaky pastry filled with raisins (flies' graveyards, Glasgow children call them) vanilla slices, and white meringues filled with cream.

"Oh Lord, I'm going to be like the side of a barn when we leave here." Gill sighed. "What if Jack is the man of my dreams? I'll be walking down the aisle in a tent."

"Jack? His name is Jack?" I asked.

"Hmm," she sighed dreamily, then stopped "What's wrong with Jack?"

"Jack and Gill?" Katie smirked.

Elbows on the table, Gill put her chin in her hands. "I know, I know. It's unfortunate, but I was already too much in love to care."

"Love, are you joking? Yesterday you were lusting after her solicitor, anyway," Katie said. "You don't have to eat the whole plate."

Gill mused, "I think you should just call me Gillian from now on."

I waited till the waitress left the table. "Stop stalling. What happened last night?" I raised my eyebrows questioningly.

Katie sighed. "We weren't keeping anything from you. It was nothing, really; it's an old house, and we were spooked by noises in the *wee sma* hours, that's all." She could see I wasn't convinced. "Look, Erica, I don't want to worry you."

"You are worrying me, by not telling me. *Just tell me.*"

Katie sighed deeply and leaned on the table. "We were idiots, that's all. Too many glasses of wine, and our imaginations were running riot. After we found you asleep, we got ready for bed. An hour later you were still sound, and we decided to just throw the quilt over you. Then there was the issue of the doors being locked. So we went together downstairs and locked the doors. Then Gill remembered the conservatory would have doors. She went through the study leading into the conservatory to check, and as she reached the french doors; she thought she saw a figure through the glass. She called me, and we both thought we saw someone in there. We were a bit freaked, so we picked up the heavy brass candlesticks and checked it out, but there was no one there."

"Did you go into the conservatory?"

"No." Katie shook her head. "It was probably the trees outside reflecting on the glass. We were just spooked by it, that's all. After that we both spent the night hearing noises."

"What kind of noises?"

"Just the house settling, I suppose, but I for one would feel happier if I had something like the walking poles under my bed."

"Great. For two people who don't want to worry me, you are doing a pretty poor job."

"Well, you did insist," Gill said. "Just as well we are all going home together on Sunday."

I leaned back in my chair. "I'm not going home tomorrow. I'll have to stay and meet the housekeeper."

"You are going to stay in that house alone?" Gill said. "No way; you just can't."

"Yes, I can and I will. I have to stay because it is my home now, remember? There are the terms of the will to consider. I will have to get used to it."

Katie smoothed her thick, brown curls behind her ears, leaned forward, and said, "I don't have to go home on Sunday. I'll phone Rebecca, and she'll take care of the shop."

We drove back to Lanshoud with a car full of shopping, warm clothes, groceries, and wine. Katie was cooking tonight—Moroccan chicken, her signature dish. We spent the rest of the day exploring the house and grounds, which were full of surprises. The cellar, which led off the hall behind the stairs, had a key hanging outside the door, I unlocked the door and switched on the light, which turned out to be no more than a light bulb on a wire and which illuminated only a small circle at the foot of the stairs. The stairs were stone and seemed to be hewn out of the thick wall. We started down, and a smell of dampness rose to meet us. There was no handrail, and as the stairs were steep, I put my hand on the wall and pulled it quickly away again. It was slimy with some kind of mould.

"Ugh, let's go back," I said. "We will leave this to another day. I can't see much farther than the end of the stairs anyway."

"Look," Gill said. "That crate there has a couple of torches on it. We didn't need to buy more."

I climbed down and retrieved the torches from the box. There were three, but one didn't work. The cellar was vast. Tools lay side by side on a table, and wood, boxes, and crates were stacked against the wall. Broken chairs and an old table, odd pieces of furniture, mirrors, and paintings were stacked in rows. Rolls of cable, insulation, and boxes of bits and pieces littered the floor. What's that?" Katie asked. "A generator?"

"Yes, I think so." I picked up a pair of wire cutters. "Well, your walking sticks were a waste of money. Not that I can't afford to waste it nowadays, you understand. Still, any one of these would be enough to clobber somebody with," I said, hefting them in my hand.

A door that led off to a smaller cellar opened onto row after row of floor-to-ceiling wine racks full of dusty bottles. "Wow. How many bottles did you pick up in the supermarket?" Gill asked, and we stepped in at her back as she picked out a bottle and dusted off the label. "I'm no expert, but that looks expensive."

Back in the main cellar, Katie cried out, startled by what appeared to be a figure under a blanket in the corner. I crossed to the figure tentatively and hesitated, not wanting to appear freaked and by association stupid. I pulled myself together and yanked the cloth off to discover another harlequin, life sized this time, made of stone and painted in red and gold diamond shapes. "That's the third one. There's another two in my bedroom, a painting, and an ornament. How strange. Somebody certainly liked clowns."

We sat in the kitchen on high stools at the centre island and chatted while Katie cooked, and Gill and I took turns finding ingredients as she needed them. We talked about the fact my little Fiat was parked outside my house in Cumbernauld, and anyway, it was not going to cope with the forest roads at Lanshoud. I would have to invest in something else if I was to drive around here.

"Oh, that's just great," Gill said. "You two get to go car shopping with an unlimited budget, and I have to go back to work."

"Don't forget Jack. Wasn't there something about him pining away?" I asked.

"Point taken. Just go and enjoy your shopping."

That night we all slept well, but in the morning over breakfast, it transpired we had all heard some kind of tapping or knocking. Gill was a bit freaked by it, but since it was probably pipes or something, we didn't bother investigating, though we had all kept a walking stick under the our beds. Gill phoned Jack in the morning and rearranged their dinner date. Then she drove Katie and I to Stonehaven, where we had arranged to hire a car; she headed for Glasgow, and Katie and I went shopping for a four-wheel drive in Aberdeen. We made the day for the young salesman working his first Sunday on the job. We bought two.

The beach in Aberdeen was packed. The morning mist had burned off, and the sun was hot but not hot enough to warm the waters of the North Sea. Children squealed with delight running in and out of the freezing cold waves as they broke on the sand. We bought fish and chips and fed the screaming seagulls with the leftovers and then ate an elaborate concoction of ice cream from the fancy ice-cream parlour on the beachfront. With nothing else to do, we sat enjoying the sea air till the sun went down. Later that night as we locked up the house, the noises started again.

CHAPTER SIX

The Tapping

It was around nine o'clock. "I don't get it," Katie said at her fourth attempt to light a fire. "People have burned down houses just because they dropped a cigarette. Yet here I am with paper, sticks, firelighters, coal, and matches, all the accoutrements required, and I have had as much luck as with a damp squib. Here, you try. I give up."

Eventually our combined efforts paid off. An hour and a box of firelighters later, we were sitting in the study toasting our toes in front of a blazing fire, smug in the knowledge that we had mastered the art of fire lighting. It was an exceptional fire, roaring up the chimney, and all our own work. The central heating was useless, and I knew that if it was like that in July, I would have to do something about it before winter; it barely took the chill off the house and sometimes didn't even manage that. The house was so large and the individual rooms so spacious with great high ceilings, that it was, in itself, unsettling, a bit like being alone in a hotel. The study, however, was cosy, and closing the door and drawing the curtains over the windows and french doors leading to the conservatory, made a comforting hideaway. There was something reassuring in the red velvet drapes, the studded oxblood leather suite, and scattered armchairs with brightly patterned cushions depicting the wonders of the world. The mellow light from the old-fashioned, heavy table lamps and the firelight played on the spines of thousands of books, giving the room a warm glow; it was without doubt my favourite room.

We talked about Paul and Ben and how our lives had changed drastically in no more than a few months. I told Katie again how grateful I was that she had been my rock when Paul died, especially since her own life was in bits at that time, with her marriage in pieces. Katie being Katie said it had helped her to take her mind off things.

She sat on the rug at the fire, her back against the leather winged armchair and talked about how Ben had been such a mouse, completely under his mother's thumb, unable to make decisions for himself. She said she had stopped loving him after the first year of her marriage, when her love had changed to pity. Then as time wore on, she learned her husband had very little honour or integrity, and the pity had turned to dislike. She told me all of this with venom in her voice.

"I didn't realise you hated Ben."

"Hated? Oh no, you need a strength of emotion to hate. It was a dawning realisation, a succession of little things. I don't hate Ben; I despise him. There's a big difference…" She stopped. "Did you hear that?" she asked, kneeling up and turning toward the window at her back. She was whispering.

"Hear what?"

"Listen."

I listened but heard nothing, only the sound of the wind in the trees around the house. "I don't hear anything."

"Shh." She put a finger to her lips. "Something is tapping on the window," she whispered.

I thought at first maybe she had heard a branch brushing against a window, then remembered there were no trees that close to the house.

After a moment she said, "Must be my imagination." She sat back down on the rug.

We sat quietly for a while, listening to the crackling and spitting of the fire, but heard nothing else. Stretching her legs out in front of the fire, Katie said, "My mother used to say if you toast your legs in front of a coal fire, you will end up with skin that looks like a road map of Britain." She examined her legs, and then drew them away from the direct heat. "You know, maybe I got it all wrong. I think Gill has the right idea. I don't think she has ever really been attached to any man for any length of time; she just uses them and moves on." Katie studied the refection of the flames on the crystal wine glass. "She is so confident. Have you ever wondered if she can play around because she is confident, or if she has become confident because she plays around?"

"Neither. I just don't think she likes men very much. Have you ever heard her talk about her father?"

"No. She did speak about her mother, though, and I met Mrs. Forsythe a couple of times."

"Did you ever meet him?" I asked.

"Yes. They were at my wedding; he seemed nice. Do you want some more?" She held up the bottle at her feet.

I held out my glass for a refill. "He used to hit her mother."

"No, you're kidding!" Katie was genuinely shocked. "I never knew that. Gill's mother didn't look the battered wife type."

"No, I know what you mean—a pretty woman, impeccably dressed, and quite sophisticated."

"Exactly. She didn't seem the battered wife type, or at least not the stereotype," Katie said.

"I don't know that he battered her, as such, but Gill said he had punched her on more than one occasion when Gill was a child. I certainly never saw any bruises. I used to stay over at their house a lot when we were students, and I stayed with them when we were in between flats. Gill told me about him, and she also told me that he was the reason she stayed away from home so much: because she couldn't stand the way her mother put up with his behaviour. Her sister has moved away too, and her mother is alone with him now."

"What does he do for a living?"

"I think he started out as a car mechanic, and now he owns a string of garages selling second-hand cars and repairing them."

"Of course. Forsythe cars, the TV advert."

"The very one. When I first met him, he was charm personified, and I wondered if Gill had exaggerated. He didn't seem the wife-beating type, but it wasn't long before I was seeing the real Ian Forsythe. He wasn't a pleasant person to be around. He used to sit at the dinner table and pontificate on subjects he obviously knew nothing about. He considered himself an expert and had narrow-minded, fixed views on everything from immigration to gay rights and global warming, yet according to Gill, he had never read anything more than a car manual. Whenever anyone disagreed with his narrow-minded, sometimes completely racist or bigoted views, or when he was actually faced with evidence that he was wrong, he refused to back down and just lost the plot. Gill's mum used to sit with a tense, fixed smile on her face, agreeing with everything he said, panic in her eyes when it looked as though someone might disagree with him. He had a quick, nasty temper that flared up at the slightest provocation. Gill said he behaved like a raging madman at times, screaming, punching doors, throwing things around, using his size and voice to dominate and terrorise his wife and children.

"Once, when I was there for dinner, he nearly got into a fistfight with Gill's sister Cara's husband Graham over the new school curriculum. Cara's husband teaches at St Benedict's. When he wouldn't listen to Graham's explanations, Graham tried to politely point out that perhaps his father-in-law had been misinformed. Well that was it, he was furious. He started shouting at Graham, calling him a stuck-up bastard. He actually got up from his chair and was pointing a finger in Graham's face, and of course Gill's mother tried to stop him, and he pushed her so hard she fell. Graham got up to face him, and it was only Cara's standing in between her husband and her father that stopped a fight. Graham and Cara left. Cara was in tears telling her mother that she was finished with that man, and if her mother wanted to see her again, she would have to come to their home. Mrs. Forsythe was crying, Gill was crying. It was awful, and I was shaking like a leaf."

Katie sat hugging her knees. "I didn't realise. She's never talked about her father to me."

"No, she doesn't talk about it. The only reason I knew is because I was living in their house. Remember during the university holidays, Gill and I were voluntary nursing aides at Beardshill Hospice. When I was on a late shift followed by an early shift, it was easier to stay with them, than travel. That's when I got to know her charming father. Gill has no time for him. When I first met her, she just said they didn't get on. Now I'm sure that he is one of the reasons she doesn't let any man get really close to her. I think she likes to reel them in just to prove she can, and then she leaves them before they can hurt her." I got to my feet and stretched. "What do you think? Bedtime? I am shattered." I yawned.

Katie yawned too and nodded in agreement. She turned again, looking over the arm of her chair at the window at her back. "Listen," she whispered. "Do you not hear that?"

I did hear it this time, a tapping; it seemed to be coming from the study window. Tap, tap, tap, a steady rhythm like the kind you sometimes hear from radiators when they are cooling down.

"It's just the radiator," I said.

"No, it's not. It's coming from the window." Neither of us moved. The tapping stopped, then started a few seconds later.

"Maybe it's rain."

"It's not rain." Katie got up and looked at the window. "It's the same as Thursday night."

"You never said anything about tapping."

"We told you there were noises. Well, that was the noise. It seemed to come from the windows that night too: Not just that window, different windows, as though someone were going around the house tapping different windows." Katie said all this without once taking her eyes off the study window. I got up and moved slowly over to look out. Moonlight flooded the ground, but the trees around the clearing were just a black wall. I couldn't see anything.

She put a hand on my arm, held a finger to her lips, and then whispered, "Listen, it's louder, coming from one of the other rooms."

It was louder now, more like a crack on the windowpane. I felt a little thrill of fear. I backed away from the window and lifted the brass coal tongs from the fireplace. Katie lifted the poker and followed me. In the hall we realised it was coming from more than one room, tap tap tap, louder and louder, from the door, from the windows, tap, tap, tap, incessant. We stood back to back in the hall, our weapons raised, then, just as quickly, it stopped. Frozen, listening for what seemed like an eternity, we waited.

I broke the spell. "My God! What was that?"

"Or who was that?" Katie whispered, and that remark served to scare me even more. We moved back to the study slowly, cautiously, trying to see out the window into the night. I lifted the telephone—my mobile, still in the hip pocket of my jeans, had no signal here. Katie followed me, keeping her back to me, poker raised.

"Erica," she whispered. "Are all the doors locked?"

"Yes, definitely."

The operator answered, "Emergency. Which service, please?"

"Police."

CHAPTER SEVEN

Molly and Alice

It seemed like eternity before the two police officers arrived from Stonehaven, and in that eternity, Katie and I stood exactly where we were, even when it was obvious the tapping had stopped. The two police officers took details and examined the house and grounds, but it was obvious from the outset that they had written us off as a pair of skittish women.

"We have checked out the grounds. There is no sign of anyone and the locks and windows have not been tampered with," the older of the two policemen, Sergeant Michael Watters, said as he wrote details in his logbook. He considered us both and said a little patronisingly. "You know, a big house like this will let you know it's settling down for the night—floorboards, pipes, the radiators maybe. I really don't think you have anything to worry about."

His tone and body language were so patronising I was annoyed and raised my voice slightly to let him know. "We are not a pair of teenagers with rampant imagination; someone was out there, and for some time, tapping, knocking, whatever you prefer to call it, on the windows of this house, simultaneously on several windows and doors. So there has to have been more than one person, and that's two nights in a row."

He raised his eyebrows and smiled, but he remained dismissive. "With all due respect, Mrs. Cameron, you said yourself you are not used to a house of this size. Old houses have their own little quirks. It could have been animals. There are a lot of deer round here. It could have been bats. I am sure you have nothing to worry about."

"What has that to do with anything?" I was exasperated.

"Old houses settle down at night. The floorboards creak, pipes rattle. It's easy when you are isolated in a big house like this to read something into these everyday noises."

"Oh, for God's sake, tapping on a window does not sound remotely like a creaking floorboard or a pipe."

"Yes, well, nevertheless, there is nothing to suggest there has been anyone outside tonight. I am sure you have nothing to worry about, but don't hesitate to call us again if you have a problem." Infuriatingly, he was still smiling as he got into the car.

Katie locked the door behind them. "So much for the strong arm of the law. What now? I think that we should check everything again ourselves." And so we went around the house, making sure all doors and windows were locked. We stayed together, still unnerved. "I can't believe their attitude and just leaving us like this," she said, and I knew how frightened she was because I was equally freaked.

"Listen, Katie, if you want to leave, we can just get in the car and go." Strangely, voicing my thoughts made me want to do just that. "But I personally don't want to let whoever is trying to get us out of here succeed. I want to stay."

She sighed, hesitated, then with resignation, she said, "Then we stay."

That night we attempted to sleep in my bedroom. I say attempted because we were straining to listen for any sound, and yes, old houses do creak and settle, and cooling pipes knock together. With the fire lit, the door barricaded by a heavy chest of drawers, all the lights on, and our weapons—the fire irons, the poker, and the walking poles—kept at hand, it was still dawn before exhaustion ruled and I for one actually fell asleep.

At exactly 9:00 a.m. the following morning, I heard the sound of tyres on the gravel outside. Looking out, I saw a battered Land Rover with a grey-haired woman behind the wheel. She got out rather stiffly, as though her hip hurt, and walked round to open the passenger door for a younger woman, whom she helped to step out. The younger woman had mousey brown hair, not soft curls like Katie's but wiry with a will of their own. Though there was at least thirty years between them, they were dressed alike, in tweed skirts and stockings and what is often referred to as sensible shoes. The younger took the older woman's arm, and they walked to the house together, arms linked, backs straight in a rhythm that made them look like a single unit. Still in my dressing gown, I went down to open the door.

Molly Johnstone had a soft, kind, rosy-cheeked face, unlined in spite of the fact she must have been at least in her late sixties, and she had a smile that lit it up.

"Pleased to meet you, Mrs. Cameron. I am Mary Johnstone. I'm called Molly though, because my mother was Mary too, and this is my daughter Alice. Alice, say hello to Mrs. Cameron." She raised her voice as though Alice had difficulty hearing. Alice looked at the ground, picking at her skirt. "Alice, love, be a good girl now and say hello."

I put my hand out "Hi, Alice. I'm Erica."

Alice had a fey look about her. Her wide, blue eyes seemed vacant and expressionless. She looked up and smiled shyly, then she took my hand and shook it vigorously. "I'm Alice. Pleased meet you," she said in a staccato voice.

"Pleased *to* meet you," her mother suggested.

"Pleased to meet you." Alice smiled her shy smile.

I held my hands up. "I'm embarrassed to be greeting you in my dressing gown. My friend and I had a bit of a scare last night and slept late this morning." I wandered through to the kitchen, and Molly and the child-woman followed me. I offered them tea or coffee, and Molly stopped me from filling the kettle, saying that was her job, and anyway Alice liked making tea.

"You want to make us a nice pot of tea, dear?" she asked. The child-woman nodded vigorously and rushed to carry out her task.

"Pardon me for asking, but you had a scare, you said?" Molly asked, surprise in her voice.

"Yes, some noises outside the house. We called the police. It was probably nothing. The police think we are couple of hysterical females."

"Not a little scare, a bloody big one," said Katie, entering the kitchen, hair still wet from the shower. "Sorry, excuse my language. I'm Katie."

Molly offered a cooked breakfast, but Katie declined, and we settled for fresh juice and toast. With Molly's motherly attentions and the fact the sun shone through the long windows that lined one side of the kitchen, the worries of the previous night seemed to fade.

Molly addressed me as Mrs. Cameron. I suggested she call me Erica and asked if she would sit with us at the table while we had breakfast, as there were some questions I would like to ask about the house.

Alice, Molly, Katie, and I sat at one end of the long wooden table. Molly explained she was contracted till the end of the month, and after that she would be available to stay if I needed her help. I instinctively liked her. There was something motherly about her. Her smile came easily, and her gentle, lilting voice was easy on the ear. I told her I hadn't a clue how to look after a house like this and that I would be very grateful if she would consider carrying on as before. She was delighted. She was a widow, and Lanshoud was her only income apart from her state pension, and she relied on it to treat her grandchildren.

"It's a big house, Molly. It seems a lot for you to manage on your own," I said.

"Well, I'm not on my own. Alice loves helping and comes with me every day. Usually a couple of times a year, a cleaning firm comes in from Aberdeen and really guts the place, and do you know about Caleb?"

"Yes, the handyman."

"Caleb is married to my daughter Lucy. He is a lovely lad and can turn his hand to most things. Caleb doesn't come every day, but I tell him when something needs done, and he sees to it, and he keeps the grounds in order. Lucy comes and helps me too. My grandchildren are both at school now. Callum is seven, and Hanna is five."

"I would really like it if you would stay, Molly, and if you could help me to run the house, I would be happy to employ someone else to give you a hand."

"Well, shall we see how it goes, and if I find it's too much for me, I'll get back to you."

"Molly, have you ever had any problems with the house?" I asked. "Or has Alice?"

Alice stared from one face to the other as each person spoke, smiling and nodding her head like one of these nodding dogs frequently seen on car rear windows in the seventies.

"What sort of problems?"

"Like these noises we heard last night."

"No." She shook her head.

Alice shook her head too and said, "No, no."

"I take it you mean intruders, or did you mean ghosts or something? It being such an old house." She looked from me to Katie.

"Anything, really," Katie said. "Has anything ever gone bump in the night?"

"Well, Alice and I leave before dark, but I can assure you I have been looking after this house for nearly five years, and I have never heard anything out of place. You have nothing to worry about, dear. There are no ghosts in this house."

"No ghosts, no ghosts," Alice repeated, shaking her head frantically from side to side.

"Molly, you said five years. Did you ever see the owner in that time?" I asked.

"I have never seen anyone except the estate agent in Stonehaven who employed me. I mean I asked, but they told me it was all done through a lawyer in Glasgow. None of the local people know anything either, but then that's not unusual in these parts. We get people who work in the oil industry buying property here and then working offshore or abroad. I had got so used to just pottering along. It was a real shock when I was asked to get the house ready for the new owner."

"Did you know the housekeeper before you?"

"Yes, I met her when I started the job. I went to see her at her home. Her name is Lizzie McIntosh, and she lives in Kincardine O'Neil. That's a village further up Deeside. In fact Lucy knows her daughter and sometimes sees her socially. Her kids go to the same school as Callum and Hannah."

"Do you know why she gave the job up?"

"No. I think Lizzie just fancied a change."

"I'd really like to speak to her. Is it possible to arrange for me to do that?"

"What I'll do then is ask Lucy to have a word."

A jubilant Gill phoned around eleven o'clock. "You are going to have to call me Gillian from now on. This is the real thing," she assured Katie, who answered the phone.

"Well, I hope you are on the road already, Gillian," Katie said. "Make sure you get back up here tonight."

"Why? What's wrong?"

"Exactly the same as the first night, only worse, and I for one am not relishing it being just Erica and I tonight again. We called the police last night."

"No."

"Oh, yes." Katie filled in the details.

I leaned over Katie's shoulder. "Look, tell her to bring with her anybody else she can persuade to come," I said. "Give me the phone. I'll tell her."

"Are you serious?" Gill asked.

"Deadly serious."

"You did get a fright."

"Yes, we did."

"Do you want me to bring Jack?"

"Definitely."

"OK, I'll ask. He's not back at work till October anyway, so it shouldn't be a problem. I was going to be there by six, but if Jack's coming, it might be a bit later. I'll let you know."

She phoned back later. Amazingly, she and Jack had bumped into James Anderson in Buchanan Street, and she told him what had been happening. She told us to hunker down because the troops were coming.

CHAPTER EIGHT

JACK

If you had asked me what a history professor might look like, I might suggest an Indiana Jones-type figure, or Gregory Peck as Atticus Finch in *To Kill a Mockingbird*, but Jack was not typical in my view. He had thick, tousled, very red hair and was short and built like a rugby player. Of Irish descent, he had a rich Dublin accent and had definitely kissed the Blarney Stone. By evening Katie and I were almost as enraptured as Gill. He made us laugh, and we forgot for a while why we wanted him there. Gill sensed we liked him, and she was pleased. Coupled with James's arrival, I for one was not as worried about the return of the nocturnal tapping.

We spent most of the evening talking over my amazing turn of fate, and Jack made a very good point. My benefactor obviously had good reason for forcing me to stay in the house. Maybe someone had an equally good reason to want me out.

"I wonder why he didn't live in it." Gill said .

"Maybe he couldn't for some reason," Jack said.

"You mean like someone who worked in the oil industry?" Katie suggested.

"Worked in?" I laughed. "They would have to own it to leave seventy-five million pounds behind."

"C'mon, James, you must know more than you're letting on." Jack filled his glass.

"No, I really don't. The will is so tightly bound legally; there is no way from our office that we could trace the benefactor. The third party is another firm of solicitors. Somebody there must know something, but getting the information from them is risky. If it was leaked that they had not honoured the conditions of will, they would be ruined."

The suggestions went from the sublime to the ridiculous: a relative who had been a drug runner; a Dutch uncle who had been a Nazi collaborator who had spirited away millions of Jewish money; my unknown godfather who was an aged Italian count who had loved my mother and, thwarted in love, had left his money to her child—that one from Katie, of course; she was a hopeless romantic.

"I just don't know where to start," I said. "I need help."

Jack inhaled. "Well, you start with your birth certificate and work back tracing your relatives on both sides. And you would have to consider your late husband being the source, so you trace his ancestry, and you research the history of this house locally and in the land records. The solicitors may be legally bound to silence, but somebody has to know something."

"Would you help me, Jack?"

"For bed and board with this lovely woman," he put his arm around Gill, and she snuggled up to him, "you have my services till October."

"Now don't say I'm not useful," Gill said.

As it grew near ten o'clock, which was approximately the time the tapping had started on the previous nights, we were quiet, listening, but the silence became unmanageable thanks to the amount of wine we had drunk, and as fate would have it, there was nothing to hear, though both men professed to be thoroughly disappointed and felt free to make sexist remarks about women and imaginations running riot. We, however, thought it might be because we had called the police last night or because the two men had arrived. At any rate, as a result we went to bed around midnight a lot happier.

We picked out a bedroom for James, Gill and Jack shared, and I went to bed with a feeling of security, smiling to myself at the Gill and Jack, Jack and Gill thing. I picked up my book, read half a page, and fell sound asleep. Another true old saying: money can't buy happiness, but it sure makes misery easier to live with.

JACK

The hammering woke me. I lay in the dark for a moment, not sure where I was, dazed from being woken suddenly from a deep sleep. I heard it again, a rhythmic pounding coming from downstairs. My bedroom door creaked open, and Katie whispered, "Erica."

I pulled on my dressing gown, lifted the poker that had been lying beside my bed from the previous night, and followed her down the steps and onto the landing. By the time I reached her, the noise had stopped. James, Gill, and Jack were already there, tense, silent, in various states of undress.

Jack and James started down the stairs, slowly, quietly. Jack had one of the walking poles in his hand. We followed the men, Katie first, Gill and I together. In the hallway James raised his hand, and we all stopped, straining to hear the slightest sound. I held my breath in the silence that was almost palpable.

"James," I whispered. He turned, and I handed him the poker.

Jack was almost at the door, his head cocked, listening. James stepped forward and carefully opened the inner door He lifted the key for the outer door and went to put it in the lock, but Jack reached out and stopped him, shaking his head in warning. We all watched the door, frozen, not daring to breathe. Suddenly a thunderous bang shook the oak doors with such violence that it seemed to threaten the very hinges of the solid oak. I jumped, and Gill uttered a cry and covered her mouth. Then, stillness so quiet that I could hear my heart beat. The men, leaning forward almost at the door, were obviously listening to something we couldn't hear. Then James stepped forward again to unlock the door.

"No." Jack stepped in front of him. He signaled, *don't open the door.*

We waited, breath held, hearts pounding. Several minutes passed. Jack put his ear to the door. There was a strange animal cry, and then the tapping again, followed by a long period of silence. We must have stood there for fifteen minutes, not daring to move.

"I think they've gone," James said. He turned and stared at Jack, puzzlement creasing his face. "Horses."

Jack nodded in agreement. "Horses." He turned to me. "The tapping you heard. Could it have been horses' hooves?"

"No, it was on the windows and the door." I looked at Katie for confirmation.

"No, it was definitely the windows," she said.

53

The study had large windows facing to the front. We followed Jack in. He and James went to the windows and looked out into the gloom. James said it was impossible to see anything because it was pitch black.

"I'll call the police," Jack said.

"Is there any point in calling the police? It's three a.m., and it takes them an hour to get here. Maybe they've gone." I looked out again, seeing nothing, only the dark night.

"She's got a point," James said. "If they had wanted to break in, they would have smashed a window. I don't know what they want, but they could have gotten in if that was their purpose. No, I think they only want to frighten us."

"Well, they're succeeding," Katie said. She was shivering. Gill and I both hugged her. We were all cold and shaking, and the house was freezing.

"Why? Would they want to frighten us, and what do you mean, *they*?" I asked James.

"There was more than one horse, and I'm presuming that they had riders. Why is anybody's guess?"

"I agree," Jack said. "There's not much point in phoning the police tonight. We might as well wait it out till morning, but I think a little brandy would help us all."

For the rest of that night, there was no further disturbance. We stayed all together, all night, in my bedroom. We lit the fire and gathered duvets from the other bedrooms. We slept on the carpet in front of the fire, on the pillows and with the duvets stolen from the beds wrapped around us. There was an unstated understanding that anything we needed, we collected in pairs. No one had actually said he or she was afraid, but we most undoubtedly were. The fire took a long time to warm us. We huddled together as much to feel secure as for warmth. I lay there thinking how much worse it could have been if it had just been Katie and I. I'm not sure anyone slept much that night.

The police came promptly the next morning. Molly and Alice fussed over everyone, cooking breakfast with endless cups of tea and coffee. Whatever James had said to the police when he called them, this time they were taking it seriously. Two CID officers from Aberdeen grilled us for two hours, interviewing us separately and together about the incident and asking about our relationship and why we were all staying in the house. They examined the grounds outside and the house inside but found no evidence to suggest that anyone, let alone any horses, had been there, and there was no fresh damage to the already scarred and weathered oak doors.

Detective Inspector Jonah Seagraves, in his fifties, a stalwart of the Aberdeenshire CID with a receding hairline and a face that looked as though it had drunk more than a few whiskies in its time and who had a husky voice that suggested he smoked too much, said he could not explain the occurrence any more than we could. Since no one had come to any harm, though I thought that was debatable, the only thing he could suggest, was that he put a constable in the house to stay with us overnight, in case of a recurrence. I had a feeling he was thinking around the lines of mass hysteria. James said it was my call, but I couldn't see us going to bed and some poor cop sitting alone waiting for phantom horses in the middle of the night, so I declined his kind offer. He then said pointedly, as though he hadn't been asking in the first place, that it would give them a clearer picture of what was going on, so I agreed. They were about to leave when he reached in his pocket and lifted out a plastic bag containing a small ornament, another harlequin.

"Does this belong to you, Mrs. Cameron? I found it outside the door."

"Yes, probably, I think the previous owner may have collected harlequins, but I don't know about that specific one."

"Do you mind if I take it back to the station? I'd like to hold onto it just now."

"Of course. Take anything you want."

We sat at the large table in the kitchen, the lack of sleep catching up.

"Maybe I should just go home. What I have never had I will never miss." I put my head in my hands.

They all reacted at once, the general opinion being that I would be mad to give this up. James suggested I go home for a couple of nights and collect the things I needed, and Katie volunteered to go with me. The thought of going home to my own bed was appealing, but I felt guilty leaving them there in case the riders came back.

"Go, Erica, even if it's just for one night," Gill said. "You will feel so much better, and you can rest easy knowing we'll have the might of the Aberdeenshire Police Force to protect us." She smiled.

Jack suggested I could pick up my birth certificate and marriage license, and we could get started researching my ancestry. It was a good reason to go, so I agreed. Katie needed clothes, and so she would go with me. The only problem was transport. The new four-wheel drives hadn't been delivered yet.

"You can take mine," James said. "Your own insurance will cover it third party, and don't worry if you scratch it. Your being a woman of means I will be sending you a hefty bill."

I laughed. "I could just buy you a new one. Maybe you're right. I suppose if the police are here, it should be OK."

An hour later we were still sitting in the kitchen. "What did you mean about the harlequins?" Jack asked. "You said you thought the previous owner collected them."

"Hmm. There is a painting and a statue in my bedroom, and there is a life-size one in the cellar."

"There is one over the mantelpiece in the drawing room," Katie said.

"There are stone harlequins in the grounds at the back of the house." Gill turned to the window. "Look, you can see the top of one there."

"There's one there behind the curtain too." Molly got up to fetch it. She put it on the middle of the table.

"Great, isn't it? The only thing we know about the previous owner is that he collected clowns," I said in mock chagrin. "That's helpful."

Jack was thoughtful. He reached over and picked up the little figure, turning it round and round in his hand, and when he spoke, his tone was serious. "Harlequins were not clowns." Jack continued turning the little figure with the half-moon-shaped hat, black face, and diamond-patterned suit.

"There are several origins of the name harlequin. The one that you probably think of is the harlequin from Commedia Dell'Arte, a form of street theatre that began in Italy in the mid-sixteenth century, characterized by masked actors. It's related to the carnival in Venice. The same characters always performed in every play, a bit like a soap opera. Though the plays were different, the characters were always the same, and the people recognised them by their costumes and masks. Harlequin was one of the stock characters of these plays. I think he was called Arlequin then or the Italian Arlequinno. His mask was always black. The notion that came to me just now is that the name harlequin is also said to come from the old French harlequins, the leader of La Maisnie Hellequin—a legendary pack of demons on horseback."

"*Demons*," Gill said. He had our attention now. I thought he must be a great teacher.

"Incidentally, his face is black because he was believed to have come straight from the devil from the bowels of the earth, from hell itself. There are numerous references in the French and medieval Latin history texts, connected to a legend that told of a troupe of spirits, who, mounted on fast horses and accompanied by noisy dogs, were condemned for their sins to ride forever until the end of the world."

"Jack, stop it. You are scaring us," Gill said.

James pushed his chair back "Aw, come on. You are not seriously suggesting there were some kind of mediaeval ghosts battering on that door last night."

"I'm not suggesting anything." Jack held his hands up.

"What do you think it could be?" I asked James. "Does *anyone* have any ideas?"

"A bunch of lunatic teenagers," Katie suggested. "So let me get it right. Is this troop of horsemen supposed to ride about in diamond-patterned, natty little outfits? Oh, this is where I miss my PC and broadband."

"Sorry, folks, I've told you all I know," Jack said. "But what about the library in the study? If the owner of this house was interested in harlequins, there may be some books there."

"I'm going to have a look." I stood up. Jack came to help me, and gradually everyone joined us in the study, leaving Molly and Alice to get on with their work. The bookshelves in the study yielded an amazing amount of literature on the subject. We gathered the books together and took them to the dining room table.

CHAPTER NINE

The Camerons

Katie and I left around one o'clock, leaving the others to do the harlequin research and to face whatever the night might bring. The roadworks on the way home were horrendous. A traffic jam stretched all the way from Stirling to Cumbernauld, but it didn't matter. I was so glad to have the familiarity of my home around me again.

The house seemed small and cosy after Lanshoud. Katie stayed the night at my house, then in the morning, she went home to her flat in Glasgow to collect some clothes and pop in on Rebecca, who was shop minding and would flat mind too, if asked. We had decided while driving down from Stonehaven that although we were home, we had both been so shaken by the events at Lanshoud that we would rather stick together. Katie would stay in the spare room till we went back to Lanshoud. At ten o'clock I phoned Gill to make sure the police had arrived.

"Are you all right? Is everything OK there? You really don't mind us leaving, do you?"

"Chill, chill, there are two policemen here, so I am a damsel in distress with four hunks. I haven't been this lucky in years. Give me a break; don't worry about me, Worry about them."

When I finally put the phone down, I turned to Katie, laughing. "She says the only problem she has is that if someone bangs on the door tonight, she won't know which arms to jump into."

That was the first night I had slept well since Paul died. Gill phoned in the morning to report the fact that the inconsiderate perpetrators of the door banging had deprived her of her chance to test which of her guardians had the best muscle and hadn't even had the decency to rattle a window overnight. And as for those policemen, well, they had left looking at them sympathetically and patronisingly reminding them to phone if there was any other disturbance. "It was just all so annoying."

It didn't annoy me; I was glad all had been quiet at Lanshoud. Long may it last.

I woke refreshed the next morning. Katie made bacon and eggs while I looked for my birth and marriage certificates, but I simply couldn't find them. I tried to remember the last time I had seen them, and I remembered it had been around the time of the funeral.

"So the last time you saw them was at the funeral, and Paul's aunt and uncle had them. Is that right?"

"Yes they registered the death and I can't remember if they gave them back."

"Well, phone them and ask. Maybe they still have them."

It was a bit early, so we finished breakfast, and at ten o'clock I dialed the number written in the leather phone book. A woman answered.

"Hello." It was a bad line, and her voice crackled.

"Hello, Gwen?"

"No I'm sorry, you have the wrong number."

I thought I had misdialed, so I apologised, hung up, dialed again, and got the same woman. "I'm sorry to bother you, but I am looking for Gwen or George Cameron, and this is the telephone number I have for them." I checked my address book again. It was the correct number.

"I am sorry, dear, you have the wrong number." The voice was elderly.

"Is this Woodsman Cottage? I have actually spoken to them at this number, two or three times."

"I'm sorry I can't help you. This is not Woodsman Cottage. I have lived here in this house for fifty years, and I don't know anyone of that name."

I persisted. "Do you know Woodsman Cottage?"

"There is no Woodsman Cottage around here." A note of annoyance was creeping in. "Why don't you try the operator?" She put the phone down.

Puzzled, I turned to Katie. "It's the wrong number. I don't get it. That is the number Gwen gave me."

"Try directory enquiries. See if they can help."

I did and they couldn't. They had no one of that name in the Inverness directory, nor did they have a number listed for the address Gwen Cameron had given me. Katie suggested Google Earth and sat down in front of my laptop, which lay open on the kitchen table, and within seconds the planet Earth was blossoming onscreen. Katie focused down on Scotland, Inverness, and then typed in the cottage address the Camerons had given me. With a sinking heart, I watched as she dragged the pegman down to street view and the cottage, or what was left of it, was revealed: a caved-in roof with weeds growing up past the doorstep, no windows, front door open and hanging off its hinges, overgrown gardens, and a crumbling wall. It was a ruin that no one had lived in for a long, long time.

My head was reeling. I sank into the chair beside Katie. "It doesn't make sense. There is no other cottage of that name, is there?"

Katie, frowning, shook her head. "It would have come up in the address pane. They have obviously been lying to you." She pondered for a moment. "You said you didn't know they existed before the funeral. Paul never mentioned them?"

"No. They turned up out of the blue the night after Paul drowned."

"So they came to that funeral for what? Possibly to steal your birth certificate and marriage lines?"

"It's starting to look like it. My God, they were so plausible. I can't believe it." Then I had a dawning realisation "It has something to do with the will, hasn't it?"

She sighed audibly. "Looks like it, unless you can think of some other reason."

I thought for a moment. "I will be able to get copies, though."

"Yes, where your birth was registered, and that was…Holland?" she corrected herself. "The Netherlands?"

"You were right the first time, I was born in Holland. Holland is only part of the Netherlands, though most people call the whole of the Netherlands Holland. My father told me the Dutch people who live in the other parts don't like it. He said it was a bit like coming from Britain, being Scots but being called English when you're abroad. I was born in Delfshaven, which is suburb of Rotterdam. Rotterdam, Amsterdam, and The Hague are all in Holland. I have never been there. I thought about it often, but my father could never be persuaded, and I felt bad going without him, so I only know what little he told me."

Katie was talking to me but typing at the same time. "Right here it is. You have to apply by sending a letter or fax with a copy of a valid ID to: Publiekszaken Rotterdam, PO Box 70013 3000 KR Rotterdam, and it says here it takes four to five weeks to process."

"Too long." I sat back in my chair. "Maybe I should just go and collect it. I wonder how long that would take. Anyway, I would quite like to see where I was born."

"You mean go now?" Katie smiled at the idea.

"Why not? If the rest will hold the fort at Lanshoud...only I have James's car. We would need to take it back first."

Katie was typing away as I spoke.

"Guess what? There are flights direct from Dyce Airport in Aberdeen to Schiphol in Amsterdam. How handy is that?"

"Perfect."

There was not much point in going over the weekend. In all likelihood the Dutch Municipal building would be closed, so it was better to wait till Monday. There was a lot to sort out, such as who would come with me? I really didn't want to go alone. How long would we need to stay? How far was it from Rotterdam to Amsterdam, and how would we get there? I kept forgetting that money was no longer an issue in my life. We took what we needed—clothes and suchlike—and I took a few personal things like the frame with our wedding photo in it. I locked up the house, and we left around two in the afternoon. It took just over three hours because we stopped for a McDonald's on the way. The others were out for a walk in the woods when we arrived, and Molly was pleased to tell us that the two new cars had been delivered and were in the garage.

CHAPTER TEN

....

The Hunt

The weather took a turn for the worse that evening. We had all considered going for a walk, but it started raining and the wind was building up, causing the tall conifers around the house to bend and sway. Gill wasn't dressed for walking anyway; she seemed to be in a party mood and was little overdressed in a figure-hugging, red jersey dress. We congregated in the study as usual, listening to the increasingly wild weather outside, but it was cosy in the study, and we relaxed sitting in the height of summer in front of a blazing coal fire, in this house that seemed to me to be perpetually cold.

Gill flirted outrageously with both men. She just couldn't help herself. The interesting thing was that Jack seemed slightly annoyed at James rather than Gill. Not so much that he said anything, just that he was a little dry. I remember thinking that he had better get used to it because flirting to Gill was like a duck to water, and she was never going to change. She sat on the sofa beside James, and every time she spoke, she stressed what she wanted to say by putting her hand on his arm and leaning closer to ask his opinion. The moves were not lost on Jack—or anyone else, for that matter.

"So did you find out any more about harlequins?" I asked, hoping to relieve what from experience with Gill I knew might develop into a situation.

Jack relaxed back in his chair. "Yes, loads. They turn up everywhere in European myths. The legends of the Wild Hunt stretch back into the distant past." He drawled a little as he spoke, and I could see he was in his element, settling back to tell a story, something he was very good at and which, I have to say, I felt a little relieved about, as it distracted everyone from Gill's antics. "The version of the story depends on when and where it originated because the little nuances in the legends are always very particular to the local people who are abducted or taken by the hunt. Depending on the area, it would be the villain or sometimes the local hero being snatched, always at night, usually in a storm, and cursed to forever ride with the hunt. In every version of the story, there are dogs and horses, always black, always with red, fiery eyes. In Denmark, Norway, and Sweden, it was called Odin's Hunt. In Germany, the Wild Hunt was said to be the souls of dead warriors riding to Valhalla. In modern Germany the Wild Hunt is also known as the Wild Army and is still re-enacted today. In England there are numerous accounts, some linked to King Arthur. In some the dead Arthur is said to be the master of the hunt." He indicated the bookshelves lining the room at his back. "There are plenty of resources in this library, for instance." He reached round and lifted a book lying among others on the tea table.

"This is *The Anglo-Saxon Chronicle* by G. N. Garmonsway." He read:

"The huntsmen were black, huge, and hideous, and rode on black horses and on black he-goats, and their hounds were jet black, with eyes like saucers, and horrible. This was seen in the very deer park of the town of Peterborough, and in all the woods that stretch from that same town to Stamford, and in the night the monks heard them sounding and winding their horns."

Jack's voice was deep and melodic, hypnotising almost. I nestled down in my chair. I could listen to him all day. I imagined he must be a delight to the history students.

"Regardless of the source of the legend, there is a common theme of ghostly hunters arriving in the night, stealing men and women to forever ride with them and sometimes throwing grisly body parts to travelers unfortunate enough to come across them."

"I found this," Gill said, leaning across James to pick up a magazine that she could have asked him to pass to her. "It's in an issue of *Mountain Thunder*." She read:

"A great noise of barking and shouting is heard; then a black rider on a black, white, or gray horse, storming through the air with his hounds, followed by a host of strange spirits, is seen. The rider is sometimes headless. Sometimes, particularly in Upper Germany, the spirits show signs of battle wounds or death by other forms of mischance. Fire spurts from the hooves and eyes of the beasts in the procession.

"You know, as I was reading this stuff, it reminded me of The Nasgul in *The Lord of the Rings*. I wonder if Tolkien got his idea from the wild hunt in mythology." She passed the magazine to Jack.

James took a folded sheet from his pocket, an A4 sheet he had scribbled on. "The hunt is recorded in Welsh mythology. In Wales, the huntsman is Gwynn Ap Nudd, the Lord of the Dead. Then there's Hern the Hunter in Windsor Forrest, and in France, of course, La Mesnee d'Hellequin. The name is thought to originate from the Norse goddess of death, Hel. All I could find in Scotland is the legend of an Arthur O'Bower and the Unseelie Court. I found an old Scottish rhyme:

> "Arthur O'Bower has broken his bands
> And he's come roaring owre the lands
> The King a' Scots and a' his power
> Canna turn Arthur O'Bower."

"What's the Unseelie Court?" I asked, fascinated.

"The opposite of Seelie. Apparently the Seelie were the good fairies of Scots and Irish mythology. Sometimes called the 'Blessed Ones,' the Seelie were seen riding the night air, visions of beauty and light. They were the helpful fairies. The Unseelie, however, were the stuff of nightmares, frightening and even dangerous. It seems to be a deeply rooted part of both Irish and Scots mythology, where the Seelie court was considered to be holy and blessed, and the Unseelie court was described as unholy and damned. The similarity is that in all accounts, the wild hunt exists for the chase. It is capable of following its prey anywhere, even across the sea. In Celtic mythology the hunt is tireless, hounding their prey until they catch it, never losing the scent, able to track over solid stone, or running water, spreading terror as they ride."

"Charming," Gill said languorously, leaning back on the sofa beside James. I could see he was conscious of what she was doing and a little uncomfortable.

"The hunt crops up just about everywhere. There is even some stuff in American literature, but that is thought to have originated in campfire tales told by immigrants from Europe. " James leaned over, easing himself away from Gill, reaching for the wine bottle.

"But apart from the Mesnee d'Heleqinn, how does any of that connect to the harlequins?" I asked.

Jack answered. "The Helequinn riders were associated with death. The creature that led the pack had a black face, thought to be because it came from the bowels of the earth and had been singed black by the fires of hell. In mediaeval times this costume was said to be made of human skin. Today, the patterned suit has turned into something much more innocent, patches cotton or silk in bright colours."

"But not all the harlequins in this house have black faces. The one in the painting by Cezanne is white," I said.

"That's just a more modern interpretation of the old black-faced harlequin," Jack said.

"Sounds like a modern interpretation of my erstwhile mother-in-law," Katie said, lightening the mood. She had been sitting on the sofa, her legs curled underneath her, raptly listening to the discourse. She rubbed her arms. "Is it just me, or does anyone else think it's getting cold in here?" She got up and looked out of the window at the wind and rain. "I'll bank up this fire," she said, shoveling the coal from the brass scuttle that sat by the hearth.

James leaned forward on the sofa and pointed to the scuttle. "Look at the moulding on the coal scuttle another harlequin." Now that he had pointed it out, it was easy to see the eyes and the nose of the clown-like face.

"There is a real chill in the air tonight," Gill said. "James, can I borrow this? You don't mind, do you?" She lifted James's sweater lying over the arm of the sofa and stretched it over her body. James, polite as ever, appeared blissfully unaware that it was all part of the seduction. "This house is always cold, Erica. You might want to consider spending some of your millions on a central heating upgrade. Listen to that wind," she said, snuggling under the sweater.

"You might want to consider wearing a little more clothes," Jack said dryly.

"Now, darling, I thought you said less is more?" She smiled a mocking smile at him.

The wind and rain battered against the study window. "It's getting wild out there," I said, getting up to have a look. But as usual, it was turning dark outside and I could not see a thing.

The talk turned to the proposed trip to Rotterdam, and as Katie shoveled more coal onto the dying fire, she complained. "It is incredible to think this is July." I felt it too, a creeping coldness around my ankles. We sat together tossing ideas around and working out details. Inevitably Gill and Katie were going to accompany me to the Netherlands, and Jack was coming along for the ride, since he had never been there and was enjoying the long university holidays. James, however, was going back to work. The four of us would fly to Schiphiol and take the train to Rotterdam, book into a hotel, and take it from there.

After dinner that evening, we gathered again in the study. The rain had stopped at last, and the storm had calmed a little. Around eleven James yawned; the warmth from the fire was making me sleepy too. I had just decided to say goodnight when I heard it—a light tap on the study window. I wasn't sure at first; it could just have been rain again, though I instinctively knew it wasn't. I caught James's eye. He was sitting still, apprehensive, listening. The others were still chatting about Holland. Tap tap tap, tap tap, it was getting louder and faster, and now everyone had stopped talking, listening, still, no one moved, no one acknowledged the sounds, and I could feel my heart thumping in my chest.

Jack and James stood up and headed for the window. I forced myself to stand, and with wooden footsteps, I followed them. They stopped, and I stepped between them. I couldn't see anything at first. I put my hand on the window, trying to peer out into the darkness. The glass was freezing, and I felt the cold seep into my flesh. I pulled my hand away, feeling a subzero chill begin to spread through my body. I turned away, saw the men were transfixed, and turned back to the window. With a dawning horror, I saw what they saw and backed away, my stomach clenching in icy cold fear; eyes, eyes everywhere; large, unblinking red eyes, malevolent in a mist of darkness, floating in a deep blackness that the moon could not penetrate.

The longer I stared, the more silhouettes I could see, grey shapes against the black, of riders on huge horses. High-pitched shrieks of dogs or wolves pierced the night air, sending shudders through my body. I was paralised with fear. In my terror I felt they were looking at me, just me, all those eyes piercing through me to my very soul, pulling, drawing me to the window. Suddenly James grabbed my arm and pulled me away, pushing me behind him as, backs to the door, we stood cowering, all aware that what stamped and howled outside the study window was not human. The lights went out, and only the firelight guided us to the door and into the hall. The hammering started on doors and windows, and we groped our way upstairs, hanging on to each other away from the onslaught. There we huddled together on the landing, shivering, listening to the raging force outside as it battered doors and windows seeking entrance.

For what seemed like hours, but in reality was probably no more than twenty minutes, we heard the horses' hooves as they thundered round and round the house. I'm not sure when it became just the wind and rain again, but at some point I realised that the faint howling was just the wind in the trees.

"I think they have gone," Jack said. "C'mon, we stay together tonight."

We stayed in my room again, wrapped in duvets at the fire, taking it in shifts to sleep until dawn.

In the morning, disheveled and exhausted, we gathered in the kitchen. We made breakfast and the men checked outside, but as before, there was no sign at all of the night riders.

"There is no point in phoning the police, is there?" I asked. "They weren't interested last time." Everyone had the same opinion. It would be pointless; we couldn't prove anything, and they would put it down as another case of mass hysteria.

I was acutely aware that we had spent the night from hell, and these people sitting round the table had no reason to stay in this house, nothing to gain—this was my house, my life, my problem. I shared what I was thinking, but no one was prepared to leave me to deal with it alone. Their reasons were different. Gill and Katie were not prepared to leave me in times of trouble. Jack said he had nothing else to do for the summer, and he was intrigued by all of this. And James said smooth transition of the estate management was part of his remit, though his senior partners might see dealing with the paranormal as stretching it a bit.

"I will see it through, though the firm, I suspect, will charge you."

My relief was overwhelming. You can be rich in more important ways than financial, and sometimes not having family isn't the worst thing in the world. Friends like these can often mean more.

Jack was thoughtful. "Your mention of the paranormal has given me an idea. I have a colleague in the Psychology Department who works with some colleagues in Edinburgh who do research in parapsychology, and this is right up their street. Would you like me to give them a call and see if they can help?" He searched his diary for the number. Nobody had a mobile signal deep in these woods. It seemed to be a blind spot for all networks.

"What ghost hunters?" I laughed. "Actually, I don't know why I am laughing," I said, remembering last night. "Yes of course, I have nothing to lose—that is, unless whoever they are manage to scare me so much that I walk away. Then I will lose it all, the house and every penny." I felt a surge of anger. "No, go ahead, Jack. You know what? If they are trying to drive me out, they will have to try harder." I had a sudden thought. "James, supposing they did drive me out. Who would then inherit?"

"Obviously you're thinking whoever would inherit is the person who is trying to drive you out. Well, it would revert back to the original solicitors who set it up, so only they would know that, and they may not be willing to divulge that information, as it would reveal the identity of the benefactor. But I can certainly try to find out. I'll phone the office and set someone onto it."

Molly and Alice arrived as we were finishing breakfast. Jack and James had left to make the calls and the others to get dressed; I sat sipping another cup of tea. The windows that stretched the length of the kitchen let in lots of light, and the morning sunshine streamed in, making it pleasantly warm.

"Was everything OK last night?" Molly asked as she tied on her apron.

"What do you mean?" I asked, wondering how much she knew.

"The storm. Don't tell me you all managed to sleep through it."

"The storm, the storm," Alice said, wide-eyed, smiling insanely, and nodding her head vigorously. She seemed more agitated than usual.

"Alice is afraid of the thunder. I have to take her into my bed just as I did when she was little," Molly said, patting Alice's shoulder. "If you don't mind my saying so, you don't look as though you slept well." She looked at me questioningly.

"No one slept well," I replied. "It was pretty bad." Which was an understatement, but I was reluctant to tell her about the night before. In the cold light of day, it sounded crazy. "Our lights went out in the middle of the storm, but they seem to be fine this morning."

"Yes, there was a power cut in the whole area, but there is a generator in the cellar. I'll get Caleb to pop over and show you how to operate it. I'll just start with the Hoover then, unless there is anything particular you want me to do."

"No, that's fine, Molly. Thank you."

Molly guided Alice to the sink. "You start with the dishes, dear, and then tidy the sink. OK, my love?"

"OK, OK." The child-woman nodded her head up and down frantically and watched as her mother left the kitchen.

I tried to chat to Alice. "So were you very afraid of the storm last night, Alice? I was scared too."

She didn't answer; she was scrubbing something at the sink in that frantic way she did things.

I tried again. "Alice, does the thunder frighten you?"

Suddenly she put her hands over her ears and started rocking. "Hate thunder, hate thunder." Faster and faster she rocked, the water and soapsuds running down her face. "Hate thunder, hate thunder, hate horses," she screamed.

Alarmed, I got up and put my arm round her, "Alice, it's OK." She was rigid, her body hard, caught in a rhythmic, spasmodic rocking, crying and pulling at her clothes.

"Alice, Alice, it's OK, Alice." She howled louder and louder, repeating her own name over and over.

"Alice, enough now." Molly's voice thundered from the door. She moved quickly and put her hands over Alice's and pulled them away from her ears. "Enough, Alice." She forced Alice's chin up to look into her eyes and more softly said, "Enough now, love."

The shudders running though Alice's body gradually lessened under her mother's calming influence. "What happened?" Molly asked me.

"Nothing, really," I replied, feeling guilty for some bizarre reason. "I just asked her about the storm, that's all."

Molly brought Alice to the table to sit. "She hasn't done that for such a long time."

"She said something about horses."

"Horses?" Molly wrinkled her brow, and Alice looked up at me.

Molly didn't look up. "Oh she is certainly afraid of thunder, but horses… you probably misheard her; it can be very disquieting when she has a turn."

She was lying. I knew she was lying, and instinctively I knew she did not want to discuss it. I didn't want to upset her, so I didn't argue.

Molly changed the subject. "Oh, Lucy met Karen, Lizzie McIntosh's daughter at the school, and explained about you wanting a word. Karen said she is bringing her over for a couple of days to take her shopping and said she would phone you. She thinks it might be good for her mum to see Lanshoud again."

"Thanks, Molly. That might be a step forward."

Jack came back with good news. Nathan Findlay and his team were prepared to help, and they could come on Tuesday. Jack asked if that was OK with me, and I said of course it was. I had an idea.

"Why don't we all go to Amsterdam for the weekend?"

CHAPTER ELEVEN

Rotterdam

Because we were anxious to be back for the University team arriving on Tuesday, we booked five seats that day on the 4:35 p.m. Aberdeen, Dyce to Schiphol, Amsterdam, which would bring us into Amsterdam at 17:05, and the return flight would bring us home at 10:15 a.m. on Monday morning. Schiphol Airport was closer to Rotterdam than Amsterdam, and it would take only twenty minutes to reach the city on the high-speed train.

We booked into a hotel near the railway station. I had a lovely, spacious corner room. There was a large picture window and window seat for me to look out, and here I hoped to get my first impression of the city where I was born. Unfortunately the view was of the railway station and tram terminal, but I could not complain because I had chosen the hotel specifically for its proximity to transport connections. James had a word with the hotel management and secured us the services of the guide and interpreter Roos de Foor, who met us over breakfast on Friday morning.

Roos was a large, solidly built girl, young, energetic, with all the enthusiasm for her country that almost always comes with the holiday tour guide. She talked incessantly from the moment we left the hotel in the minibus that James had also organised, so that by the time we reached Delfshaven, we were fully educated on tea shops, the Red Light District, windmills, cheese, wooden shoes, bikes, and miscellaneous Dutch traditions. She included of course the Dutch people themselves, their history, habits, how they eat, drink, think, and live. She suggested we taste liquorice; a stroopwafel, a sort of syrup waffle; herring; a nice glass of liquor or Dutch gin; and of course the cheeses.

Roos was enthusiasm personified. We left the others at her personally recommended best teashop in the area, and Roos and I went to Delfshaven City Hall. Roos explained in Dutch to the very friendly lady clerk that I required a copy of my birth certificate. The clerk took my passport as ID, and while we waited, she searched the database.

About fifteen minutes later, she told us my birth had not been registered in Delfshaven. The pleasant older woman, oozing sympathy based on whatever Roos had told her, also searched online to see if my birth record was held in the City of Rotterdam. She finally spoke to me in Dutch with a painful expression on her face, and it was not difficult to understand that she was telling me that there was no record of my birth or that of my father anywhere in the Netherlands. Through Roos I protested there had to be some mistake. I told the woman I was born in Delfshaven and been taken to Scotland when I was three months old and I had a Dutch birth certificate, which I last used when my husband registered our marriage in Glasgow.

"There is no mistake, I think," she said pityingly. "Your father's details—you see there is also no one in the Dutch registers of that name and date of birth, neither are there any records of the marriage of your mother and father. I am so sorry I cannot help you. Perhaps if you knew where they were married, a church or a civil ceremony, that place may hold a record."

I turned to Roos. "My mother told me they were married in Laurenskerk Church in fact; I noticed it on a tourist guide at the airport." I had remembered it when driving to Lanshoud for the first time with Gill and Katie. I had noticed the signpost for Laurencekirk and remembered my mother telling me about St Laurenskerk in Rotterdam.

She nodded. "Yes, the Grote Kerk, in Rotterdam. When were they married?"

"In nineteen sixty-five and my father would be seventy if he were alive now."

"Then they could not have been married there," Roos said. "It is one of only a few buildings that survived the Blitz during the Second World War and is one of the oldest buildings in the city. The church was heavily damaged during the bombings of 1940; only the tower and most parts of the outer walls were left standing, and the reconstruction was only finished in 1968. Today it's a concert venue. The yearly Bevrijdingsdag ceremony, to celebrate the liberation from Nazi Germany on May the fifth, 1945, is held here." She looked at me closely and said kindly, "It is unlikely it was there they were married."

The clerk spoke again, and Roos said, "Your passport, Erica, she points out, if they took you out of the country, you would have had a Dutch passport. Your passport now is British. The British authorities may have some details."

"Yes." I nodded, dismayed by the dead-end. I thanked the clerk for her help.

We stepped out into the brilliant sunshine, and again the old surges of anxiety were making me feel dizzy.

"We should join the others, yes?" Roos guided me toward the teahouse.

What we had seen of Rotterdam was mostly industrial and modern, but Delfshaven, a suburb of Rotterdam, was more what I expected Holland to be like, being a little more picturesque, with pretty houses, canals, and fishing boats. Roos became the tour guide again, telling me the Harbour was the one from which the Pilgrim fathers set sail in 1620 before going to England, where they changed ship to the larger Mayflower and that the Oude Kerk, which was the church near the teahouse where we had left the others, was the last place they had prayed together in Holland before setting sail. She pointed out the eighteenth-century windmill that still ground flour. She was so passionate in her love of her country that I tried to appear interested, but my head was still reeling from the latest revelations.

Katie looked up as we reached the table. "So did you get it?"

I shook my head and sat down beside them. Roos ordered tea and cake, and I told them what I now knew of the missing documents.

"Where were you actually born?" James asked. "Was it a maternity hospital?"

"No, I was born at home, delivered by the local midwife, but there would still be a birth certificate."

"Yes," Roos said. "The midwife would give your parents a notice of birth, which your father would take to register your birth, but perhaps for some reason he did not do so." She thought for a moment. "Yet they would have needed one to get a passport for you. To take you as a baby from the Netherlands, they would have needed a passport."

"So," Gill said, "if you could get access to the midwifery records?"

"I will find out." Roos left the table to make some calls.

I felt so lost and confused, as if I didn't know who I was anymore—this rich widow sitting in the sunshine with the sound of church bells and bicycle bells, the little boats on the canals, my friends sipping tea in a Dutch tea house. I was a million light years away from the woman who nipped into the Tesco store at Craigmarloch after work, to pick up something quick for dinner, the woman who knew who she was.

Roos came back. She clapped her hands, delighted to impart the news. "It is unbelievable. The midwife, who delivered the babies in Delfshaven, when you were born, still lives in the same house. We may go to see her, but not until Monday, I am afraid. She is at her daughter's and will not be back until then. Her son lives at the same house, and he said she kept her own records of every baby she ever delivered."

"Thank you, but that's no use. We go home on Monday," I said.

"Change the flights. I will go back and meet Nathan Findlay," Jack offered. "You stay and sort out the midwife."

"Why don't I stay with you?" James offered. "The others can keep the scheduled flights. It will be easier to change just two seats."

Gill raised her eyebrows and gave me a knowing look. "Sound like a plan to me."

On Monday after the others had left for the airport, James, Roos, and I drove to Delfshaven to the home of Maartje Hartevelt. Her son greeted us and showed us into the room where the elderly lady sat on a chair beside the window. She did not smile or acknowledge our entrance in any way, but sat looking at the floor. She was dressed all in black, and her white hair was neatly braided and wound around her head. Her face was round and soft and had few wrinkles, but when she raised her head, I found myself being scrutinised by the most piercing blue eyes. I handed her the bouquet of flowers that we had brought for her. She took them and smiled. She smelled their fragrance and thanked me.

"*Mevrouv Hartevelt, dank u voor het zien van ons Ik whave komen om te vragen voor uw hulp*," I asked carefully for her help in the few Dutch words I had learned over the weekend. I wanted to make the effort but since that was the extent of my Dutch, Roos took over. With Roos translating, I explained that I was trying to find a record of where I was born and had been told that it was on this date, in Delfshaven. I handed her a slip of paper with the date and my parents' names, and I explained that my birth certificate had been lost and I had been unable to obtain a copy from the authorities. The old lady picked up spectacles lying on the small round table beside her and looked at the date; she told us that she had kept a record of every baby she had ever delivered. A large ledger-type book also lay on the table. She reached over, struggling to lift the book. Roos knelt down beside her to help, and together they found the only entry of a birth that matched my details. The only baby Maartje Hartevelt delivered that week was a baby girl born to a nineteen-year-old French girl called Marianne Belliere.

"Roos, tell her please that I don't expect her to remember the birth, but if there is anything she can remember, I would be very grateful."

Roos translated. "She says to the contrary, she remembers that particular birth very well."

For a few moments Mevrouv Hartevelt was silent. She tilted her chin and gazed out of the window as though she were daydreaming. When she spoke, it was to me, and Roos kept pace with her.

"I was midwife in Delfshaven for thirty years. Over half of the deliveries in my journal were domiciliary, the rest were hospital. I provided antenatal and postnatal care for all of them. The ones who still live here I remember. The others I have forgotten, but the French girl was different. I remember her very well.

"I was called in the middle of the night to a hotel where a young girl had gone into labour. She delivered twenty minutes after I arrived. She was a tourist traveling with her parents. The baby, they said, was four weeks premature. She had gone into labour in the car, and they had no idea where the hospital was. They saw the hotel and took her there, and the staff called me. I arrived just in time. The birth was uneventful, and the baby was a good weight and healthy, but I explained she should be checked at the local hospital. The mother refused. I was not happy because I knew nothing of her medical history, so I left her to get some sleep and said I would return in the morning. In the morning they had gone, left before dawn. The night porter had not seen them leave and did not know how he could have missed them. He was very anxious to reassure me that he had not been asleep, yet he had seen no one. We called the police, but in the excitement they had not registered, so the hotel staff had no passports or record of the registration number of the car. In fact no one had even seen the car. The police never found them; there was no trace of them or the baby."

James asked if Mervrou Heartfeldt had given the child's mother a notice of birth before leaving the hotel that night. She said she was very thorough and would never leave without doing so. James turned to me. "Then the birth could be registered under another name. You need to go back to Delfshaven City Hall. They would have had to get a birth certificate in order to take the baby out of the country."

I asked one more question: "Did you know the baby's name?" She looked at me kindly.

"No, I am sorry. The mother had not named her yet."

We took our leave, thanking her profusely for her help. I was very touched when she asked if she might give me a parting kiss on the cheek. She said she just knew I was one of her babies. Now at least I had a name and an address to go on, and maybe I was Marianne Belliere's baby, and maybe, just maybe, my name was not Erica. As we were leaving, Mevrouv Hartevelt stopped Roos. She said something else that was strange about that birth, about the girl's parents. The girl was French, and the mother seemed more English than French and seemed very young to be the girl's mother. When she, Mevrouv Hartevelt, had asked, she was told the mother had lived in the UK for many years. The father, however, was Dutch.

The same clerk was on duty, and again she searched the database. This time she came up trumps. "Camille Belliere, born to Marianne Belliere. Yes, there is a record here."

"Is there a father listed?"

"No, I am afraid not."

"Is there a place of residence?

"The residence is given as 2 Rue de Fleur, Lyons-la-Foret, Normandy, France. She explained that she could not give me a copy of the birth certificate. For that I needed proof of identity and relationship since the birth in question was under forty years ago."

I turned to James. "So what can I do now?" I wasn't actually asking him; I was just thinking out loud.

"Normandy maybe, to the address Marianne Belliere gave. Look, Erica, you don't even know if that baby was you."

At least I had a name and an address to go on, and maybe, just maybe I was Marianne Belliere's baby.

CHAPTER TWELVE

Lizzie McIntosh

James and I flew back to Aberdeen on Wednesday morning. We recovered our bags from the carousel, cleared customs, and walked into the arrival hall to find Gill waiting for us. Delighted to see us, she gave me a hug, and obviously not wishing to leave James out, treated him to one that lasted just that second or two longer than necessary. He grimaced over her shoulder, so I guessed he wasn't enjoying it—which I have to say was unusual, as most men, I had observed, quite liked Gill draping herself over them. She was incorrigible, but I was glad to see her too.

The weather in Aberdeen was awful. Gill drove carefully through the deluge while the windscreen wipers struggled to cope with the sheets of rain that poured down from a dark sky. She told us about the parapsychology team and how they had set up their equipment and kept watch all night but had not heard even a mouse squeak. I was both happy that there had been no return of the night riders, but I was equally disappointed that these people had come all the way from Edinburgh for nothing.

We told Gill all about the meeting with Mevrouv Maartje Heartfeldt.

"So what are you saying? That baby might have been you?" She turned to look at me.

James, in the back seat, called out to her. "Gill, watch the road. There's some sheep there."

Just in time—as one of them chose to wander in front of the car—Gill put her foot on the brake and crawled behind the five sheep, who in the custom of sheep, instead of going back to the verge, ran up the middle of the road in front of the car, forcing Gill to reduce her speed to five miles an hour.

"It's a possibility I can't rule out. I might have to face the fact I am not who I think I am. The hardest thing to believe is that my mother and father, who brought me up, who gave me everything, and whom I grieved for, were not my real parents."

"But you don't know that for sure," Gill said in a sympathetic tone.

"I think," James said, "Erica has to consider it as a possibility." He paused. "There are some undeniable facts. For instance, she has been told categorically by the people who brought her up that she was born in Delfshaven, in Rotterdam. Her birth certificate, forged or otherwise, was Dutch. It would have been easier to change the baby and the mother's name than to forge the whole certificate.

"There is also the fact her marriage certificate has disappeared, last seen in the possession of a couple who equally cannot be traced. She has been left a fortune by an unknown benefactor, and to cap it all, someone is trying to scare the living daylights out of her. Adding some sort of caretaker parents to that would be in keeping, don't you think?"

The sheep finally decided to make for an open gate and left the road, allowing Gill to speed up.

"So how on earth could you find out?" Gill mused, watching the road.

"We could get a DNA sample," James said.

"DNA? You mean ask the police to be involved?" I asked.

"They are involved already, but now with money no object, there will be some lab willing to do it for you," James said. "Were your parents buried or cremated?"

"Buried."

"Well, you would need a court order anyway to exhume the bodies. DNA evidence is becoming an increasingly popular means of resolving probate disputes. With people leaving larger amounts of money in their wills and the level of relationships breaking up, the number of complex probate disputes has risen through the roof. It's not uncommon these days for DNA analysis to be used as a way of identifying family relationships."

"Couldn't I get it from hair samples?" I asked.

James was amused. "Why? Have you got hair samples?"

"I have a box of personal things." I tried to think. "I have my father's cap. He always wore it when it rained. It's how I will always remember him, and I have a silver hairbrush belonging to my mother. There might be hair in these things."

"I think it has to be a complete hair with follicle intact. I am sure broken hair is no use. The DNA, if I remember correctly, is only in the hair root. It shouldn't be a problem though. Standard DNA, paternity or maternity testing, usually involve testing mouth swab samples from the individuals to be tested, and these samples are collected at sampling appointments at GP surgeries. However, in cases where one of the parties who's DNA requires analysis is dead, collecting the samples is usually done from close personal objects belonging to the deceased. I have been involved in a case like that before. Our firm works with a company called Genocel; I'll phone them and find out what we need."

As the car turned into the gravel courtyard in front of Lanshoud, Katie, with a man at her side, appeared on the steps. James lifted the cases from the boot, and the man came over and lifted both cases.

"This is Caleb," Katie explained, giving me a hug.

"Hi, Caleb, nice to meet you at last."

Caleb, a big guy with the ruddy complexion that comes with working outdoors in all weathers, nodded a shy smile and carried the cases into the house.

Molly was in the hall to greet us, with Alice standing at her back wringing her hands. "Welcome home, Erica."

I had the strangest feeling that I was the lady of the manor returning home, when in fact, I had only been gone a few days from a home I hadn't even known existed a fortnight ago. There is no doubt in my mind now that truth is stranger than fiction.

Nathan Findlay and his crew were well settled in, and their monitoring equipment was everywhere. A lecturer in psychology with special interest in parapsychology, he was in his late forties, tall, and sandy haired and he wore round, wire-rimmed spectacles. His colleague, also a psychology lecturer, Jessica Alexander, was an older woman with grey hair. It was difficult to guess her age, but I thought late fifties. They had brought two students, Toshiro Wantanabe, known as Tosh, and Patrick Dempsey, Paddy to his friends, both so keen on their hobby of ghost hunting that they spent all their spare time on it.

Nathan shook my hand vigorously; he was obviously in his element and thanked me profusely for letting the team investigate. He said he had a good feeling that this might be the case they had been looking for, for years. He was as excited as a child on Christmas Eve and kept pushing his spectacles back up his nose, from where they descended of their own volition every five seconds.

When Jack introduced us, I felt the need to apologise for the fact they had had a fruitless watch the night before, but both Nathan and Jessica protested that they were the ones who needed to apologise, for littering "my lovely home" with their equipment.

They called it, my lovely home. That was the second time that morning Lanshoud had been called my home. Funny, but at that point, I still didn't think of Lanshoud as being my home. My clothes hung in the wardrobe, and I had scattered family photos and some personal things around the house, but they seemed out of place, and I even felt as though I was intruding in someone else's home.

Nathan and Jessica gave me a tour of the equipment. They had night vision video cameras, thermal imaging equipment, audio recorders, and extra sensitive microphones. There were wires, cables, and cameras everywhere, and a bank of monitors was set up in the dining room.

"Someone will man the monitors twenty-four hours a day." Nathan showed me which monitors were connected to which cameras. The cameras were pointing inside and outside the house.

"I hope this is all right with you. Jack assured us this is what you wanted, though your housekeeper was a bit put out by the mess," Jessica said.

"Oh, don't worry about Molly. She means well. I am very glad you are here, but I feel bad for you. You must have been disappointed. Gill told me that it was a quiet night last night."

Nathan shook his head. "Not at all, we are very glad to be here. Not everyone takes us seriously, I'm afraid, and yes, it was quiet, but that's not unusual. Spirit activity is not always a nightly occurrence."

"So you do think it could be some kind of spirit?" I felt silly even asking.

"Well, Jack and Katie certainly told us a tale, but we'll wait and see, shall we? Best to reserve judgment," Jessica answered.

"Presuming you believe the story Jack told you—and I feel it seems so outlandish in the cold light of day; the police, I think, were laughing all the way back to Stonehaven—but if, let's suppose there is something, why is it not every night?"

"That's not uncommon," Nathan said. "It's well documented that people have sat in for several nights on location before there is a manifestation, if at all."

At that point we were interrupted by the telephone. Katie answered and brought it to me, saying it was Karen Drennin. The name meant nothing to me, but it turned out to be Lizzie McIntosh's daughter. She was staying with Karen, who wondered if she could bring her over at some point. We agreed that two o'clock that afternoon would be convenient.

I went to arrange lunch for everyone, and I heard the laughter as I walked into the kitchen. Molly, Jack, and the Japanese student Tosh were howling with laughter, and Molly was wiping the tears away with the edge of her apron.

"Can I join the party?" I asked from the door.

"Oh, Erica, come and sort these two out. They are pulling my leg something terrible. They offered to help me make lunch, but they are just making a mess."

"Now we love cooking, woman; you would think you be grateful," Jack said. "My mother would be turning in her grave if she knew you didn't appreciate the culinary education she gave me. I do a mean toast and beans."

"Grateful? You're like a pair of small boys," Molly scolded. "Look at them stealing the scones before they are even cool. Now go away." She shooed then with a tea towel. "Get out of my kitchen, the two of you."

Tosh grinned happily, blowing on a scone Jack had tossed him, and Jack said, "We're going, we're going" as they backed out of the door, leaving Molly and I alone in the kitchen.

"They smell delicious." The aroma of hot scones cooling on the wire trays wafted upward and made my stomach grumble.

"Help yourself, dear," Molly said.

Lanshoud

"Thanks." I sliced the hot scone open, and my mouth watered as I spread the butter thickly and watched it melt. "Lizzie McIntosh is coming over after lunch."

"Oh, good, Karen got in touch then," she said, cutting large slices of ham from the bone.

"Yes, thanks for sorting that for me. Can I help? I'll butter the bread, shall I?"

I gathered bread and butter and started layering the sandwiches. There was no point in beating about the bush.

"Molly, the other day in the kitchen, you were obviously uncomfortable when I mentioned horses to Alice."

"Uncomfortable? I'm not sure what you mean." She looked at me as if she was surprised, and for a split second I doubted myself, but I decided to push on.

"I don't want to upset you, but it seemed to me that Alice reacted to my mention of horses."

She put the knife down and sighed, and then she looked at me as if deciding what to tell me. "I'm sorry I lied to you. It's been bothering me since. It's just that Alice gets so upset, and I tell her it's just her imagination. I'm only trying to protect her."

"Her imagination, so she has seen horses?"

Molly sat on a chair at the kitchen table "It was terrible. She used to scream for hours, imagining she had seen horses."

"Seen them where? Do you mean only here, at Lanshoud?"

"Yes, but she really only saw them once, and she was so frightened she had nightmares for months. It was awful. That's why we always leave here before dark."

"But you were with her. Did you look out the window? Did you see anything?"

"No, there weren't any horses; it was just a storm, a terrible storm. We had stayed behind changing the beds; we were taking dust sheets off furniture because I had been told a new owner would be arriving soon and that I might only have a day's notice. It had been overcast all day, and the storm started up so quickly. I decided we would be better to wait till it died down. I had always taught Alice not to be afraid of thunder and lightning. She was watching the rain out of the window, and she thought she saw horses. She was terrified, and it took weeks for her to settle down again. I'm really sorry. I didn't want you thinking Alice was unstable because she's not usually." Molly wiped her eyes.

"It's OK. I understand you didn't want me to think badly of Alice, and I don't," I hastened to reassure her.

Molly looked at me earnestly. "Tell me it's none of my business, but it's not hard to see there is something going on here. Tosh obviously thought I knew, and he told me he was a parapsychologist, a sort of ghost hunter, he explained, and the state you were all in the night after the storm. It wasn't just vandals, was it?"

"It may have been, Molly, though the police have not found any trace. It could also have been some elaborate hoax to get me out of here so that I lose the estate." The memory of that night came clearly into my mind again, the hellish eyes, the cold, the fear coursing through my body. "The reason I asked is because there were horses. We didn't see them, but we heard them."

"I see. Maybe I wasn't being fair to Alice. Maybe she did see something."

"I think maybe she did, and hopefully Dr. Findlay and his team will find out what it was she saw." I stood up and looked out the large kitchen window onto the peaceful gardens, where Caleb was digging in the borders. The rain had stopped, and it was turning into a lovely day. "C'mon, Molly, I'll give you a hand with the rest of lunch. Let's get these people fed."

Lizzie McIntosh and Karen arrived promptly at two o'clock. Lizzie was younger than I expected. She must have been in her late fifties, early sixties maybe. She was definitely younger than Molly and fashionably well groomed in a smart trouser suit. Alice brought us tea in the drawing room, and we chatted for a while about the ten years she had spent as housekeeper at Lanshoud.

Lizzie looked around the room. "Nothing has changed," she said, smiling. She was looking intently at my wedding photo on the mantelpiece. "May I?" she asked, standing to get a closer look.

"You were a beautiful bride," Karen said.

"Thank you. Unfortunately, my husband died six months ago."

"Oh, I am so sorry," Karen said. "I didn't realise"

There was an awkward silence. Lizzie said nothing and was still standing at the mantelpiece with her back to us. I thanked her for coming and was about to tell her why when Karen interrupted.

"Mrs. Cameron, I have to tell you that my mother is here under duress."

"Under duress, really? You didn't want to come here, Mrs. McIntosh? Why is that?" I looked at Lizzie, surprised. Lizzie was obviously annoyed at her daughter; I looked from one to the other. "I am sorry. I don't understand."

Lizzie turned to look at me. Her face was tense and her manner abrupt. "No, Mrs. Cameron, I don't expect you do, and Karen had no right to tell you that." She glowered at Karen. "It was a mistake to come here, and I would like to go now. I am sorry to have wasted your time." She put the photo back on the mantelpiece.

Karen was equally annoyed and raised her voice. "Oh, for God's sake, Mother, stop it; this has gone on long enough. Erica is the owner now. Are you going to live with these ridiculous fears for the rest of your life?"

She turned to me and said, in a softer, almost pleading tone, "My mother has had a phobia about this place for years. For a long time, she blankly refused to even drive down the Slug Road. If we were going to Stonehaven, she would go via the Netherly Road or not at all. You're asking to see her out of the blue was a godsend. It is the perfect way to sort this out once and for all."

"I'm sorry you feel like that, Mrs. McIntosh. In that case I am even more grateful to you for making the effort to come." I had butterflies in my stomach and a sense of excitement. She knew something, and I knew she did.

"Would you be willing to tell me what you were afraid of? You see, I asked you to come because my friends and I have had some unpleasant experiences associated with the house. Quite frightening, really."

Her expression was hostile, I thought. She looked at me long and hard. I held back a bit, telling her only that on more than one occasion we had heard noises in the night and tapping at the doors and window, and we thought there might have been intruders outside. I explained that it was so frightening we had called the police, but they had found nothing.

"Mother," Karen shook her head. "Tell her...please."

Lizzie looked at me as if still considering carefully whether to tell me anything.

"Please, Mrs. McIntosh. Tell me what happened to you."

She retorted sharply, "I'm sorry I can't help you. I have never heard any knocking, or any noises for that matter." She headed for the door.

Karen jumped up and blocked her exit.

"No, Mum. I am asking you, please, you can put this behind you."

I was frantically thinking of something to say that would stop her.

"Mrs. McIntosh, please don't leave like this." I stepped in front of the door so that she would look at me. I made a quick decision. I indicated the chair. "Please give me a few more moments, and I will tell you the whole story." She hesitated, and then sat down again.

I asked for their agreement that what I told them would be in strictest confidence. I didn't want Lanshoud to be the talking point of the whole area. I started with the day of the letter and glossed over inheriting the house, the unknown benefactor, and the night riders. They both listened intently, not interrupting me.

Lizzie remained silent through the whole story, and when I had finished, Karen pleaded with her again. Without looking at Karen, looking only at me, still unsmiling, she began to speak.

"I took this job after answering an advert in the local paper. In all the time I worked here, I dealt with the same man. His name was Stephen Roberts. He was a handsome young man, suave, sophisticated—an educated Scot I thought, immaculately dressed, never a hair out of place, a bit like a tailor's dummy. I asked him one day about the owner; he was charming, chatty, and he said the owner of Lanshoud was a very rich and powerful man, and he managed projects for him. He told me he was employed on a long-term project at the moment based near Glasgow. He laughed and said it had its moments, but it was very boring. It kept him busy, and it was difficult to travel far, so he couldn't get to Lanshoud very often. I heard him on the phone once, speaking to the owner. He called him Sir."

"Can you remember anything he said?"

"He spoke about a woman. He actually said..." She thought for a moment. "He said he was *keeping her very happy*. I would have said he was every girl's dream, but there was something about him I didn't like. Nothing I could put my finger on. I used to tell Karen about him, about how he gave me the creeps."

Karen nodded. "That's true. She did. She used to come home at night and say that he had been at the house again. Something not right about him, she would say. Nothing she could put her finger on; she was always saying he was just too good to be true."

Lizzie continued. "He called monthly in the summer, but sometimes it could be two or three months over the winter. He stayed overnight, I think, but he was always gone in the morning. There was one afternoon I had left my shopping bag in the kitchen. I hadn't gone very far, just as far as Durris, and I had meant to tell him about the problems I had had with the gas supplier, so I turned and went back. The front doors were locked, so I used the back door key and came in through the boot room.

"I saw the cellar door was open, and the lights were on. I called his name, and as I reached the door of the cellar, from the top of the stairs I saw him walk into the wine cellar. I called his name again, but he didn't hear me. I went down the stairs. I stopped at the entrance to the wine cellar and called him again. I thought maybe he was checking the stock, maybe concentrating, and didn't hear me. I looked between the wooden shelves, looked along the rows of bottles. It was freezing, really cold. I mean it's always cold in that cellar, always damp. I never liked having to go down there unless I absolutely had to. I wandered round to the back wall; it was so cold I was actually shivering. He wasn't there. I couldn't understand because he couldn't have passed me. There was no other way out, and there was a strange smell, so strong I thought I was going to vomit. It was a metallic smell like blood, but with decay or rot overriding it. I wondered about a dead rat or something, though there would have to be more than one to cause that stench. I felt dizzy, as though I would faint. Then I heard whispering. It got louder, lots of voices whispering, I couldn't make out what they were saying. It didn't sound like English. I couldn't make out where the whispering was coming from. It seemed to be all around me, but I couldn't see anyone. I was so afraid and shaking with cold, I was sick and frightened at I don't know what, but I managed to make my way upstairs and left without my bag. I got into the car, and my hands were shaking so much I couldn't get the key in the ignition. I was terrified, and I can't even tell you why. I drove home like a mad thing."

Karen moved over to sit beside her mother. She put a comforting arm around her shoulder.

"Did you ask him about it when you saw him again?" I asked.

"No. I never went back. I didn't want him to know I had even been back there that day. He didn't know I was there, and I had such a bad feeling about it I didn't want to tell him. I pleaded ill health and didn't even work out my notice."

"Have you ever seen him again?" I asked.

"Not until today," she said and looked up at my wedding photo. "The man you married is Stephen Roberts."

CHAPTER THIRTEEN

Jonah

I stood at the large drawing room window and watched the car turn out of the clearing and onto the lane. The taillights disappeared, and the last vestiges of Erica Cameron disappeared with them. I had nothing left to cling to, not even my memories, for they were nothing more than a sham. Holding myself together as best I could, I had grilled Lizzie McIntosh, and she held out under my grilling, describing more and more the man who had been my husband—his voice, his manner, his clothes, his car. There was not a shadow of a doubt in my mind that Stephen Roberts and Paul Cameron were one and the same man.

I had that feeling of panic again starting at the pit of my stomach. I had difficulty breathing, and the tears were rolling down my face. Standing rigid at the window, unable to move, finding it more and more difficult to breathe, I was gasping for air, and my heart was pounding. There was ringing in my ears. I felt dizzy and about to faint. I was swaying and falling into the familiar black hole when suddenly someone was pulling me, strong arms turning my head into a shoulder, calling my name, shaking me, shouting at me, telling me to breathe. I choked, gasped air into my lungs, and collapsed sobbing into James's arms.

"Erica, my God, what happened to you?" He held me against his shoulder, his hand stroking my hair.

I couldn't speak. My tears soaked his shirt, and for a few moments, he let me cry it out, saying nothing, just holding me. When I became calmer, he sat me down and poured a glass of Brandy. "Here, drink this, don't sip," he ordered. "Down in one." The liquid burned my throat, but I drank and almost immediately felt the warmth spread through me.

"Was it something to do with the old housekeeper and her daughter?" he asked softly, taking the glass from my trembling hands. "I saw them leave." He filled the glass again and put it back in my hand. "This time sip."

I leaned over and picked up the wedding photograph I had thrown across the floor. Through the shards of glass, I pointed with a trembling hand to the man who had been my husband. "Apparently the man I married is not Paul Cameron," I said, "but Stephen Roberts, the estate manager of Lanshoud." Through eyes blinded by tears, I told him all that Lizzie had told me, how she had described the characteristics and mannerisms of the man I had loved so much. There was no doubt in my mind that it was the same man, and the obvious conclusion was that I had been the "boring, time-consuming project in Glasgow." I was the woman who was being kept happy.

"Who am I, James? I don't know who I am; I don't know who anybody really is." The panic rose again. "I had a family, a mother, a father, a husband, but it's as if they never existed. Can you imagine how I feel right now? Everybody I knew and loved and thought loved me was lying, and I don't even know who they really were." I laughed and gulped air. "Look at me, the grieving widow. I have been dying inside," I stabbed at my chest, "at losing someone who was nothing more than a cheat and a liar. He lied to me for years. What kind of fool does that make me?" I stood up and walked away from him, "And what about you, James? Are you another plant? And Gill, Katie, Jack—all of you—are you all part of the project too?" I laughed a little hysterically. "It goes on and on and on, doesn't it? How will I ever be able to trust anyone one again?"

James stood up and turned me round to face him. "Don't be ridiculous. Look at me," he said, and his voice was soothing and gentle. "You are not alone. I'll help you. We'll get to the bottom of this. For what it's worth, I swear to you, you can trust me." I looked into his eyes, and they calmed me more than the brandy, of which I had now drunk just a little too much. I swayed a little.

"C'mon, I think you should lie down for a while. I'll help you upstairs." He led me like a child into the hall. Molly came out of the kitchen as we reached the foot of the stairs, her face creased with shock when she saw my red eyes and tear-streaked face. James held his hand out, warning her not to ask. He took me up to the bedroom, made me lie down, and threw a rug over me. Sitting on the edge of the bed, he said, "Try to sleep, Erica. I'll sit here for a while." I rolled onto my side, and the effects of alcohol and emotional exhaustion took their toll. I fell asleep.

I woke my head feeling fuzzy and thick and closed my eyes again, hoping everything had been just a bad dream. I lay there, weary, a little sick, a little scared, not wanting to face the world downstairs. Memories of other mornings waking like this crowded in, when I had lain tormented with grief, thinking about Paul, the little scar on his neck just under his shirt collar, the way his hair felt through my hands, how the beat of his heart felt through my fingers, the lingering scent of Bleu de Chanel on his clothes. Those were the memories that had caused me so much grief and loss, but now, like a butterfly fighting its way out of a chrysalis, I was free. What I thought I had lost I had never really had. I felt liberated. All that heartache that had sucked at my soul was gone, and now I was angry, furious, and exhausted all rolled into one. Thanks to this latest revelation, I had undergone a metamorphosis.

At around six o'clock there was a knock at the door. It was Katie, come to tell me that Detective Inspector Jonah Seagraves was downstairs asking for me. Two minutes later Gill followed her with a mug of tea.

"Molly and Alice have gone home. Molly was fluttering like a mother hen. It was all we could do to stop her waking you," Gill said. "You know it beggars belief. That bloody swine had us all fooled. What a piece of shit. I can hardly believe it, the sleepless nights you had nursing him, the crying you did when he died. I mean you just went to pieces. Look at the hours we spent trying to hold you together, and for what? I hope the bastard rots in hell."

She was rattling on; verbal diarrhoea was notably her strongest trait in times of crisis, when Gill always seemed to have the knack of opening her mouth and saying exactly the wrong thing. She saw the coldness on my face. "You are sure, aren't you? Paul and this other guy Stephen somebody? What a bastard."

"Oh for God's sake Gill, SHUT UP!" Katie turned on her just in time to stop me from saying something more vitriolic.

"What's your problem?" Gill retorted.

I sighed and sat back against the pillows. "It's Paul, OK?" I sipped the scalding hot tea. "Paul and Stephen Roberts are one and the same person."

Katie sat on the bed. "James told us what happened, and I am sure that you feel you can't trust anyone anymore, but you know, don't you, we will always be there if you need us. James said you were devastated, which is probably an understatement." Katie's eyes were moist, and she watched me carefully. I think she was seeking some kind of reassurance; I couldn't answer. I had no reassurance to give her. A moment later she asked, "Are you coming down for something to eat? James has made a curry."

I wasn't hungry, and the thought of facing everyone at dinner was more than I could bear. I wanted to go home, but I didn't even know where that was anymore. When I thought of going back to the house in Cumbernauld with all the memories that entailed, Lanshoud suddenly seemed a better option. "I'll get changed and be down in a minute. Wait for me, will you?" I got up and headed for the dressing room.

Jack was sitting at the kitchen table and stood up when we came in. "Are you all right, Erica? A hell of a thing for you to find out, what a nightmare."

James was standing at the sink in Molly's apron, and the kitchen reeked of garlic and spices. I sat down in the chair beside Jack. "I'm fine, thank you. Where's the policeman?"

"Checking out Nathan and company," James said.

I smiled. "You know your apron's ruining your street cred."

"I haven't got one to ruin."

"So where are the others? Are they not eating?"

Gill answered. "They are eating as we speak, glued to the monitors in the dining room. They are eating James's curry." She spoke in the tone of a mother praising her child. She added, "James has a hidden talent. He can cook. That curry you smell is his own chicken curry recipe, made from scratch, would you believe, thrown together in minutes and not a jar in

Jonah

sight. So you have to eat, or he'll be offended. Won't you, James?" she said, looking at him coquettishly. James declined to answer. He dished up, and we sat round the table. Jack opened a bottle of red wine and poured it into glasses.

"Jack, really, let it breathe," Gill censured him.

Jack took a large swallow. Unsmiling, he said, "I prefer to give it mouth-to-mouth resuscitation."

I ate the curry, and they made small talk, obviously skirting sensitive issues that might upset me. James broke the ice. He told me he had spoken to the Genocel people, and they were sending a pack with instructions on how to collect samples from clothing, etc. They usually had a maximum three-week turnaround, but it could be as little as three days.

Katie told us that she had been to see the estate agent in Stonehaven and had discovered that the man they had dealt with also fitted Paul's description, the same Stephen Roberts. "The woman in the Stonehaven office was obviously taken with the charming Mr. Roberts. She did know that he worked for the firm of solicitors that managed the estate."

James shook his head. "Hang on, that can't be right. Galbraith and Anderson have managed this estate for years."

"Which means," Jack said, "that you employed him."

"Yes, it would mean Adam Galbraith or my father, who incidentally is the Anderson of Galbraith and Anderson, would have employed him."

"Can you find out?" I asked.

"Sure. I'll give my father a call right now." James left to use the landline.

"So we know what he looks like, and we have plenty of photos of Paul to show around. Maybe someone else knows something about him, maybe someone from his work?" Katie looked askance at me.

"No, Paul was a freelance surveyor...supposedly. I never met anyone from any of the jobs he worked on. He traveled to sites all over the UK, and in hindsight I suppose that gave him his excuse to come up here to Lanshoud. I never contacted him on a landline. It was always his mobile. For all I know, he never did any surveying for anyone."

"I asked the estate agent for the contact number she had, and she gave me this mobile number." Katie put a slip of paper on the table. "I rang it, but the line is dead."

"Just like he is," Gill said. She was bombarded by looks of disapproval.

A few minutes later, James came back into the kitchen, with Seagraves at his back. "Detective Inspector Seagraves would like a word with you, Erica."

"Come in, Inspector. What can I do for you?"

He sauntered in, "Good evening, Mrs. Cameron."

"You're working late, and you drove all the way out here to have a word. It must be important. Have a seat. I would like my friends to hear anything you have to say. Would you like something to eat or some tea?"

"Food smells good," he said, and Katie went to get him some.

"Any luck with your father?" Jack asked James.

"My father recognised the name all right, but it was probably Adam Galbraith, in fact more likely just Laura, Adam's secretary, who dealt with him. I'll try her in the morning."

Seagraves sat down in the chair opposite me at the table. "I actually wanted to speak to you about the statue or figurine whatever you prefer to call it, the one I found on your steps."

"You found a figurine? Oh yes, the harlequin you found outside the door. I'm sorry, there has been so much going on I completely forgot about it. You took it away. I'm intrigued, you didn't give me the impression you believed anything we told you," I said, and he almost smiled. It must have been an effort, I thought, because he didn't have a face that seemed to be in the habit of smiling.

"I believed you all right, but there was just no evidence to back up your story. Let's face it; horsemen tearing round the house in the middle of night, hammering on doors and windows, seem a bit farfetched, eh? But it's also a helluva story to make up. Quite frankly I couldn't see what you had to gain by lying. So I sent the little statue to forensics and had a most interesting report." He took some papers from his inside jacket pocket. "Normally the lab can trace, if not fingerprints, then at least something on the object. However, this one..." he read from the report:

"No fingerprints, hairs, cosmetics, plant fibers, mineral fibres, synthetic fibers, glass, paint chips, soils, botanical materials...

"Nothing to indicate where it had come from or how long it had been lying there; in fact, the guy I spoke to at the lab said it looked as though it had been completely sterilised before being popped into the evidence bag. Now here is a photo of where it was lying when I found it on the step outside your front doors." He put the photograph on the table for the others to see, the little harlequin with the blue-and-white diamond costume and the blue face. "The forensics guy couldn't explain it any more than I could, especially considering the violence of the storm that night. There should have been at least some dust on it. He told me about something called Locard's Exchange Principle." He read out:

"'Wherever he steps, whatever he touches, whatever he leaves, even unconsciously, will serve as a silent witness against him. Not only his fingerprints or his footprints, but his hair, the fibers from his clothes, the glass he breaks, the tool mark he leaves, the paint he scratches, the blood or semen he deposits or collects. All of these and more bear mute witness against him.'

"There was no witness against whoever left this on that step." He stabbed the photograph with his figure. "There was no trace evidence on that statue, not even microscopic. Yet someone has to have dropped it, and what, wiped it clean first? Why do you suppose there was there no dust on it? You, Mrs. Cameron, were very airy-fairy about it when I asked you. To be precise, you said it may or it may not have come from the house, and there is one more interesting fact. I had an antiques expert look at it. The material this little figurine is made of is something he called true porcelain, Italian in origin, he said. You can tell by the way it's decorated in only blue—in fact, he got very excited about it." He was directing this whole dialogue at me, raising his voice. "This guy said that though Meissen is usually regarded as the first European porcelain, Medici porcelain of the sixteenth century was actually the first. It is only decorated in blue, and there is only a handful of surviving specimens. And guess what? The only two pieces he had ever seen sold went into the millions." He raised his eyebrows, watching me for a response. "Now how about that for something that may or may not have come from your house?"

"I would like to say I'm surprised, but the truth is, Inspector, nothing surprises me anymore. All I can tell you is whoever owned this house collected harlequins."

Jack said, "Well, it certainly ties up. When we were researching harlequins, I read something about porcelain and that date. In one of the books from the study, there is a photo of an illustration by the Italian Giovanni di Paolo, in the sixteenth century, of Arlecchino and other demons handling souls from the pit for Dante and Virgil. Remember, Arlecchino is thought to be one of the possible origins of the harlequin, and a bit further on, there's a chapter on porcelain in Italy. It says that it was first successfully made at the court in Florence in the 1570s. Previously they relied on porcelain shipped in from China."

"Oh, so you were researching harlequins, is that right? Now, somebody want to tell me what's going on here? Tell me why a surgically clean object worth millions is lying about in your front yard, Mrs. Cameron, especially since you don't seem to know who it belongs to." His tone was louder than I liked, and there was a hint of aggression in it that I didn't like either.

"I would if I could, Inspector," I retorted in kind, just as loudly, standing up and pushing my chair away. "We could have an exchange of information. You might want to tell me who I am, or where my home is, or who my husband was? Who is battering down these doors at night, and maybe then we can swap answers, and I can tell you something about your little doll." I turned to James. "Will someone else please tell him what he needs to know?" I had had enough for one night. I stormed out of the kitchen and lifted my jacket from the hall stand, I needed fresh air.

It was dusk, and the night was still and cloyingly warm. There was a pressure in the air and a distant rumble of thunder. I looked up at a sky full of dark clouds, no moon in sight. A rich scent of pine emanated from the forest, but it was pitch black among the trees, a deep darkness that I found a little menacing. There were no outside lights in the grounds, a strange oversight on the part of the previous owner. I remember thinking I would have to do something about that. It was getting dark, so I stayed near the house, taking benefit from the floodlit windows. I strolled round the perimeter of the house, listening to the light wind stirring only the very tops of the tall conifers, making the leaves rustle and whisper. The gravel crunched at my back, and I turned to see Katie.

"You OK? Do you mind if I walk with you? It's so warm inside the house tonight."

"Yes, I felt it too. That must be a first." I looked up. "Strange weather, there's definitely another thunderstorm on the way."

"Yes. Even though he brought his own generator, Nathan Findlay is a cross between fretting that we might have a power cut and hoping that it might bring the riders." She paused. "I think Seagraves will stay put till he finds out more. Now there is evidence of fraud, it will be a criminal investigation."

"How is it fraud? Nothing's been stolen. Even if Paul was using an assumed name, what harm did he do? The riders left nothing behind, not a mark on the doors or windows, not a hoof print in the earth. What can he do? Arrest a ghost?" I was still looking up at the trees and the sky. "It's strange."

"What's strange?"

"There are no birds. They usually sing like mad at this time of night. It must be the thunder. Do birds sing when there's thunder?"

"I can't remember." Katie persisted. "Your birth certificate appears to have been fraudulent; that's something he could check out."

"Like I have a choice. He just annoys me, that's all. The guy's so arrogant."

"Yes, and he smokes and eats too many doughnuts by the look of him, but that doesn't mean to say he can't help, does it?" She sighed. "I just worry about you."

"Well, don't. Listen, Katie, stop worrying about me. I have been selfish. You have lost someone who at least loved you, and somehow I have managed to forget that."

Katie shook her head. "The difference was, I suddenly realised I didn't love him. I didn't even like him by the time we split up, so I have no regrets. It was good riddance to bad rubbish."

"Funny, isn't it? Ironically, we are both in the same boat."

The wind was rising, lightning flashed, and a few minutes later, thunder boomed overhead. "I don't like this. I think we should head indoors."

"Me neither," she said. We made a dash for the door.

CHAPTER FOURTEEN

The Team

We met James in the hall. He had been about to come looking for us. I asked him how much he had told Seagraves.

"He knows most of your story now, and Gill's been embroidering the edges for him," James said in hushed tones, in a house that was still and unusually quiet. "You had better come in here." He indicated the dining room, "apparently there was something on one of the monitors."

Everyone was in the dining room. Nathan, Jess, Tosh, and Paddy were frozen in silence over monitors. Gill and Jack stood behind Paddy watching intently, and Seagraves was absorbed in watching something that Nathan was pointing out to him. Curry-stained plates with forks and glasses with various cold drinks were scattered about the huge dining room table.

Jess signaled to me to come and look at the screen, she stood at. "Orbs," she whispered, tense and excited. "Look, there must be twenty or thirty of them: I have never seen or heard of anything like it."

I looked and saw the bright circles of light moving around in the darkness. Some were higher than others, and when they moved, they left a trail of light behind them.

"Look." She held up an instrument. "The temperature is dropping." She smiled at me, eyes wide, delighted, excited.

I could feel a familiar chill tickling my skin. I looked at James, and he squeezed my arm reassuringly. It was all starting to kick off again.

"It's dust particles. The lightning will be affecting them." Seagraves looked at Nathan, not convinced.

"Oh no, it's not. I've seen plenty of dust particles in my time, certainly enough to know the difference." He held up his fingers. "Number one, they are too large and too bright to be dust particles. Two, they are leaving a trail, and dust particles don't leave trails. Three, the temperature has dropped drastically and four they are grouping and not moving with the wind but within their own space." His glasses had slid to the bottom of his nose again. He pushed them up and stabbed the screen with his forefinger. "What you are seeing there, Detective Inspector, are genuine orbs."

The thunder boomed overhead. I could feel the chill spreading up my spine, and I moved closer to James, who put his arm round my shoulders. The lightning flashed again, and the lights went out.

"Don't panic," Nathan called out. "Everyone stay just where they are. The generator will kick in, in a moment." Paddy and Tosh switched on lamps and torches, in the light of which Nathan could be seen pressing the buttons on the generator. There was a gentle hum, and the generator roared into life. Immediately the monitors came on, and the orbs could be seen spreading out almost in a line two levels high.

"Some of them are grouping round the door, the front door, and the rest are spreading out," Nathan said. We waited the tension in the air almost palpable.

Katie heard it first. "Over there."

The tapping had started on the windows of the dining room. Nathan moved to the monitor of the camera focused on the left side of the house. A couple of orbs were visible. We watched in horror as the wispy, grey-and-white form of a man and a horse took shape.

Jess was enraptured. "Oh," she whispered, "it's amazing."

Tosh and Nathan had gone to the window but said they couldn't see anything. As we watched from a distance, the lightning flashed again, and then we all saw them: three riders, their large horses stamping the ground. It was momentary, but the image that flashed into my brain was the shape of men on horseback, one man holding a pole toward the window. At the same time, an almighty and deafening crash sounded at the front doors.

"Stay still," Nathan said. "They are spirits. They cannot harm you." Seagraves headed for the door. James followed him into the hall and grabbed his arm. "Hang on. We don't know that."

Jack, Nathan, and I followed him. "He's right," Jack said. "Don't go there. With all due respect, Nathan, you said yourself that you had never seen anything like this."

Seagraves hesitated. The doors pounded again with such force that they seemed about to burst, and the vibration caused a vase on the console table to crash onto the floor. A pulse of noise vibrated through the house on every door. On every window of the ground floor something tapped, knocked, beat, or drummed. The noise was deafening, and the pounding on the doors increased. The howling started a few minutes later, wailing and screeching like some tormented creatures from hell, hounds baying and scratching at the doors. I trembled with fear as I could hear quite clearly the sound of horses galloping round and round the house.

No one moved. In the torchlight we seemed frozen like statues, fear etched on faces deathly pale. The noise of the wild hunt, for that is what I felt it must be, was a cacophony of screeching and wailing, a discordant, deafening sound that attacked the ears of anything unfortunate enough to hear it and by virtue of the horror it suggested, struck terror into the soul. I'm not sure how long it lasted, as the storm outside raged and crashed until we could not distinguish between it and the riders. Only when the storm calmed and the orbs could not be seen on the monitors did we believe they had gone.

The house was freezing. We went through to the study and lit the fire. Jack opened a bottle of brandy and offered a little in a glass to everyone. No one refused. For someone who had never tasted brandy, I was developing a liking for it. Jess, who was trembling like a leaf but still smiling, whispered to me, "How wonderful." Gallingly I realised she was serious.

Seagraves was the first to pull himself together and again headed for the door. James and Jack followed him. Nathan was white as a sheet, and he spoke nervously, pushing his ever-mobile spectacles up his nose.

"I am going to suggest we get some more help here," he said, grimacing as the brandy burned his throat. "I am out of my depth, I mean, this is mind blowing. This is going to keep us funded for the next twenty years. I am going to suggest we get the help of a clairvoyant. What do you think, Jess?"

Jess nodded vigorously. "Yes, I agree. This is momentous. When my heart rate returns to anything near normal and my hands stop shaking…" she held up her glass in trembling hands, "I intend to work out which bit of my defective personality drove me to put myself in this situation."

"Do you know anyone, Nathan?" I asked.

"I know a few, but there is only one I really trust. He's brilliant, but he may or may not be willing to help. He may have to be persuaded."

"You mean Emilio? Persuade him. Call him now," Jess said.

"Money is no object. He can name his price," I said.

"It's one a.m." Nathan looked at his watch.

"Just call him, Nathan. We need him tonight," Jess said.

"They may not come back. It's not been every night, has it?" Nathan was reluctant to phone this man in the middle of the night.

"No, but they will come tonight because Erica's here," James said from the doorway.

"What?" I turned to look at him.

"I'm sorry, but it's pretty obvious that they only come when you're here."

"So what are you saying? It's me they're after?"

"I am not saying anything," James said. "Other than we need to try to find out."

Nathan made the call. Fifteen minutes later a jubilant Nathan told us Emilio Mendez would be joining us as soon as he could get here.

"Where's Seagraves?" I asked.

"I'm here, and no, there is nothing to indicate anyone, let alone horse and hounds, has been visiting tonight."

"So Nathan, was it worth coming up here?" Jack asked.

"Oh, definitely worth it. I owe you one. My God, just think what a breakthrough, if we could prove the existence of the Wild Hunt."

Although Gill was as shaken as the rest of us, she sat down on a cushion near the fire, stretching out her figure to best advantage, fooling everyone but Katie and I. Her long, black hair was tied in a ponytail that showed off her high cheekbones and large brown eyes. Nathan was captivated.

"Why do you think they are only here when Erica is here, Nathan?" she asked him, wide eyed.

"He stared at her for a few moments before he realised she was speaking to him. "I...I..." he stammered. "Sorry, I have no idea. It may just be coincidence. I am hoping that Emilio Mendez will help us with that."

"I don't think it's coincidence. I think it has something to do with whoever left me this house and made it in my best interest to stay in it, but I don't know who or why, so I hope this medium can help."

"Emilio Mendez is one of the best clairvoyants in the world," Jess said. "He came to live in the UK because he was hounded by people in Spain needing or just wanting his help; he is practically in hiding here. He refuses to do it commercially, but he has helped us in the past. They just don't come any better than this guy."

"When do you think he will get here?" James asked Nathan.

"He's intending to leave at seven. Allowing for the morning rush hour, he should be here around ten."

By about three a.m., we had all gone to bed. Nathan and his team bunked down in sleeping bags in the dining room, taking it in turn to watch the monitors just in case the riders returned.

CHAPTER FIFTEEN

Tosh

I woke around nine and showered and got dressed before going downstairs since Emilio Mendez would be arriving at ten. Nathan was so exuberant in his praise for Senor Mendez that I dared to hope the clairvoyant might provide some answers. As I came down the stairs, I could hear the hum of voices and the scrape of cutlery on plates. In the kitchen, the rich smell of coffee filled the air, and sunlight poured through the windows. The warmth from the sun and the comforting smell of coffee brewing helped to chase away the chill left from the night before. James, Tosh, and Jonah Seagraves were already in the kitchen sitting round the table, the remnants of a cooked breakfast on their plates. They were talking about taking a look at the cellar and about the story Lizzie McIntosh had told. They were all casually dressed; Seagraves, in jeans and a sweatshirt, had evidently brought an overnight bag with him.

"Good morning," I said, taking in the scene where the three men round the table were obviously getting on well. It was strange. A couple of weeks ago, I didn't know them, and they didn't know one another, yet they had bonded, as I had with Jack and James. I think it had something to do with the fear we had experienced and the animal need to be in a pack. In lightning quick time, we had accepted one another, warts and all.

"Sleep well?" James asked.

"I feel as though I haven't slept at all. I could have slept on, but with Emilio Mendez arriving at ten, I thought I had better make myself presentable." I declined the offer of coffee and filled the kettle for a pot of tea.

"You could have slept on. Emilio phoned Nathan; he has been stuck at the Auchenkilns roundabout for over an hour. There has been an accident, and some truck has disgorged chemicals all over the motorway. He says he will stop somewhere for lunch, so we can expect him around two."

"Shouldn't a world-famous clairvoyant have been able to predict that one?" Jonah asked, smiling.

"I don't think it works like that," Tosh said jumping to Senor Mendez' defense.

"Oh, really?" Jonah sat back in his chair, rubbing the stubble of his beard with one hand. "How does it work then?"

"Ignore him, Tosh; he's just looking for an excuse to poke fun at you," I said.

"Hey, that's unfair. I'm just looking to be educated here—or should I say enlightened." He grinned.

"I did not sleep well either, Erica," Tosh said. "I spent the night spooked by noises."

"A ghost hunter spooked. Now that's funny. Maybe you're in the wrong game, pal." Seagraves laughed.

"No, I'm in the right game; I would not have missed last night for the world," Tosh answered, grinning, not fazed in the slightest by Seagraves's ribbing.

"Answer some questions for me, Tosh. Why was Jess so excited at the drop in temperature last night?" I asked.

"Because it is a good indicator that something may be drawing energy from the living in this house and using it to manifest itself. We came here, Erica, not to prove there was a supernatural presence in or outside your home, but rather to disprove it. A big old house in the middle of woods, rattling hot and cold pipes, mice, maybe even rats, loose window frames, birds or animals tapping on windows, all appear to be unexplained phenomenon when you are afraid."

"So you came disbelieving even though we saw them, the shapes in the dark, the red eyes?" I said.

"Yes, but prior to that, you were already scared. It could have been autosuggestion. The more people in the house, the more chance of group hysteria," Tosh answered.

"Is that what you really think, Tosh?"

"Not now. Nathan and Jess were ecstatic last night. They really believed that something supernatural had manifested," Tosh said.

"She's right, you know. Nathan was rubbing his hands all the way to the bank," Jack said. "He might actually get his funding this time."

Tosh leaned over. Elbows on the table, he shook his head and spoke softly. "A manifestation is more than he expected, but Nathan will still be conservative with his report. He must be rigorous, for more than any other field, parapsychology is subject to ridicule, and Nathan has been subjected to ridicule many times. It is what he has come to expect. After last night, Nathan and Jess, well…" he put his hands up. "I believe that they may at last have found what they have been searching for: evidence of something truly supernatural. It is the only reason Nathan would have asked for help from Emilio Mendez, and whatever he said to him on the phone must have been very convincing for Mendez to become involved."

"A superstar is he, this Mendez?" Jonah asked. "Are we going to be subjected to a diva?"

"He's the best in his field and a very private person, almost a recluse," Tosh said quickly.

"You don't have to be subjected to anything, Inspector," I said. "You don't have to stay."

"Mrs. Cameron, please, I wouldn't miss it for the world. So how did you get into this ghost hunting lark anyway?" Seagraves asked Tosh. "Is it a sideline for all psychology students?"

"I study modern languages. Parapsychology is my hobby."

"Some hobby," James remarked. "You study modern languages do you? Tell me, what do you make of the name Lanshoud?"

"Jack asked me that already. It does not mean anything to me. It's not a Scots name, not associated with anything local, and it's not English."

"It's not Lanshoud either." Seagraves took a pen from his pocket and scribbled on a paper napkin. He turned the napkin round for me to see. "The name is on the lintel over the door. The stone is really worn, but if you look closely, you will see there is a *t* at the end, very hard to see because it's almost obliterated. It must have originally been Lans Houdt."

I turned away from the teapot and the mug I was filling. "Say that again." He did.

"That's Dutch. I don't know what it means, but I am sure it's Dutch." Tosh agreed, especially given my background and connection to the house.

"Why don't you ask Roos De Foor?" James suggested. "I have her mobile number."

Seagraves asked if I was OK with his staying over. I was tempted to say no, but I told him I felt the house was less threatening the more people there were in it. There might be safety in numbers. He reiterated the fact that there was no evidence of any intruders; these phantoms hadn't even left a footprint. Tosh reminded him of the video footage from the monitors, but Seagraves said it would take more than few blotches on a video to convince him there was anything supernatural out there. There was no hostility in Seagraves's voice, but it was heavily laced with cynicism. He said he didn't know how they were doing it; maybe it was lasers or something and sound devices.

"And the pounding on the doors without leaving footprints?" James asked.

"Really, Inspector, you should not dismiss so quickly something you have no experience of. I was once just as sceptical as you are," Tosh said.

"Really, and what changed your hold on reality?"

Tosh was not amused: "The death of my grandfather a few years ago."

"And?" Jonah raised his eyebrows.

"What, Inspector! You are interested in a ghost story?"

Jonah smiled. "It'll pass the time."

"Tell us about it, Tosh," I said.

Tosh was silent for a few moments; he seemed to be considering whether opening up to Seagraves was a wise thing to do. I have no idea why he trusted us with something I later realised was a defining moment in his life.

"I was very close to my father's father. I was the eldest grandchild, and we spent most of every day together, fishing, reading, and tending his beloved garden. He felt it was his personal duty to turn me into a good Japanese boy. He was a karate expert and taught me how to defend myself. He read to me every day the best of Japanese literature, and he told me endless stories of his own boyhood. I adored him. He became very ill during my final exams, and my father phoned me telling me to come home because my grandfather had been asking for me. If I had gone back to Japan at that time, I would have missed the last two exams of my degree. So I decided the best thing to do would be to finish my exams and then go home. As fate would have it, by the time I had boarded a plane, it was too late, and I returned to Japan just in time for the funeral.

"My father was unforgiving. He said my grandfather had asked for me repeatedly before he died, and my father told him over and over again that I was coming. My father in his grief was furious and said he would never forgive me. He accused me of putting studies before my family, which of course is exactly what I had done. I was upset and very guilty; I loved my grandfather and would not knowingly have caused him any distress. The whole extended family had dropped everything and traveled from far and wide to see him when he lay dying, yet I, to whom he had given so much love and attention, had failed him.

"To understand, you would have to know my father. He lives and breathes all the old traditions of Japan. He could not look at me. He was shamed by the fact his son had put studies in the West before family. He said the old man's spirit would not rest, as he would go to the spirit world sad that I had not loved him. My family is Shinto. I don't know if you know much about Shinto. It is a belief that all living things have a soul, a spiritual essence. In Shinto culture we have rituals to purify the dead, to ensure that the souls of our loved ones do not return to the earth. In Japan if someone dies harbouring rage or jealousy or guilt, it is believed that person's spirit will return, often a vengeful spirit that will haunt the people involved in those trapped emotions. Though I have lived in the West for many years, America and the UK, I have never lost my belief in the Shinto way of life, though I did draw the line at spirits returning to haunt the living.

"I was dreading the whole funeral thing. Our extended family traveled from all over Japan to our home in Okinawa. Everyone was painfully polite, but I felt they were all judging me, and I was ashamed at my shortcomings as a grandson. The Shinto funeral was a long, drawn-out affair spanning over two days. Part of the funeral service involved a ritual cleansing, where each family member was required to symbolically wash the body. My grandfather lay before the Shinto altar, and we were each provided with a wet tissue, with which we were to cleanse his hands and face, only a token wash, as the body had been cleansed thoroughly by the funeral home. It was at this point that we were to say our final good-byes. I was dreading it. I walked forward to where the body lay before the altar. I could not look at his face. I washed his hands and steeled myself before washing the face. When I did look, I was quite suddenly overwhelmed with grief. I could feel the hot tears running down my face at the sight of this lovely old man who must have died thinking I no longer loved him.

"From where I stood over the body, no one could see me. I closed my eyes for a few moments to compose myself. When I opened them again, my grandfather's eyes were also open."

Tosh looked at us individually; we were riveted. He said "I froze, the adrenaline chilling my body; I dropped the cloth in fright, I cried out. I stared into his smiling eyes, and then he winked and smiled. It was the most amazing thing. I was staring at the face that seemed alive and glowing, the face of the old man I remembered. I cannot expect you to believe it was any more than an illusion, but I believe it was more. I was the last person to say my good-bye and when I stood too long not speaking, the men came to place his body in the casket. That broke the spell. I looked up, and when I looked down again, it was the cold white face of a corpse.

"I believe my grandfather's spirit came back to let me know that he understood and he forgave me. A few years ago, I would have laughed at such a tale, but like most people who have experienced something supernatural, I have changed the way I look at life and death, and I realise there may be more things in this world than science can explain. Since that day I have been searching for some kind of explanation."

There was a pause. "That's quite a story, Tosh," I said.

"It certainly puts your paranormal interests into perspective," James said.

Seagraves didn't comment. He was watching Tosh intently. "What about Paddy? Is he one of Nathan's students?"

"Yes, and he has always helped out on assignments. He and I share a flat, which is how I became involved. Paddy has his own story."

"Which is what?" Jonah asked.

"Ask him," Tosh answered.

Jonah studied Tosh for a few moments and then he turned to me. "Do you mind if I take a look at your cellar, Mrs. Cameron?" I suggested he call me Erica. I wanted to take a look too, but I also wanted to phone Roos first.

Roos answered on the second ring. She was very helpful; yes the name Land Houdt was Dutch. The best translation she could give was Lance Hold or Lance Keep.

The cellar, with its woefully inadequate lightbulb, was cold and dank. Jonah and James were shifting boxes and looking under dust sheets. I stood and watched as they poked around, lifting dust cloths and checking out crates, which were mostly full of old tools, rolls of cable, electrical fittings and oil cans. One contained a box radio from the 1940s; another had bits of a mangle and gears from a kitchen pulley. Jonah checked out the life sized harlequin. He scraped a little of its surface into a small plastic bag which he put in his pocket.

I showed them the wine cellar and James asked me to tell Jonah exactly what Lizzie McIntosh had said. I followed Jonah around, telling the story while he picked up bottles, brushing off dust to read the labels; he gave no indication that he was even listening, but when I stopped in mid-sentence, he turned round, looked at me surprised, and said, "Carry on." He tapped each of the barrels and ran his hand along the walls. He went back out into the main cellar and came back with a plank of wood, which he banged at intervals along the walls, concentrating on the back wall where Lizzie McIntosh had said she heard whispering, but there was nothing. There was no change in the sound, and he nodded in agreement when James said the walls were solid stone and it seemed unlikely there could be a concealed room.

Hands in his pockets, Jonah lay back against the wine cellar wall. He looked around at the walls, the floor, the ceiling. He said nothing for a few moments, then, hands still in pockets, he bolted back upstairs, saying, "I need a word with your housekeeper."

"He's a strange one," James said.

We followed Jonah and found him in the kitchen, where he had cornered Molly; Molly was flustered. Her answers were obviously not convincing Jonah.

"Let's just go over this again. When I interviewed you, you said you never went down to the cellar."

"That's right," Molly said "I—"

He cut her short, took his hand out of his pocket, and held it up to stop her speaking. "Let me think." He looked up at the ceiling, and then looked back at her. "I'm going to quote you: 'Alice doesn't like the cellar. We don't go down there. In fact Alice has never been in the cellar.'" He gave Molly a wide-eyed, quizzical look. "That is what you said, right?"

Molly nodded. "Yes, but…"

He cut her off again. "Where is she?"

"She's upstairs changing towels in the bedrooms."

"Get her, please."

"Now?"

"Yes, now."

Molly protested. "Look, Inspector, Alice has to be handled carefully. I don't want you upsetting her. She has a routine, and if I don't keep her to it, she gets stressed."

Jonah raised his eyebrows and said slowly—and rather menacingly I thought: "Mrs. Johnstone, I'm getting stressed, and I would be grateful if you would go get your daughter from the bedrooms and bring her to the kitchen, now, please."

Molly wiped her hands on her apron and left hurriedly. She returned a few minutes later with a confused and agitated Alice.

"The policeman would like a word with you, dear. You sit here." Molly eased Alice into a chair at the kitchen table and glowered at Jonah.

"Could you get me a sheet of paper, please?"

Molly reached into a drawer in the centre island and handed him a ring binder with sheets of blank paper. Jonah sat down opposite her. "Hi, Alice. You remember me, don't you? I'm Inspector Seagraves."

Alice, almost crying, said she had to do the rooms. She tried to get up, but Molly eased her back into the chair. "It's all right, Alice. We'll do them together later. We don't have to clean anymore. Remember, the ladies from the cleaning firm are going to come in and do it." She turned on Jonah. "What do you want, Inspector? You can see she's upset."

He lifted his hand to silence her again. He put the paper in front of Alice and handed her a pen. "Alice, can you write your name for me?"

Alice looked up at me through tear-stained, blue eyes.

"Can you do that, Alice?" I asked her softly. "Can you write your own name?"

Alice nodded. "Alice can write Alice."

"Will you show me? Alice, please," I asked her.

Alice looked at me and smiled. "I show you, Erica." She took the pen and slowly and carefully scrawled *Alice* in big, childlike letters across the page. She looked up at me for my approval.

"That's very good, Alice. Well done."

"What's this all about, Inspector? Why are you making Alice write her name?" Molly put her arm around Alice.

Jonah ignored the question and turned the paper round to study it. A moment later he turned to face Molly.

"So your daughter never goes to the wine cellar. OK, so explain to me why *ALICE* is written exactly like this on the dust on the shelves of the wine cellar."

Molly froze. She looked at Alice for a moment, and then turned to Jonah. "My daughter has never been in that cellar. She has been terrified of it since ever she first looked through the cellar door."

"What scared her then?" Jonah asked.

"I don't know." Molly shook her head, "Probably the dark and the damp smell. There was nothing to scare her then. She just looked down the stairs and blankly refused to go down them."

"Why did you want her to go down them?"

"No particular reason. We had just arrived here, and I was looking around. I opened the door and switched on the light, and Alice backed away. She got upset, the way she does, and refused to go down. There was never any reason to force her, and even if there had been, I wouldn't have forced her anyway. Since then, anytime she has seen the door open, she just backs away."

Jonah Seagraves continued to question Molly but got nowhere. Molly was unshakable in her assertion that Alice had never been in the cellar. She could not explain how Alice's childlike scrawl was in the dust on a shelf in the cellar. She couldn't explain it, and there was no way Jonah was going to get any information from a troubled and flustered Alice.

CHAPTER SIXTEEN

....

Emilio

The rain was pouring down again as the BMW crunched onto the gravel at the front of the house. Emilio Mendez had presence. The poise, the air of confidence, the self-assurance, that indefinable quality that makes you look up, look away, then look again when someone who has it walks into a room. Senior Mendez exuded "I am here" out of every pore in his body. Senor Mendez owned the space he moved in, and lesser mortals stepped back.

He was in his fifties, with black hair peppered with grey at the side, sallow skin, and dark eyes. He was immaculately dressed in a brown corduroy jacket and beige trousers. He reminded me of a tailor's dummy in an expensive gent's outfitters. By chance Alice had opened the door to him—Alice, who was the complete opposite, a victim of circumstance, never in control and always at the mercy of her environment. Alice, wearing her blue floral coverall that she used to protect her clothes when she was working. Her tweed pleated skirt and grey jumper made her look older than her thirty years. She was immediately flustered.

Emilio Mendez smiled at her. "Hello, Alice," he said in a deep hypnotic voice with a soft Spanish accent.

Alice's eyes widened in surprise, she was already in the flow of discharging her well-rehearsed greeting. In the faltering speech that characterised her, she rattled out, "Hello, I'm Alice. Pleased meet you." Then surprised, mesmerised by this stranger with the piercing gaze: "Alice...yes...I'm Alice...." Then, "You know... You know I'm Alice?" She wrinkled her brow, confused that he knew her name.

"Yes, I know you are Alice, and I am Emilio and very pleased to meet you. Nathan told me you make better coffee than anyone he knows." Emilio turned to indicate Nathan, who was carrying a bag at his back. Alice nodded, turning her chin down and looking up, shyly smiling at him. Then she turned to see me standing behind her.

"Alice, I'm sure Senor Mendez would like some of your delicious coffee. Nathan and I would like some tea. Could we have a pot of tea and some cups, please, in the morning room?"

Alice nodded and smiled shyly again at Emilio Mendez before scurrying off happily to make the tea and coffee. Molly came to take his coat, and Jess appeared from the dining room. "Emilio! It's wonderful to see you again."

"And you, Jess," he said, air kissing her on both cheeks.

Nathan put the case down and introduced me. "And this is Mrs. Cameron."

In beautifully modulated English, typical of someone for whom English is a second language, Emilio Mendez said, "Mrs. Cameron, it is a pleasure. Thank you for inviting me."

I held out my hand in greeting. "Please call me Erica, and thank you for coming." He didn't take my hand.

He bowed slightly. "Forgive me, please; it is the nature of my curse—or gift, as some would see it. Nathan has not told you of this?"

"Oh sorry, no, I should have said something." Nathan explained, pushing his specs back up his nose, "Emilio sometimes gets overwhelmed by psychic images when he touches people."

"And so I live alone, and I try not to touch anyone." He looked at me with soft brown eyes, smiling, and I thought...how sad.

We walked toward the morning room, and as we reached the door, Emilio suddenly stopped, turned, and stared along the hall. Then he closed his eyes. Nathan, Jess, and I followed his gaze, but there was nothing to see. We stood watching him in silence.

He opened his eyes and asked, "The last door on this side—where does it lead?"

"That's the cellar door," I said. "Is there something wrong?"

He shook his head. "I do not know yet."

"Come with me, Emilio," Nathan said, indicating the dining room. "Paddy and Tosh are eager to meet you; they are through here manning the monitors."

Jonah had been to the police station to pick up the results of DNA tests he ordered had on items belonging to my parents. He was waiting in the morning room with James and Katie. He asked to speak to me alone, but there was no point. In the room, which was warm and inviting because Molly had lit the fire against the chill caused by the damp weather, with James and Katie as my cushions, I received the not-unexpected results. The man and woman who had raised me were not my biological parents. The three of them watched me, gauging my reaction. The concern etched on their faces was strangely irritating. I wasn't sad. I was many things—angry, frustrated—but not sad.

"It's OK. I have been expecting that. I'm all right." I took a deep breath and asked Jonah, "So who am I?"

"I am afraid it only proves who you're not," Jonah answered.

"Where do I go from here then? How do I find out who my parents were?"

"We may have to go back to the baby born in Delfshaven. Interpol are helping with that, and I already have a trace on Paul Cameron and Stephen Roberts. It's just a waiting game. I take it that was the clairvoyant arriving." I nodded yes. "So this guy is going to do what exactly?" Jonah asked.

James answered, "According to Nathan he is the best in the world. Apparently he doesn't do it for profit anymore, and according to Jess, who is his number-one fan, he is so good he had to leave his native Spain years ago because he was hounded by people who wanted his help." James sat relaxed, one arm resting on the back of an overstuffed sofa.

Jonah leaned forward. "Look, I get it. He's popular. Fine, but what does he do exactly? Read palms? Crystal balls? What?"

"Neither." Emilio, Jess, and Nathan stood in the open doorway. "I see, sir, you are a sceptic, and that does not offend me, as I find most people are extreme one way or the other. To answer your question, I have a sixth sense, as sharp as hearing and sight, but where I can choose to listen to music or look at a beautiful woman…" he inclined his head with a smile at me, "my sixth sense is not so selective, and sometimes I hear and see things I would rather not have seen or heard."

I stood up, as did James and Jonah. "Senor Emilio Mendez, may I introduce Detective Inspector Jonah Seagraves, my solicitor James Anderson, and my very good friend Katie Armstrong." Both men and Katie nodded in greeting; apparently I was the only one who hadn't known about the handshake thing. Alice appeared with the tea and coffee; she put down the tray on the marble-topped coffee table and glanced in the direction of Emilio, smiling, blushing, and smoothing her wiry hair with one hand, with a poise and confidence alien to the Alice I had so far seen. I was amazed at the effect he had on her.

"I didn't intend to offend you," Jonah said. "I have been told you are a psychic or a clairvoyant or…"

"Or a freak of nature, some would say, Inspector."

"No need to be paranoid. I simply would like to know how your sixth sense works. How exactly you think you may be able to help in this situation?"

Emilio sat in the pale brocade chair with the Queen Anne legs, his legs crossed, arms relaxed on the chair arms. He instantly looked right at home. Jonah didn't faze him in the slightest. "Tell me, Inspector, since you have been investigating, what is your explanation for the phenomena that you have all been experiencing? The tapping, the noises? Do you consider them to be caused by feral youth? Perhaps tricks of the weather? Let me think… mass hysteria? You have come to some conclusion, yes?"

"Touché," Jonah acknowledged. "Of course you know already that we have no rational explanation, or you wouldn't be here."

"Then that is what I do Inspector. I can sometimes, though not always, provide an explanation, but I must warn you that it may not be rational in your eyes. All life has a soul, and each soul has a spirit form that surrounds it. On death of the body, unless influenced by evil, the soul and the spirit will seek to return to the Light. Sometimes these souls, now spirit forms themselves, are trapped; they can be stuck, tied to something or someone from the lost life. I see them and I hear them."

"Emilio has the most amazing ability to interpret observable happenings, incidents, and facts that we cannot make sense of," Nathan said, pushing his ever-sliding specs back up again.

"He has been immensely helpful to our department in the past. Emilio can provide an explanation for the inexplicable," Jess said animatedly. It was obvious that Nathan and Jess formed the fan club that Alice had quickly become a member of. In my newfound distrust of everyone, I reserved judgment.

"So," James said, "where do we go from here?"

Emilio stood and walked to the window. He looked out for a few moments, and then turned to look at me. "Mrs. Cameron, Erica, I can tell you that you have nothing to fear within this house. There is something very powerful in your cellar, but it is not, in essence, evil."

We all reacted differently, and everyone spoke at once. For some strange reason, I believed this man instantly, and though there was nothing to substantiate it, I had an overwhelming sense of relief.

Jonah smirked, leaned back, and rubbed both hands over his face. "What does that mean?"

"What do you mean 'something powerful' in the cellar?" James asked. "And if that's true, how do you know she has nothing to fear?" James had a habit of sounding like a lawyer every time he asked a question. "What are you basing your opinion on? You haven't seen anything yet. With all due respect, you've only been here five minutes."

Emilio rubbed his forehead, and again he directed his words to me. "There are protective forces all around this house, which for me was like walking through an invisible force field and from your cellar, there emanate waves of power like nothing I have experienced before."

"I don't understand. Where are the protective forces? We searched the cellar and we found nothing," I said.

"The protective forces are all around the house. Someone who knows what he or she is doing has used ancient signs or rituals to erect a barrier around this house. Look for them scratched into the stone. It could be talismans buried under the doors and windows. With your permission, Nathan told me your story. I suggest to you that whoever caused you to move to this house and made it difficult for you to leave it did so for your own protection."

"A barrier against what?" James asked.

Again without taking his eyes from me, he said, "Perhaps against the hunt." I felt my blood chill, that crawling feeling in the skin that my mother used to say was someone walking over your grave—except she wasn't my mother."

"Why now?" Katie asked, moving to sit beside me. "She has lived all her life without these barriers. There were no riders in her life until someone left this house to her."

"I am sorry; I cannot answer that. At this moment all I can tell you is that the intensity of the power that originates from your cellar is beyond anything I have experienced before, and were it malevolent, I would not have crossed your threshold. I have been left close to death by lesser manifestations. That is all I can tell you just now. Perhaps after tonight I will know more. I have been told they come every night."

"Every night Erica is here," James said.

"So then, perhaps tonight," Emilio said.

"Do you intend to just wait till the tapping starts?" Jonah asked. "Or would you like to take a look at the cellar?"

"In truth, neither, but I will go with you to the cellar."

We finished our tea, and Jonah led the way. James, Nathan, and I followed and watched the change in Emilio as he stood outside the door of the cellar looking stressed and pale. Jonah opened the door, switched on the inadequate lightbulb, and led the way down into the cold and damp. We stood under the light in a circle waiting for Emilio to comment. When he didn't speak, James said, "We have been over it with a fine-tooth comb and couldn't find anything."

"The walls are solid, centuries old, and there's no space behind them, but if I have understood you correctly, you think there is something down here," Jonah said.

Emilio stopped at the door of the wine cellar. "You should have asked Alice. She knows."

"Knows what?" Jonah asked with a tone that suggested he was getting irritated.

Emilio closed his eyes, and we waited. Then he said, "She is like me."

"Could you be a little less cryptic?" Jonah asked.

Emilio didn't answer. He was standing, eyes closed, at the entrance to the wine cellar. He started to sway a little. He was deathly pale, with beads of perspiration on his forehead. He turned. "I am sorry. I cannot do this, not now, perhaps later."

Emilio

We returned to the morning room. Jonah asked Emilio what he'd meant when he said, "Alice knows."

"Alice has a gift, Inspector. She is aware of things you do not understand. Alice will have felt the power from this cellar almost as surely as I did. It would have drawn her to it as soon as she entered the house." He turned to me. "You were not aware of this?"

"No." I shook my head. "I don't think anyone is."

Jonah breathed in audibly. "Well, that might explain her fear of the cellar, though I am not saying I believe any of this."

The phone rang, and Molly came to tell me it was Gill. I took the call in the hall. Gill said she and Jack were staying in Aberdeen for dinner, but they would be home before nightfall.

I went through to the kitchen to tell Molly how many there would be for dinner that night. Now that the cleaning firm came two days a week, Molly made us a simple lunch and an evening meal each day. James followed me through to the kitchen and asked me how I was holding up.

"I'm fine."

"I've been looking for a chance to tell you. It was Adam Galbraith who interviewed and employed Stephen Roberts. Adam said he had good references both by letter and word of mouth from his contacts. Jonah's team has checked out the addresses and the contacts, and they were all genuine. Stephen Roberts did actually live where he said he did and worked for several years for some of these firms listed in his CV." When I didn't answer, he said, "Paul Cameron has been very clever. There are no loose ends."

When James left the kitchen, Molly, who was rolling out pastry, put down the rolling pin and wiped her floury hands on her apron. "He is very a nice young man, dear. He is obviously very fond of you."

"What! Oh, you are havering, Molly. It's his job to look after me just now, that's all."

"I think it's more than that, and I think you know it. I think you like him too." She smiled at me knowingly.

I shook my head in denial. "No, it's not what you think. He really is just doing his job; it's in the will that the solicitors take care of things during a settling-in period."

She started rolling her pastry again "Do you feel it's too soon after your husband?"

I laughed. "You don't give up, do you?" I sat at the island beside her. "I don't know how I feel just now. It's all very complicated. I just try to concentrate on getting through each day and the revelations each day brings, without caving in."

"I know. I have been where you are now. Only where you have just found out your husband had faults, I lived with mine for nearly forty years." She didn't look up from her work.

"Were you not happily married, Molly?"

"Oh, I suppose I was on the outside, as much if not better than the next person, but my early married life was difficult, and I was miserably unhappy. It wasn't an arranged marriage as such but just as restrictive, two neighbouring farms and two families expecting us to wed. He wasn't even a childhood friend; I mean I knew him well enough, but not to call a friend."

"So you never loved him? Is that what you are saying?"

"I am not saying anything. You don't need romantic love to make a marriage work, as long as at least one of you works hard at it. I have lived long enough to know there are many, many marriages that have survived on that."

"That's quite sad."

"Och, I was happy at times, latterly anyway. My husband professed to love me. When I was young, he was obsessively jealous, but there was still something missing. The something I can see in you and James when you look at each other." I told her she was way off kilter, but she ignored me and continued. "My husband had a violent temper, though he never lifted a hand to me or the children. I learned to live with it, and I learned how not to provoke him, for the sake of the children. He was selfish, thoughtless, and insecure, and I always felt I had three children to look after instead of two."

"Was there no one else?"

"Yes, but it was too late for us." She looked into my eyes and said pointedly, "It's not too late for you."

I didn't want to go down that road, so I changed the subject. "Did you know that Emilio Mendez told us today that he thought—no, that's wrong—he actually said with absolute conviction that Alice is psychic?"

"No!" Molly sat down heavily into a chair. "My Alice! Never." Unsure, she asked, "Did he say what he meant by psychic?"

"I asked him that. He said she is a sensitive, she is intuitive, and she has a strong sense of things outside our knowledge. He said he connected to her at the door and that she recognised it in him."

"You know, it's funny you say that. She has been acting a bit strange this afternoon," Molly said thoughtfully.

I continued. "Jonah, of course, jumped on it straight away because Emilio said she would have been drawn to the cellar. Jonah is now convinced that Alice has definitely been down there. I told Emilio that Alice was afraid of the cellar; he said of course, she will feel the power coming from it but won't understand it. Have you never seen signs of it in Alice?"

She didn't answer at first but looked out the window, her eyes unfocused, remembering. "Years ago, when we moved into our own cottage, when she was a little girl, she had an imaginary friend called Bella who lived in her bedroom. We discovered it first when she started carrying an old rabbit she had found somewhere. It was mink- coloured velvet, worn, with shabby ears and beady eyes. She took him everywhere and said that Bella had given him to her." She turned back to me. "At first because we had just moved in, we thought Bella was a real child, but it wasn't long before we heard her talking to Bella in her room, and of course she stopped the minute we opened the door. She played with Bella and Bun all the time. That's what she calls the rabbit; she still has him, you see, Bun."

"What about Bella? Does she still speak about Bella?"

"At first we didn't bother because it made her happy. Because of her learning disabilities, Alice had difficulty making friends, so we thought there was no harm in Bella and Bun. But then it used to scare people, other family members, other children, when she spoke about Bella, so in time we stopped her from speaking about it. One time, when she was about nine, Lucy had gone to a neighboring farm to have dinner with a school friend. Bob, my husband, was due to go and pick her up when Alice came screaming down the hall saying that something had hurt Lucy. She was so distraught that we couldn't console her. Twenty minutes later we were told that Lucy's friend had taken her to see the bull. That bull was unpredictable at most times, and the children had been told to stay away from him. But bairns will be bairns, and they had dared each other. The children had teased the bull, the bull had smashed the wood of its enclosure in the barn, and a large splinter went into Lucy's leg. Fortunately her friend's father heard the screams, or it might have been worse. I was sure then that somehow Alice had known about the bull. When I asked her how she knew, she said Bella had told her."

We chatted for a while, and just as I was about to leave the kitchen, Molly said, "Wait, I'm sorry, Erica. I should have said…you should know that Alice…well, it's not just Bun she speaks to. Alice still speaks to Bella."

CHAPTER SEVENTEEN

Bella and Bun

Molly and Alice left before dark, as always, and we were having dinner in the kitchen—everyone, that is, except Paddy and Tosh, who ate in the dining room while maintaining their constant vigil on the bank of monitors spread out on the dining room table. Molly had excelled herself as usual, and we tucked into her delicious Beef Wellington. We talked well on into the night, the conversation light as we chatted about Emilio's impression of living in Scotland as opposed to his native Spain and of Nathan and Jess and how they had become interested in parapsychology. They joked with me about how I should spend my newfound fortune, and James regaled us with hilarious stories of going into business with his stuffy father and friends. On the whole it was all very lighthearted, and for a while, I for one forgot what lay in front of us, what the night and the dark might bring.

I brought up the subject of the DNA and asked Jonah to elaborate, assuring him that I was among friends and had nothing to hide. Jonah went over the information we had, which was the incontrovertible proof that I was not the natural child of the parents who had raised me. Jonah said we should assume the Dutch passport I had come to the UK with was false, but he also said it was likely that the Vansterdams had been truthful about my being born in Delfshaven because we knew that the baby born to the French girl on that day in Delfshaven was a girl and the people with her were said to be an English woman and a Dutch man. He suggested my mother must have had contacts in the UK. She came to Scotland married to a Dutchman and with a new baby; no one would have questioned it. He said if I had not heard that story from them, I might have heard it from someone else, so they prepared the ground by telling me some of the truth. "Consider Paul Cameron. If we start from the premise that Paul Cameron married you to keep an eye on you, it could have been because that originally had been the job of the Vansterdams, who had died suddenly. When Paul Cameron died, whoever is behind this had a problem. They had to get access to the original birth and marriage lines before you tried to use them to register the death. It's possible that they were afraid that you would find out they were fake. So the aunt and uncle turn up and take over the funeral."

"Who identified the body?" James asked.

"They did. It was several days before Paul's body was found. It had been damaged by fish and battered by rocks. Even though I wanted to see him, the Camerons convinced me it was the wrong thing to do. They begged that they be allowed to do it. Gwen Cameron said, "Paul would not want you to remember him like this. For his sake and yours, remember him as he was.""

Katie sat back in her chair. "I was there. I remember the police officer saying that it would be better for Erica if she identified the body; it would help her to accept Paul's death. His aunt said it was a horrendous thing to expect any young woman to do, and she would not allow it. Erica was too distraught to interfere."

"And so," Jonah said, "they successfully prevented you from seeing the body, and they managed to remove your birth certificate."

"Then just disappeared," James said.

Jess, who had been listening intently, asked, "Could the French girl be traced?"

"Interpol are helping with that," Jonah said. "There is an address in Normandy, but it's more than likely a dead end."

We sat tossing over possibilities, biding our time. Occasionally someone would look at the window, each of us very aware that it was dark. I turned to Emilio. "I had a conversation with Molly today, about Alice. You were of course right, Emilio; Alice does have a history of sorts. It turns out she had an imaginary friend called Bella, whom Alice believes gave her a stuffed rabbit she calls Bun. According to Molly, Alice still has Bun and still talks to Bella."

Emilio had been sitting quietly, just listening to the conversation. "Alice knows a lot about this house. She would be able to help you. She may not be able to explain what she knows or what she can remember easily, but with time and patience, maybe."

"So Bella is her spirit guide?" Nathan asked him.

"Possibly," Emilio answered.

"What exactly is a spirit guide?" Katie asked Emilio.

"Different things to different people: Sometimes it is someone who has died and who was very close to you in life and chooses to stay with you, like a guardian angel. You are familiar with this concept? Yes?"

"Yes," Katie nodded. "So that would mean that Alice must have known Bella."

"Not necessarily. A lost or lonely earthbound spirit will sometimes attach itself to someone who attracts it. Alice was a child when Bella made contact. I suspect a very innocent child. Bella would be attracted to the light emanating from Alice. Had they just moved into a new home, Erica?"

"Yes," I said surprised that he had guessed that. "Molly told me they had moved into an old cottage."

"Well, there you are. Perhaps the spirit haunted its old home," Emilio said.

"Sometimes they haunt an object that belonged to them," Nathan said.

"Like the rabbit, Bun," Jess said.

"Yes, like the rabbit." Emilio nodded.

"There is no way we are going to get more information from Alice," James said. "She disintegrated when Jonah tried to question her already."

"And Molly will flip if we even try," I said.

Emilio asked Jonah why he had tried to question Alice in the first place. Jonah told him about the writing in the cellar and Molly's vehement denial that Alice had ever been in the cellar.

"Alice will be aware of things in this house that you are not. She has perhaps learned as a child not to share the things she knows with others. People who do not understand a child with sixth sense are afraid and will..." he hesitated. "*Regañe al niño*. I am sorry, I do not know the word."

"Scold the child," I suggested.

"Ah, yes, scold," he said. "They may have scolded Alice for telling stories."

"Molly did suggest that to me, though she did say that she knew Alice still talks to Bella."

It was at this point Emilio stopped and looked toward the window. His manner stopped us all; instinctively, no one spoke. He closed his eyes, and when he opened them, he said, "They are here."

CHAPTER EIGHTEEN

The Riders

It was an hour before the onslaught was in full swing. Through windows that rattled with their knocking, we could see spectral shapes of riders racing around the house. The oak doors threatened to burst with their pounding. Frozen in terror by the hellish noise, we could do nothing but listen and wait. Grouping together over the monitors in the dining room, Katie and I stood with James between us, holding onto each other, watching the infernal display on the screen.

Emilio, as before, sat very still, his eyes closed. When he opened his eyes, he said, "They seek entry, but they cannot pass the barriers. Do not be afraid. We are safe within this house."

Thunder crashed overhead, the nightmarish specters shrieked and howled, and the dogs bayed. The cacophony of screams and discordant howling lasted almost two hours and had become almost unbearable when suddenly, it stopped. The sudden cessation of the attack and the ensuing silence was as appalling and as terrifying as the clamour had been.

When they were gone, when we were sure they had gone, Nathan and Jess turned to Emilio. "Emilio, can you help us?" Jess asked.

"Can you tell why they are here, what they want?" Nathan asked.

Emilio stood, gripping the back of a chair so hard his knuckles were white. "They are not human."

"Not human? Do you mean they are ghosts?" I asked.

"No, they are not ghosts, at least not what I think you mean by ghosts—that is, they are not earthbound spirits of the dead. They are not human, and they have never been human. They are not of this world. Do you understand?" His hand shook a little as he took the glass of brandy held out to him by Nathan; he downed the brandy in one.

"What do you mean then? What are they?" James asked.

"They are demons."

Now, even considering what we had just experienced, which, without exception, had scared the living daylights out of us and therefore should have engendered a degree of belief in the supernatural in all of us, including Jonah, still there was no escaping the derision in Jonah's voice as he challenged Emilio. "Demons! Oh, gimme a break. Ghosts were hard enough to swallow."

Emilio was cool. "Ah, I see you are able to make the distinction between the two. You know something of demons, Inspector?"

"Oh, yeah. In fact, I have a few of them myself, but that does not explain what is happening here."

"Most certainly it does explain it. I think perhaps you are ignorant of what you are dealing with, or the tone of contempt with which you couch your question and make your statements would be absent." I think Emilio was getting just a little rattled, but then, Jonah had that effect on most people.

"You have got me wrong, pal." Jonah spat out the words. "Until I find a rational explanation, which I will find, I have an open mind."

Emilio shook his head, almost laughing. "You know, sometimes I find your arrogance astonishing, delusional even." Annoyance rising in his voice, he said, "Your mind is not open, Inspector; you reach denial very quickly." He walked away from Jonah and waved his hand in the air. "But that does not matter. In this case, what you believe or do not believe will not alter the outcome."

"Which you think is? What?" Jonah asked.

"Not think, know, as do you, that the creatures seek entry to this house. There is something here that they want, and they will not give up. These are creatures of darkness, dwellers of the forest. To confront them is foolish and dangerous. To communicate with them is risking your life and your soul."

"Isn't that what you're here for, to confront them, to get rid of them?" Jonah eyes, wide, challenged Emilio.

Emilio raised his voice. "I am a clairvoyant, not an exorcist. I cannot, will not, risk confronting them."

"Demons? How are they different from spirits, ghosts?" I asked, more to defuse the tension than anything.

Jess answered. "First let me say that there is, as yet, no scientific evidence that either ghosts or demons even exist. There are, however, many texts from ancient civilisations and in all religions that describe them in detail and group them into types; they are thought not to ever have been human in the first place. Depending on what religious text you read, they exist on a different plane, another dimension from ours. They are thought to be fallen angels, denizens of hell. Destructive, malevolent eaters of souls able to posses and destroy human life."

"Charming," Jonah said.

"Do not be afraid, Erica. Someone has gone to great lengths to protect this house. Someone was expecting them, your house is surrounded by protective forces, and you are safe within it," Emilio said again.

"Where are the protective forces?" I asked.

"They could be anywhere—amulets, talismans, religious icons; they may have performed a ritual. There is also the power that emanates from the cellar. I can perhaps locate the source, but tomorrow, not in the hours of darkness. They have gone for now. We will need strength; we should sleep." He turned to Nathan. "There is one other thing. You said they have become more visible on your monitors."

"Yes," Nathan said. "They started as orbs, and now you can see strong shapes of dogs and riders. We have taped it from the monitors. Look, you can see for yourself."

"Then they grow stronger," Emilio warned.

It was almost dawn, and we were heading off to bed when Katie asked me, "Gill and Jack, have you heard from them again? They didn't phone back, did they?"

"No! Oh my God, I forgot about them. I'll give Gill a call. It's funny she didn't phone back."

"There is no point. The line is down again," Katie said. "Anyway it's four a.m. it's too late to call. It was probably getting dark, and they wouldn't have risked running into the riders. Don't worry. They will be all loved up in a hotel somewhere in Aberdeen."

Jonah, who had gone into the study to look out the front window, called back. "They're here. I can see Jack's car." At that point someone hammered the big knocker on the front door. James went to answer it, and I followed him. He unlocked and opened the door to a wet and bedraggled Jack and Gill standing on the doorstep.

"Where have you been?" I asked, stepping past James. They stood stock still on the doorstep, both smiling. Later, I thought that it was funny how your primal instincts kick in because then, subconsciously, on some subliminal level, I knew there was something not right. I started to say "Come in out of the rain," and only got as far as opening my mouth when Emilio yelled from the dining room door. "No! Close the door! Don't invite them in!"

Before I had time to think, James pushed past me and slammed the heavy oak door shut. Immediately a high-pitched, blood-curdling howl broke out from outside the door. "Gill!" I screamed, trying to open the door again, with James pulling me back. "They are hurting her."

James dragged me back from the door, and Emilio stepped in front of me. Katie, who had heard the commotion, was being held back by Paddy, who had grabbed her when Emilio shouted.

James held me fast. Jonah, who was heading toward the door, stopped when he heard the authority in Emilio's voice. "Erica, look at me, look at me," he shouted. I stopped struggling. "Remember what you saw: They did not follow you into the house because they could not."

I stared at the door, and a picture rose in my mind of the two smiling faces, the memory of the black circles in bilious yellow eyes; red, red lips; and pale, drawn faces. I knew he was telling the truth, and nausea swept over me.

"They were waiting for you to invite them in. They cannot cross the threshold, cannot penetrate the psychic barrier erected around the house unless you invite them in." Emilio spoke slowly, gently. "Those were not your friends, Erica; you know this."

I felt bile rising in my throat, and I swallowed it quickly. "Gill...what's happened to Gill?"

Paddy finally let go of Katie. She threw herself at me, and we clung to each other. Emilio didn't answer me. He said, "It is almost daylight. We can do no more tonight. We must sleep."

"Sleep? How can we sleep while Gill is out there?" Katie cried. "Those things—what will they do to her?"

Emilio looked at her pityingly. "Those were not your friends; your friends are not here. You are exhausted and can do more until morning. Please, rest. We may all need our strength for what tomorrow may bring."

I was in bed by five a.m. and was startled awake a few hours later, feeling I had just closed my eyes. I heard someone screaming, then the sound of uncontrollable sobbing. I fell out of bed and ran out to the landing to find Katie pulling a dressing gown over her pyjamas and James already halfway down the stairs with Jonah at his back. It was daylight, but I was stupid, my head fuzzy with lack of sleep and sudden awakening. I leaned on the banister and watched as Katie raced downstairs. From the landing I saw her fall to her knees, her head in her hands before the open front door. My heart racing, adrenaline coursing through my veins, I ran downstairs. Jonah and James stood in front of the door, blocking my vision. I could just see the top of Molly's head. Then James turned to lift Katie to her feet and pulled her onto his shoulder, turning her away from the scene before him, and as he did so, I saw what they had seen. Two bloodied heads, severed at the neck, one with long, black hair, one with red hair, facing each other in the parody of a kiss. Gill's hair was artfully arranged around her butchered neck, before them a pair of severed hands, fingers entwined. I saw no more. Everything went black.

Molly and Alice had found them. It was Alice I had heard screaming. I woke on the couch in the morning room with Jess holding a cold cloth to my head. Sitting up, I pulled the cloth away as the memory of the horror flooded back. "Gill?" I asked Jess.

Jess bit her lip, eyes brimming with tears. She shook her head. "I'm sorry." The tears rolled down her cheeks, and her lips trembled. "I'm so sorry."

It was real then, not the bad dream I had thought when I opened my eyes. Beautiful, vibrant, funny Gill, my friend, almost a sister, her life gone because she tried to help me; I dissolved into tears, and Jess sobbed with me. The door opened, and Katie came in. She couldn't speak. With eyes red and swollen from crying, she knelt down beside the couch and put her head in my lap.

We sat there in silence. There was nothing we could say. There were no words that could have brought even a whisper of comfort. Even hard-bitten, experienced Jonah was subdued, and James's eyes were shadowed, bloodshot.

Molly had pulled herself together, her need to comfort a distraught Alice masking her own distress. Nathan and Emilio had found a blanket and thrown it over the heads on the doorstep, closed the doors, and locked them. The telephone lines were down, and we had no mobile signal. No way of contacting the police. And Emilio said that by taking even temporary possession of Gill and Jack, the demons had become strong enough to attack in daylight. There was no going for help, no communication with the outside world without risking our lives.

CHAPTER NINETEEN

The Cellar

Paddy and Tosh made tea and coffee and laid out the fresh croissants Molly had brought on the coffee table in the morning room. No one could eat, but we sipped the hot liquid.

"Until we know what they want, we are in danger. We have to find what they are looking for," Emilio said.

"Then if you are right, it's the cellar," Jonah said. "But we've already searched it, top to bottom."

Emilio looked over at Alice, who was sitting on a sofa beside Molly, rocking mechanically back and forth, her mother's hand on her shoulder soothing her. "She knows something," he said. "I need to question her."

Molly reacted in anger. "No," she protested. "No, you have to leave her alone. Look at the state she's in."

Emilio sighed. His voice was soft, mellow, soothing. "Molly, you trust me. I can help Alice. She is in torment, and she is maybe the only one who can help all of us."

Molly was agitated. "You'll push her over the edge. No, I won't let you."

Emilio stood up. He walked over and knelt on one knee in front of Molly and Alice.

"Molly, you must let me speak to her. She is in a world of her own just now; she cannot hear or maybe even see you. I can help her; if you love her, you must trust me."

Molly was beside herself with worry, but then she looked into Emilio's soft brown eyes and burst into tears. "I don't know, I don't know what to do." She looked around at all of us. I moved over beside her and put my arm around her shoulders.

Then the first actual admission came from Jonah that he was feeling out of his depth. He said firmly, "Molly, we don't know what these things are, but they have killed tonight and might kill again. I don't know what Emilio's doing either, but I don't think he can make it any worse. I say let him try."

Molly looked anguished, I suspected her need to protect Alice was clouding her ability to trust anyone.

Emilio spoke again. "She needs help, Molly."

Molly nodded her assent.

Emilio acted quickly. "I need two dining chairs, facing each other." Paddy and Tosh, who were nearest the door, brought chairs from the dining room and placed them in front of the tall fireplace, "Close together, facing please," Emilio said, and Paddy moved the chairs closer, with a little space between them. "I ask you all to be very quiet now." Emilio knelt before Alice, who sat with her arms held tight across her body and was still rocking back and forth violently. "Take your hands from her, Molly," he said, and Molly let go of Alice. Emilio placed both his hands on Alice's shoulders and on contact jolted backwards as though he had been shocked with electricity. He recovered, stood, placed his hands on her again, and called loudly, "ALICE!" Alice continued to rock. "ALICE!" Louder he called her name, commanding her attention. Suddenly Alice stopped rocking. He knelt in front of her, willing Alice to make eye contact. Alice looked at him, and Emilio held out both hands to her. Very slowly Alice unfolded her arms and placed her hands in his. Emilio stood up, raising Alice with him. Without letting go of her hands, he took her to the dining chairs and sat her down. He then sat in the chair facing her. Alice's face relaxed; the strain seemed to melt away.

"Alice," he said gently. "Is Bella with you?"

--- The Cellar ---

Alice's face relaxed. She turned her head, her chin down, and looked up coyly at Emilio. She smiled, raised her chin, and licked her lips, then, to my amazement, in a normal adult voice, unlike her normal halting speech Alice said, "Bella won't come here."

"Why will Bella not come here Alice?" he asked.

"She is afraid of this house."

"Is she afraid of the house or of the riders outside of the house?"

"Both."

"Why is Bella afraid of the house?" Emilio asked.

"She is afraid of what lies in the cellar."

"Do you know what lies in the cellar, Alice?"

"No."

"Does Bella know what it is?"

"Yes, but she won't tell me."

"Why not?"

"I don't know."

Emilio drew his breath in and sighed.

"But I know where it lies," she said quickly, a new husky tone to her voice.

Emilio sat up again. "How do you know where it lies?"

"Bella told me. I went to see, but then I didn't want to look." So she had been in the cellar. Jonah had been right.

"Will you show me where it is, Alice? This thing that frightens Bella."

"Uh huh," she said coquettishly.

Still holding her hands, Emilio stood. He let go of one of her hands, pointed to the door, and said, "Show me where it lies."

Never taking her eyes from his, still holding his hand, Alice rose. She faced him, smiling. "Come with me," she said, letting go of Emilio's hand. She waited for him to open the door; he opened it, and she walked through into the hall.

Emilio signed for the rest to stay, but James, Jonah, Nathan, and I followed them. In other circumstances it would have been comical, for Alice walked straight and tall with a gentle, seductive sway of her hips that was incompatible with her tweed skirt, thick woolen tights, and brown lacing shoes. With a confidence that belied this was actually Alice, she took the key and unlocked the door, switched on the light, and walked carefully down the dimly lit stairs. Jack and Jonah lifted two large flashlights from the foot of the stairs and followed them.

Alice turned right into the wine cellar; stopping in front of the shelves, where earlier we had seen her name written on the dust. Looking at Jonah pointedly, she raised her eyebrows and pouted her lips. Then with a gait that would have done credit to a 1930s Hollywood diva or a catwalk model, she walked to the end of the shelves, turned, and with both hands pushed the shelves backward. She strained a little, putting all of her weight behind the effort, then, grating on some kind of mechanism, the heavy oak shelves full of wine bottles slid back. They moved until they almost blocked the entrance through which we had come, exposing a trap door in the floor beneath. Alice leaned back, and with the same knowing smile fixed on her face, said in a husky voice, "This is what you are looking for."

At her feet lay a trapdoor with a large iron rung. Jonah stepped forward, grabbed it with both hands, and with effort pulled, heaving the trapdoor up to reveal stairs winding down into darkness.

Emilio turned to Alice, took both her hands in his, and said, "Thank you, Bella."

Bella, of course, I should have realised the behavior so alien to Alice was not that of Alice at all. Somehow Emilio had brought Bella out in Alice, and it was Bella, not Alice, who had led us here to this underground place. Emilio had no sooner spoken Bella's name than the face before him crumpled. She looked wildly round her. "No, no," she cried. "Mummy, Mummy," she called for Molly.

I put my arm round her. "It's OK, Alice," I said. "Everything's all right."

Nathan took her from me. "C'mon, Alice, I'll take you to your mother." He led her away.

Jonah flicked a switch he found underneath the trapdoor, and we looked down into another, deeper, dimly lit cellar. Walking in single file, we went carefully down the narrow wooden stairs into a room about forty feet square. The only thing in the room was a long metal chest or box some fifteen feet long by four feet wide, about the depth of a coffin.

It lay directly on the centre of the floor, surrounded by iron rungs like the one on the trap door, each of which was embedded into the floor. There were thick iron chains crisscrossing the chest, looping through the rungs, and each corner rung was padlocked. We stood looking at it, bewildered, speechless for a few moments.

"It is from this chest the power emanates," Emilio said in a strange detached voice.

"What is it?" I asked.

"Whatever it is, we are going to have a hell of a job finding out," Jonah lifted the nearest length of chain. "These rungs are nearly an inch thick and solid iron."

James lifted a padlock. "This is the weakest point," he said.

I was horrified. "Wait a minute; you are not seriously going to open that? You have no idea what's inside. It could be dangerous. I've seen the movies, you know the ones where people open the sarcophagus of an Egyptian mummy and the corpse comes out to meet them."

James smiled "I don't think we have a choice, but I think it would be better if you go back upstairs."

"I agree," said Jonah. "We have to open it, it's the only clue we have to what's going on here, but in case there is a problem you should join the others."

"I'm not going anywhere. If you insist on opening it, I want to be here."

"Erica, it could be dangerous" James said.

"I just said that to you. You're the ones about to open it and I'm not leaving."

James looked at Jonah and sighed, "There might be something in the cellar upstairs we could break the padlocks with." He went to look, and Jonah followed him.

"Do you think it's safe to open it Emilio" I asked. Emilio hadn't moved he had been standing staring at the box in silence; I watched as he began rocking slightly on the balls of his feet, almost trance-like. Suddenly his face contorted, and he moaned a deep, primordial, agonised sound, as of something in terrible pain or fear. The sound chilled me to the marrow; my instinct was to run, not to help him; I wanted to run away, but I couldn't move. He started to cry, to sob; it was the most horrible sound I had ever heard. My heart and my mind could not compute that this man, so strong, so self-composed, was wailing in abject despair.

The horror of the moment was broken by James and Jonah returning with a pair of bolt cutters they had found. Emilio turned to face them, anguish still showing on his face. He almost bumped into a surprised Jonah as he stumbled towards the stairs. Jonah said. "Is he OK?"

"What's wrong with Emilio? What happened?" James asked.

"Nothing, I don't know." I was clutching my arms and shivering. "He started moaning...it was awful." I looked at the chest, "It has just reinforced my feeling we shouldn't be opening this."

"You're shivering," James said, taking his fleece off and putting it around me.

"Ready?" Jonah asked as he put the jaws of the bolt cutter round the hasp of the first padlock.

"Wait... wait a minute," I cried. "Are you just going to open it, shouldn't we think about it first? I mean we don't know what's in there. Emilio... he ran away, you saw the state he was in. He picked up something, he was terrified."

James shook his head. "We have to open it Erica we can't just walk away and pretend we never saw it. I think the answer is in there."

"We have to do this" Jonah said, he hesitated for only a moment, and then he looked at James who said, "Do it".

I had chills running up my spine as I watched while the lever mechanism of the bolt cutter sliced through the old iron easily, and the padlock snapped. "Well, that was easier than I expected." Jonah continued until all the padlocks had been cut. James pulled the chains through, and the two men, using the bolt cutters, levered the lid. It took the three of us pushing to slide the heavy iron lid off the box until finally it clattered to the floor. Inside lay another box, almost the same size as its housing. It was made of old, broken wood, rotting in places, not manufactured but sliced straight from the tree. The ill-fitting lid lifted off easily, and James shone his torch inside. Lengths of natural-coloured linen-type cloth, old and faded, covered what lay in the box. There appeared to be three packages. The first was round, the second was smaller and square, and the third was long and took up the entire length of the box. Jonah carefully removed the cloth from the round package to reveal what looked like interwoven branches of some kind. They looked a bit like bramble branches, layered, pleated to form a circle, about the size of a human head.

"What in God's name is that?" Jonah asked, turning it carefully in his hands.

James was staring at it, then he turned and looked at me, wonder in his eyes. "'God's name' might be the operative words."

"Well," Jonah said, examining it, turning it, his voice faltering, the macho tone fading, realisation dawning. "Any ideas?" he almost whispered.

There are no words I know of that could tell you, could describe, the awe that gripped all three of us as we gazed at the Crown of Thorns.

CHAPTER TWENTY

Paddy

Jonah stood uncertainly, his usual command of the situation gone. He seemed lost for words. James reached into the box and lifted the smaller package; he carefully unfolded it in his hand and exposed three large, thin iron spikes.

"Looks like some kind of iron pins," Jonah said.

"Or nails," James said. "I think the black stuff on them might be old, dried blood."

Jonah put down the circle of branches and opened the last package. A long wooden spear lay nestled in the fold of the cloth. It consisted of a wooden pole about six feet long fastened onto an iron shaft. The shaft ended in a sharp point. On the head of the spear was the same black staining as on the branches and the spikes. We stood, the three of us, not speaking for what seemed like eternity. I felt strange, awed, upset, confused, drunk with emotion. I backed toward the stairs. "I'll go fetch the others. They should see this."

In the morning room the fire blazed. Alice lay asleep on the sofa, and Molly sat beside her. Nathan sat with Tosh and Paddy. They were locked in conversation about demons. Katie and Jess sat together, Jess listening intently. In other circumstances it would have been a cosy scene, but Molly looked stressed and worried. Katie's eyes were swollen and red with crying, and everyone looked in need of sleep.

Even with James's fleece wrapped around me, I was still cold. I moved to stand by the fire. "We have found something in the cellar." They waited for me to explain, to tell them more.

Then Nathan said, "What?"

"You have to go see for yourself. I think all of you should go."

Molly looked at Alice.

"Leave her, Molly," I said. "Let her sleep. She won't come to any harm." Molly was unsure. "You have to see. Come, it will only take a few minutes."

"I will stay with her." Emilio had appeared at my back. He was perfectly composed.

Katie hung back. "What is it? Why the mystery?"

"Trust me. Go see for yourself, make your own mind up."

I took them to the top of the underground cellar and left them to go down to James and Jonah. Back in the morning room, Emilio sat and Alice still slept. I moved the two dining chairs from the front of the fire and shoveled coal from the brass scuttle onto the fire. "You're not going to ask me, Emilio? I would tell you what was in the box, but I think you already know." I hesitated.

"Why? Because I ran away?" he said.

"No. Actually, I was going to say…You saw something…I mean, felt something."

Emilio leaned forward, elbows on knees, hands clasped, and stared into the fire crackling and spitting in the hearth. "Yes, I saw something." I waited for him to speak again, thinking I won't ask him; if he wants to tell me he will. Finally he said, "I saw…a man…tortured." He twisted his hands, stood up, and began pacing the floor. He gesticulated in the air. "When I see things, when I touch a person or an object, it is for me like watching a movie, but this was different. He looked straight at me, this man, in pain, bleeding…looked at me as though he knew I was watching him."

I carried one of the chairs over to the wall by the door. "We opened the box; we found another inside made of roughhewn wood and three objects wrapped in cloth. Branches twisted into a crown, iron spikes with pointed ends, and a spear with an eagle on the shaft. There were black stains on all of them. James said it's blood." I moved the other chair. "They are real, aren't they?"

"Real? Are you asking me if that box contains the instruments of death used to take the life of Jesus Christ?"

I didn't answer. It was too momentous a question; I could hardly believe what I was thinking. The cold shivers ran down my back again. I sat down, mostly because my legs felt shaky.

"Are you Christian?" he asked.

"I was brought up a Christian. If you are asking do I go to church, no, I don't, haven't, not for years. If they are real, do you think could be what the riders want? Could there be a connection?"

"They are real," was all he said. "The wood of the box is the wood of the cross."

They came back together, all subdued; no one spoke. Molly took her place beside Alice. Nathan, Jess, and the students stood together. Tosh and Nathan were energized, excited. Paddy and Jess were quiet. Katie sat down beside me. "Do you think they are real? Maybe they are fakes?"

"What would be the point of going to all that trouble to hide fakes?" Jess said.

James stood beside the fireplace; he looked cold too. "Whoever put them there certainly thought they were real."

Jonah had walked to the window and was scanning the grounds. "It's still and quiet out there; too quiet." He looked at Emilio.

"They are still there," Emilio said. "I can feel them."

Alice woke. She looked around and smiled at everyone as though nothing had happened. She made to get up, but Molly stopped her, asking her where she was going. Alice told Molly it was time to make tea. Molly said, "Later, Alice. We will both go make lunch, OK?" Alice whispered in Molly's ear, and Molly said, "OK, but I'll come with you, and we might as well make a start on lunch." She turned to me. "Something hot, or sandwiches?"

"You don't have to, Molly. Just sit with Alice. We can all make our own."

"No, we will be fine, won't we Alice? I find it's better if we keep to a routine." Molly took Alice's arm and walked her Siamese fashion to where Tosh held the door for them.

Emilio answered my thoughts. "She does not remember anything."

"So Emilio, they are the real McCoy, are they? Those instruments, for want of a better word, you think they might be genuine?" Jonah asked.

"Genuine? Ah! What exactly are you asking me, Inspector? Have you come round to the possibility of a spiritual world? Remember I did not see the things you saw. What were they? Erica tells me you found a spear, a crown of thorns, nails. Perhaps you can get DNA from the blood on them. You do agree it is blood? Can you collect DNA from two-thousand-year-old samples, Inspector?"

"Cut the crap, Emilio. You know what I am asking you."

Emilio capitulated. "Yes, I believe they are genuine."

"Do you think the riders could be after the spear?" Nathan asked Emilio.

"Why just the spear?" Jonah asked.

"Have you never heard of the Spear of Destiny?" Nathan asked Jonah.

"I know, Emilio, that you believe they are real, but how can that be?" Jess said. "The Spear of Destiny, the lance that pierced the side of Christ? That is in a museum in Vienna."

"Allegedly," Paddy said. He was still leaning against the wall, his hands inside the pockets of his hooded sweatshirt. "There is another with a claim to authenticity in the Vatican in Rome, and one in Armenia, and at least one other kicking around."

"You know a lot about it," Jonah said.

"I spent five years in a Roman Catholic seminary before I decided the priesthood wasn't for me."

"Five years!" Katie exclaimed. "Does that not make you a priest?"

"No, not even nearly. After high school it takes eight years of study, and that includes a bachelor and master's degree. Even then it's up to the bishop to decide if a candidate is suitable."

"Paddy has a degree in theology," Jess said.

"Good," Jonah said. "That makes you useful. You can throw some light on this. What do you know about this spear?"

Paddy, still leaning against the wall, hands in his pockets, studied his trainers for a moment. When he looked up, he said, "Historically the Jews didn't like crucified criminals to die on the Jewish Sabbath, so the practice was to break their legs to ensure they were dead. Instead, unwittingly perhaps, but nevertheless fulfilling an ancient prophesy, a Roman centurion pierced Jesus's side with his lance, and it is written that blood and water flowed out. Check out the Bible. There is probably one in the study; there's everything else in there."

"Why would the riders want it?" I asked Paddy.

"Why?" He paused again, considering his answer. "Because the Holy Lance has great occult and historical significance. There is a legend that the one who possesses the spear will be invincible in battle, able to conquer and rule the world. Some of the most powerful dictators and generals in history searched for and found and lost a spear they believed to be the Holy Lance. Constantine the Great, Barbarossa, Charlemagne. Even Napoleon attempted to steal the spear but failed. It's one of the most precious archaeological pieces in the world. Myths and legends have circulated for generations about the spear's mystical powers. Hitler was supposed to have been obsessed by it. In 1938, when Hitler became the chancellor of Germany and annexed the state of Austria, he ordered the entire Habsburg collection, including the spear, to be moved to the city of Nuremberg. He secreted the spear in a church where it was found by the Americans at the end of the war and reportedly returned to the museum in Vienna. It was recovered on the same day that Adolph Hitler shot himself, the day that Germany surrendered to the allies. Interestingly, that fulfilled another legend that whoever held the spear would die on the day he lost it. That lance, which is still in Vienna, is believed to contain a nail from the cross. The nail and the lance were carbon dated not that long ago. The nail was from the correct period, but the lance was dated seventh century. So there has always been a question as to whether it was genuine in the first place, or did Hitler substitute it with a fake? There are some conspiracy theorists who suggest the Americans handed back a replica and kept the real lance. They point out that since the Second World War, America has become the most powerful nation on earth."

"So is there a possibility the one in the cellar is the real one and that is what the riders are looking for, valuable antiques?" Jonah asked.

"Not for their value in money, Inspector. Something that took the life of Jesus Christ would be a powerful weapon in their hands," Emilio said.

"Because it killed Christ," Nathan said.

"But it didn't," Jess added. "He was already dead. Remember, the centurion pierced his side to confirm death."

"It is still covered in the blood of Christ," Paddy said. "An evil entity might want to use the power of that blood."

"Yes, exactly. The occult significance is enormous. The demons that ride outside tonight may well have been sent by Satan to collect it," Emilio said.

"Why? Is he an antique collector too?" Jonah sighed. "Oh lord, I feel as though I am living in Fairyland."

"That would be about right, Jonah. Fairy-tales are full of corpse heads on doorsteps. Sorry, Erica." James looked an apology in my direction. "What's your problem? You don't have to be a Christian or believe Jesus was the Son of God to accept that this man who died more than two thousand years ago is still influencing millions of people around the world with his teachings."

"Teachings that have caused wars," Jonah said.

"Teachings that have been corrupted by man for his own gain and so caused wars," Paddy said.

"I am not an historian," Jonah said, "but even I know that the Gospels have been called into question. Weren't they written well after the death of Jesus, and aren't there plenty of documents to say they are inaccurate?"

Paddy shook his head. "The writings of the early church say that the stories from the life of Jesus were told to the writers of the Gospels by word of mouth, by eyewitnesses. You have to take into account that the people, who wrote the Gospels and preached the word of God at that time, had nothing to gain and a lot to lose. They had no financial gain, and they were persecuted, imprisoned and put to death just for spreading Christ's words of peace and love."

James said, "Eyewitnesses, Jonah, the most powerful weapon against crime. The most likely way to get a conviction, to have a jury believe what the lawyer wants them to believe, is the testimony of an eyewitness."

"OK, let me get it right: you're asking me to believe not only that there are devils or demons whatever you want to call them, riding round the house, but that they are doing it just to collect some old Roman weapons. That is pretty hard to swallow."

Paddy said, "You know, Jonah, evil not only exists, it thrives today, thanks to disbelief and apathy. Take a look at the world around you. There was a documentary on TV the other day. In Uganda, voodoo is thriving. Witch doctors are again sacrificing children, fueled by the belief that child sacrifice will make them rich. The growing upper classes are having children kidnapped from poor villages. Then witch doctors are burying them alive or beheading them. The story circulated for a long time, and no one really believed it until the journalist collected the evidence. Watch the news, Jonah. Satan is alive and doing nicely. The more good men are incredulous, the more of a hold evil gets."

"OK, right. Let's suppose you might have a case. Where do you suggest we go from here?" Jonah asked.

"We go for help, that's where we go," Katie said.

"No," Emilio answered. "That would be suicide. They are out there, and because they have killed, they are now stronger. They are able to manifest in the daylight. It is too dangerous; we would never make it out of the woods. Anyway, what kind of help are you going for? Who would believe your story? The police? Look at Jonah, who has been with us, who has experienced what we have, and yet still he doubts the truth. No, there is no one. We are on our own here. If the riders want these things, these weapons instrumental in the death of Christ, it must be to use them to kill or destroy someone they cannot kill or whose soul they cannot possess any other way. Perhaps they seek the one who set the psychic barriers around the house, the one who has drawn Erica here. The answers are here in this house, and if we want to survive, we had better find them before nightfall."

CHAPTER TWENTY-ONE

Caleb

"Find out how? I mean where do we even start?" I asked Emilio.

"We start by leaving it outside the door," Jonah said.

"Leave it outside the door? You want to leave The Spear of Destiny lying on the doorstep? That is preposterous," Jess said.

"So preposterous you'd rather they killed you first and then took it? Remember what they did to Jack and Gill," Jonah reminded her. "You need a reality check."

"You are right, Inspector. Give them what they want. Leave the spear on the doorstep and see what happens," Emilio said.

I jumped when a bell in the hall rang. "That's the kitchen doorbell," James shouted as he and Paddy ran for the door. "Molly doesn't know. She'll open the door."

We ran after them and watched as James burst through the kitchen door, but it was too late. Molly had already opened the outside door. As I reached the kitchen I heard her say, "Come on in, son, I'm so glad to see you." She stood wiping her hands on her apron, pushing her grey hair back into place, smiling at the man in the dungarees who had stepped in at her invitation and quickly pushed the door closed behind him. She turned, surprised at the commotion behind her. "It's all right. This is Caleb, my son-in-law." She turned back to him, anxiety returning to her face. "We are so glad to see you, Caleb. You'll never believe what's been going on in here. We thought we couldn't get help. People were killed last night, horribly. We need help. Someone has to go for the police. There's no phone, and we were scared to go for help, and…" She was babbling. She stopped and followed his gaze to Alice. Alice was backing away from her mother and Caleb, shaking her head. "Alice, what is it?"

"Come away from him, Molly," Paddy commanded. "It's not Caleb."

I realised what was happening and pulled Molly's arm. "Molly, come away from him." She turned to look at us and back to Caleb, confused. "What are you talking about? This is Caleb," she cried.

"No, it's not," Paddy said from the doorway.

Caleb spun round, his face contorted. "Ah, it's the little priest," he spat out. "What would you know, little priest? You cocksucking little bastard," he screamed. "You don't believe in all this shit anyway. Isn't that right? Patrick?" he spat.

Smirking, hands in his dungaree pockets, Caleb strolled around the floor. He stopped, leaned over, stooping, then lifted his face up, his shoulders still hunched over. He grinned, and his voice changed to a woman's with a strong Irish accent. "Patrick, darlin', you have to have faith. Your mammy knows what's best for you, son. You go and be a priest and make your mammy proud." He tottered forward as though he would fall, then stood up straight. He laughed at Paddy.

Paddy turned pale, but he didn't answer.

"But you didn't, you little shit. You let your mammy down, didn't you? You didn't believe all this crap she fed you. Now she's with us in hell, and the old cunt doesn't have a fucking little priest to babble his filthy prayers for her."

Molly was stunned, horrified by what she was hearing. She backed away, reaching for Alice.

"Remember, it lies," Paddy said.

It turned on Emilio, "Oh oh oho whoop e do, and it's the fortune teller. Let's hear it for the Asshole—EMILIO MENDEZ, con artist extraordinaire." It growled a deep, throaty, gurgling sound. The voice had changed to an American accent. "Hey, Emilio, we can make a buck or two here, conning old ladies. Hey, Emilio, old buddy, it's me, Frankie. I'm rotting in hell…and I'm keeping a place warm for you. No more conning old ladies for me." It…Caleb…laughed a guttural, harsh rasping sound.

"Don't communicate with it. Don't listen to it," Paddy said.

The thing that was Caleb stood salivating in the middle of the floor. There was a horrendous smell, and faeces ran down its legs, pouring out its trousers, fouling the floor. I covered my mouth and nose as the overpowering stench made me retch. "Oh my God," Jonah cried, covering his mouth and nose.

"God," it hissed at Jonah. "GOD? You haven't got one. What the use of askin' that freak for help anyway, Mister Polis Man? You don't believe in him, remember? It's too late for you, waaaaay too late, you is joinin' us in our little special place where we eat the flesh of little polis men like you." It slavered, shooting its tongue back and forth.

Alice whimpered, "No. No." She shook her head, covered her ears, and backed against the wall.

"Hey, hey, fucking stupid a-a-a Alice, come over here now. You come to Daddy. Come see what Daddy's got for you." It stood pumping its hips toward Alice.

"Molly, take her out of here." James pushed Molly and Alice toward the door. Katie stepped forward and helped Molly pull Alice out of the kitchen. It made to follow them, but Paddy grabbed a carton of salt that Molly had left on the work surface and poured it in a line across the kitchen between the creature and us.

"Ohhhh, think you're smart, asshole?" it hissed at Paddy.

"We need to contain it," Paddy said. He seemed to stand taller, and in a perfectly controlled voice, he said, "The demon has taken over Caleb's body. Caleb is still alive. Get into the hall. It won't leave, and it can't cross the salt line."

I couldn't move. I was so terrified of this spitting, foul thing that my legs had stopped working, but Jonah pushed me toward Tosh, who pulled me out the door into Jess and Nathan, who were watching from the hallway. Emilio and Paddy followed, and James pulled the door, slamming it shut behind him.

It was surreal. We stood in the lovely hallway of Lanshoud, with its cream flock wallpaper, gold framed prints of highland glens, and solid oak doors, lit by elegant lamps on highly polished tables. The scene in the hall was one of elegance and normality while in the kitchen, Molly's son-in-law howled like an alien from another world, like some fetid organism from a nightmare, snarling and growling like a demented animal.

"Tell me you know what you're doing," Jonah asked Paddy. How does the salt work?"

"How is a long story," Paddy answered. "Let's just say it should keep him contained—for a while anyway."

Should; I personally would have preferred it if Paddy had sounded a little more convinced. No one else one said anything. If I were to hazard a guess, it would be that everyone was thinking, *Should* keep him contained. Does that mean it might not?

Molly, tense and anxious, stood cuddling Alice. "But what about Caleb? We can't just leave him there." She looked anxiously at Jonah, who I think was still trying to get his head around the salt. And he wasn't the only one, because James then asked, "What about that salt? Are you saying it won't keep him in there?"

"No it won't keep him there. He can still leave the way he came. He just can't, I hope, cross it to reach this door," Paddy snapped.

"I asked you how it worked," Jonah barked at Paddy loudly enough to make Nathan jump. "The salt thing."

A clearly unnerved Nathan must have felt he should intervene in what seemed to be a tense moment. He blurted out, "Salt represents life. It comes from the ocean, where life began. The water evaporates, leaving salt behind. It cures meat, flesh, it prevents decay, keeping it edible long after it's shown to have rotted. Scientifically, it's supposed to have something to do with electricity, electrical currents that exist in matter. It's thought to ground spirits." Jess was nodding frantically in agreement.

Jonah didn't even look at Nathan; he had not taken his eyes off Paddy. "Somehow I don't think he was taking the scientific approach, were you?" he asked Paddy. Jonah's tone had a hint of derision in it that I found strange in someone who was supposedly asking for help.

Paddy seemed to consider him for a moment before he spoke. "From ancient times, salt has been used both to identify and to protect from the presence of evil. In the Roman Catholic rite of Baptism, salt was applied to the lips to exorcise the devil. In other cultures too; in Sweden it was put under the infant's tongue, in Germany, in the Balkans, in Southern India, they do the same. In Thailand, women wash with salt after childbirth to protect themselves from demonic assault. In the North of England, it was the custom to tuck a small bag of salt into a baby's clothing on its first outing, to protect its innocence from evil. The fact is for centuries salt has been used around the world, to ward off demonic attack." Paddy hesitated. "The truth is, I didn't even know if it would work. There are other things stronger, but they weren't lying about the kitchen table."

Emilio had been listening intently. "This conversation is pointless. Caleb is possessed, and you are not going to get any information from him. Not from Caleb, and not from the spirit who possesses him."

"Possession? Well, there you are. It seems you and Emilio are on the same wavelength. It's your call, Paddy, but I think you should at least try."

Paddy held his hand up and stepped away "Whoa, Jonah. If you're suggesting what I think you are, forget it. I am way out of my depth here; I can't carry out an exorcism, and even if I were willing to try, in all likelihood Caleb would not remember anything."

"Well, we won't know till you try." Jonah challenged him. "You're almost a priest, aren't you? Isn't that what you do? You seemed to understand what was going on in there. Why can't you do it?"

"Because *almost* is the operative word. Look, I spent some time with an exorcist. I have seen this before, but I am not an ordained priest. I was only there because the bishop thought it would renew my faith. Instead all it did was make me realise I was not cut out for the priesthood. I wasn't good enough. Do you understand? If one of the hunt has taken possession of Caleb, then you are talking about a spirit of considerable power."

Jonah was not giving up. "You've seen it before, you've played at this game before. That means you must have some idea what to do." It was a statement, not a question.

Paddy was furious. "It's not a game; it's dangerous. The man I studied with was an expert chosen by the Vatican because he was a good and holy man; I can't do what he did. It's ludicrous. It's out of the question."

James appealed to Paddy. "You may have to, Paddy, because you are all we have got. What choice do we have? They are out there now circling. In the night they will be stronger, and if one of their number has possessed Caleb, isn't there a chance it might kill him?"

"Kill him," Molly cried, her face drained. "Oh God no." She turned to Paddy. "Please, please help him if you can," she pleaded.

I put my hand round Molly's shoulder. "Paddy, where else are we going to get help? And that is a man in there. We can't just leave him like that."

"Could you at least try to communicate with it, find out what they want?" Nathan asked.

Paddy shook his head. "There is no point. It will just lie."

"Erica…Erica…" a voice called from the kitchen, wheedling, enticing. Chills ran up and down my body, instant recognition causing a vice-like fear to grip my stomach. The voice was singsong. "ERICA. Kom naar Papa schatje."

I stared at the closed door; shivers ran up and down my spine. I was listening to a voice from the grave, the voice of Aalbert Vansterdam. James tried to stop me, but I pushed his hand away and walked toward the door, mesmerised I pushed it open slowly. Immediately my senses were assaulted on all fronts, by the horror in the chair, the sight, the smell, the voice. Caleb sat sideways on a kitchen chair, his legs crossed, relaxed, checking out his fingernails. Fingernails that had grown long, yellow, and dirty in the space of an hour. He gestured for me to come to him, but the voice that was chilling my blood, was that of my dead father.

James stepped in front of me. "Don't go in there." His voice was muffled by the hand he used to shut out the nauseating odour.

I whispered, "It's what my father called me—*Schatje*. It's Dutch. It means little sweetheart."

Paddy caught my arm and pulled me back from the door. "Erica, it's lying to you. It's not your father."

Caleb laughed. "Yes, you fucking bitch. You should listen to the little priest, you stupid cunt," it screamed, shooting off the chair toward us, but it was brought short, snarling and spitting to a halt by the salt on the floor. "We want your father!" it howled in fury at me. "Bring him here. We are WAITING," it screamed. Caleb's face was changing, growing older, his skin coarser, wrinkled, and jaundiced-looking; the stink was overpowering. Nauseated, I backed away into the hall, and James closed the door.

"We want your father. What did it mean?" I asked no one in particular.

"It means nothing. It will say anything to get your attention," Emilio said.

"No," James mused. "I think she's right. We might be missing something. Aalbert Vansterdam was not Erica's father. She doesn't know who her father was. Maybe that's what, or rather who, they are here for. Obviously her real father could be the unknown benefactor. Maybe it's not the relics they're after. Maybe it's Erica's real father."

"What? You mean he is here in this house somewhere?" Emilio asked.

"I don't know. I'm clutching at straws," James said

"All the more reason why we need to question it, find out why they are here, get some answers." Jonah turned to Paddy. "If you could do that—question it, I mean—what would you need?"

Paddy drew his breath into a kind of incredulous laugh. "You don't know what you're asking. Did you listen to a word I said?"

"Yeah, yeah, I heard it all. I heard the important bits like you were apprenticed to an exorcist and you've had a crisis of confidence, you're think you're not good enough, something like that; I got it all," Jonah said, waiving his hands dismissively at Paddy. He was not about to take no for an answer. "Well, right now you are all we've got." He got just too close to Paddy, confrontational. "So I'll ask you again: What do you need?"

They stared into each other's eyes in some kind of standoff; they were both angry. It was a few moments before Paddy answered.

"I have what I need. I have a crucifix, holy water, and the Roman Ritual."

"What? You brought these things with you?" Jonah asked, surprised.

"We came here to a supposedly haunted house, though I never really intended to use them."

"Paddy, I think you have to do this," James said. "I will help you if I can."

Paddy stood looking at the kitchen door through unfocussed eyes. We waited for his decision while the thing that was Caleb growled and muttered obscenities in the background.

"We need rope or something to restrain him, and I will need someone, not you Emilio because you are a sensitive; you would be a target, and not you, Jonah, because it will feed on your scepticism and disbelief...James?"

"Anything. What do you want me to do?"

It is for anyone hard to imagine; it was for me unbelievable, that in this day and age we were contemplating talking to a demon. It would be laughable in any other circumstances. Until a couple of weeks ago, we were a group of normal people getting on with our ordinary, everyday lives. For most of us, the biggest worries were financial or emotional. Now we were tired, exhausted, balancing on the edge of fear. With communication cut off from outside, our world had been reduced in size to the walls of Lanshoud and was suddenly populated only by the people in that house. How crazy that my life was in the hands of people I hadn't even known existed last month, and now they were in peril because they came to help me. The human race in its finest hour can be extraordinary. Outside there were people shopping, cooking dinner, going about their everyday business; but here we were, reliving a scene from the Middle Ages. Emilio had been right when he said there was no point in going for help, for who would believe us?

I wanted to be there, to watch, to help, but Paddy was adamant that there would be just he and James; he said it was far too dangerous. He did not say "for a woman," but it was implied. I stood my ground I wanted to be there, whatever happened. I pointed out this was my house, my problem. I would not leave them to face it alone. I was as determined that I would be there as Paddy was determined that I would not. I could see no reason why James should be there and not me.

James opened the door of the study. "Can I speak to you for a moment?"

"If you are about to lecture me, save your breath. I make my own decisions, James," I warned him, but I went in anyway.

I folded my arms and turned to face him. He closed the door and grabbed the back of a chair, white knuckled.

"I'm not disputing that this is your house and your decision to make, but Paddy is putting everything he believes in on the line. He has told you it's dangerous, he has told you he is not sure he is up to the task, but he is going to try anyway. It's Paddy that thing will attack first; you know that. I know he said Jonah and Emilio will be targets, but you, Erica, you are a prime target. There were no riders round the house when you went home, and there were no riders when you went to the Netherlands. As you said, it has something to do with you. You are asking Paddy to put you at risk. He won't do that; don't ask him to." He was angry. "It's selfish and irresponsible."

He left the room noisily. I was humiliated. I felt like a chastised child. I knew deep down he was right. I thought about going after him, but if I did, I would have to concede he was right, and that might seem as though I was acknowledging his mental superiority and good sense. No way was I going to do that, but I did find Paddy and tell him that I would take his advice and stay out.

We needed food—not from the kitchen, because who would even consider going in there for food, even though Caleb had stopped growling and there had been silence for some time. There was the larder beside the kitchen, and I knew we would find something to eat there. Katie came with me, and we found Long Life Milk, bottles of cola and lemonade, biscuits, and cheese. There were tins of corned beef, salmon, and ham. We couldn't use the salmon, as it didn't have a ring pull and there was no tin opener. We had no dishes or cutlery, but there were display cabinets in the dining room with expensive china. We rinsed them in the sink in the boot room, where we also found an old picnic basket with some plastic cutlery. Tosh gathered coal from the bunker in the boot room. He filled as many containers as he could find and lugged them through to the morning room, where the fire was still lit.

No one had much of an appetite. Still everyone, in the interest of trying to keep our strength up, tried to eat something—all except Paddy, that is, who declined all offers of food. I met him coming down the stairs. "Paddy, I just wanted to say I'm sorry if you feel pressurised. I know you have doubts, and I understand that. My head's all over the place. I try to rationalise, to find some other explanation for what has been happening here because it seems madness to even consider that Caleb is possessed by an evil spirit, but…"

He cut me short. "You have no need to apologise. I have no doubt about what it is we are dealing with, Erica; only my ability to control it." Paddy sat on the stairs, and I sat down beside him. "And that is not a lack of faith in God, but a lack of faith in myself. When I first met Michel de Biere, the Vatican-appointed exorcist, I seriously doubted the legitimacy of exorcism. The people he saw mostly had had extensive psychiatric investigation and had either been diagnosed as split personalities or were deemed delusional by experts in that field. All of them had failed to respond to traditional treatment. It was almost always a relative who called for help when they realised that the traditional treatments weren't working and the patient's condition was deteriorating. I was already having a crisis of faith, and watching these people didn't help me. I felt that some of them were duped almost, that they had been led to believe they were possessed by something and were just acting out the part. It was all very theatrical. I just wasn't convinced. My faith was not strong enough.

"I had decided to go back to the bishop and tell him I was definitely leaving the priesthood. Out of courtesy I went first to tell Father De Biere of my plans. It was on the same day he was asked to see a young girl called Natalie. He asked me to assist him with this last case, and I agreed. I don't want to discuss it in great detail with you. To ask you to believe me would be to ask you to comprehend the incomprehensible. The things I saw were unbelievable: a fifteen-year-old Italian girl screamed obscenities at us in Latin and in Aramaic, the language of Palestine at the time of Christ. Furniture was flung by unseen hands across the room, her bed levitated, she spat volumes of spittle at us. Have you ever seen the movie *The Exorcist?*"

"Yes."

"Well, this was the real thing. I experienced terror even more than you have experienced here. It left me with a belief in God and the ancient wisdom handed down for centuries by the church. It also left me with absolutely no doubt that I was not good enough, and my instincts were to get as far away from it as possible. The fact is there are some entities that resist exorcism; only the extreme holiness of Michel De Biere enabled him to overcome it. If the riders around this house are demons, if it is the Wild Hunt that races around this house and it's those of the legend that has terrorised the human race for centuries, they will be powerful spirits who will resist any attempt to remove them."

"You're saying you ran away."

He nodded yes.

"Yet you didn't because you are here now. Why did you become involved in ghost hunting if you were trying to escape? Why are you with Nathan and Jess?"

"I wish I knew. I ask myself that all the time. It never left me, the fear. I had difficulty sleeping, I lost weight, seemed to always be ill. I went back to see Father De Biere, I had been told he was ill. He understood. He told me once I had opened my eyes, there was no turning back. He said evil walks the earth disguised. Its aim is to corrupt, alter, and damage all that is good, to discredit and deceive and win over to the dark side those who follow the teachings of Christ and other teachers of goodness. He said always remember that demons are the ultimate liars. They can pretend to be the dead, pretend to be family, friends. In the spirit life, they prey on the weak and vulnerable. He said to me 'Watch the news, Patrick. Watch it with new eyes, and you will see that they walk the earth today, and they are more prevalent in our secular societies than they have ever been. Masters of disguise, they feign friendliness to lure in the suggestible, the thrill seekers, but it is ultimately part of a plan for seduction and corruption. They are entities sent to destroy the human race and its belief in a benevolent god. Pretending they don't exist will not give you peace of mind.' He was right.

"Michel De Biere was a good, devout, and holy man, and the light shone from him. If you met him, you would understand what I'm saying. Believe what you will, but I was there when he called on St. Michael the Archangel to defend us and in the name God to cast the demon back to where it came from. He succeeded in casting it out and giving that girl her life back, though it almost killed him. He was ill for a long time afterward.

"Father De Biere taught me how to look beyond just the mental changes in those poor, demented souls. How to look for the physical changes, the speaking in tongues, their singular terror of religious objects Often it turned out they had been involved in the occult in some way, playing with Ouija boards, that kind of thing. Michel De Biere said, 'Patrick, never seek out the face of evil, it will see you, but when you know it has penetrated this world and you recognise it, don't allow it took take hold. Stamp it out. Do not allow it to deceive others.'

"Maybe I wasn't cut out for the priesthood, but when I started studying psychology with Nathan, I found myself looking for that other world, and so I got caught up in Nathan's hobby. So do you understand my reluctance? The thing about Caleb is I know it's the things racing around this house that are using him. I have agreed to try only because I can see no other way."

There were footsteps. I turned to look. It was Jonah, and in his familiar drawl with a hint of sarcasm, he said, "I wouldn't worry. You won't have to. You had better come and see him."

Caleb was sitting on the floor, his back against the fridge. He looked dazed and bewildered. James helped him to drink some water, then Emilio and James helped him onto a chair. Perplexed, I scanned the kitchen. The outside kitchen door was closed and locked from the inside. The key was in the lock. The strong stench had gone, the mess on the floor had been cleaned, and Caleb looked as he had when I first met him.

The coarseness of his features had gone, and the long, yellow fingernails were normal again. Only the faecal staining on his clothes and the smell remained. He had seemed not to have any recollection of what had happened, which in hindsight I thought was just as well. Caleb was shocked and confused, but he asked for Molly. I told him not worry, that she was here, and Katie went to fetch her.

Katie came back with Molly, who, with relief flooding over her face, cradled her son- in-law's head in her arms. "Thank God you're all right, son," she said to Caleb. Then to me she said, "He's frozen. We need to get him through to the fire." She suddenly realised the faecal mess had gone. "Who cleaned the floor and Caleb?" I shrugged my shoulders. "How is that possible?" She looked from me to James. James shook his head and opened his hands in a who knows? gesture.

"We don't know either, Molly. Give me a hand, Tosh. We'll take him through, and I'll get some fresh clothes for him," James said, helping Caleb onto his feet. Caleb stood on unsteady legs, and with an arm round each of their shoulders, James and Paddy supported him as he walked slowly out of the kitchen.

As he passed Emilio, Emilio said, "Wait, what's that?" He reached forward and pulled a piece of folded paper sticking out the pocket in the bib of Caleb's dungarees. It was an A4 sheet torn from Molly's kitchen folder, folded in four. Emilio held it out for us to see. "Erica," he said gently, "I think this is meant for you."

In a beautiful cursive hand, the word *Camille* was written in black ink.

CHAPTER TWENTY-TWO

Luke

"Camille?" Jonah asked. "The baby born in Delfshaven?"

I nodded. I had a king-sized lump in my throat. I opened the letter and read it out to the others. It said, simply:

Do not be afraid. I am the one they want. No harm will come to you.

It was unsigned. Jonah held out his hand, and I passed him the letter. My mind was in turmoil. All I could think of was *Camille*. The assumption was, of course, that the letter was addressed to me, which meant that I was the baby born to the French girl in the Netherlands. Who then had brought me up? Who were these people who had given me a loving home, and who was the man who had written the letter? It said they had come for him, and the thing that had possessed Caleb had screamed, "We want your Father" at me. I took the letter back from Jonah and looked again at the elegant handwriting. I felt a thrill that this might be the hand of my real father, and if so, if he was here in this house, then I surely would meet him. And where in the house was he hiding, and why was he hiding from us?

"OK, supposing we didn't notice this before and it was stuck in Caleb's pocket for Erica, where did he go? Not out here." James checked the locked outside door. "He has locked the door from the inside."

Nathan hadn't left his post outside the kitchen. He had listened for almost an hour to Caleb shouting obscenities and had strained to hear when for a long time afterward Caleb had been silent and he couldn't hear any movement. When Jonah returned with rope intended for Caleb, together they had opened the door and were baffled to find Caleb on the floor, laid in the recovery position and the floor cleaned. They looked out the window, but there had been nothing to see, just an impenetrable thick, white mist.

James and Jonah helped Caleb to his feet and half carried him through to the morning room. There, wrapped in a brightly chenille rug and sitting at the fire with Molly fussing around him, Caleb, who was still deathly pale, told us what little he could remember. He had no memory at all of arriving at Lanshoud that morning. The first thing he did remember was waking up in the kitchen with a man holding onto him and the feeling he described of something being pulled from every corner of his body. It was dark, he said, and someone was screaming. He thought it might have been him screaming, and then everything went blank. Jonah asked if there was anything he could remember about the man—what he looked like, whether he spoke. But Caleb only remembered the voice. Jonah asked where he had come from. Was it the outside door? He couldn't have gotten past Nathan. But Caleb shook his head.

"If the outside door was locked, and he didn't get past Nathan, how did he get in?" Jess asked.

"It wasn't locked; nobody locked it after Molly let Caleb in. It would have meant crossing Paddy's salt line," Nathan said.

Emilio stood in that way he did when he was feeling the atmosphere, sensing, almost smelling the air. "The house feels different, clean somehow. I think they have gone. The riders, they have definitely gone. Nathan, is there anything on the monitor?"

Nathan and Tosh had been checking the monitors for any sign of the riders. "There is nothing on the screens," Nathan said. "Not yet, anyway."

Jess got up from the sofa and walked to the window. She folded her arms, rubbing them up and down with her hands as though they were cold. Looking out, she said, "It's getting dark so quickly, and it's impossible to see a thing in that mist." She turned to us, almost pleading. "We should try to leave now, don't you think? Get help while we still can before it's dark." She was almost pleading. The mist was darkening, grey and thick, as though the world outside had vanished, and it was eerie, deathly silent.

Jonah joined her at the window. "Help from where? Anyway, do you intend to go out in that? You wouldn't be able to see an inch in front of your nose. No, we have to wait through another night and try and get out of here tomorrow when it's daylight."

It was at this point the phone rang. We all jumped, startled by the sound, and for a moment no one moved. I went to answer it; it was Lucy looking for Caleb. Keeping my voice as normal as I could, I told her we had a problem, and I would call her back in a few moments. I asked her about the fog, and she said there was none.

"Caleb will have to stay here tonight, Molly. We all will. He's in no fit state to go anywhere, and it's already dark. The fog is thick, and it's only here. Lucy says there is no fog or mist where she is. He will have to stay. Could you make some excuse?" I asked.

"Like what?" Molly was incredulous. "What am I supposed to tell her? Lucy will want Caleb home."

Jonah was dismissive. "Tell her we have lost power, and he is trying to fix the generator. Tell her anything you like, just convince her that he has to stay here tonight. Molly, do you understand you say whatever it takes to convince her. Caleb can't leave tonight. It's too dangerous, and she mustn't come here."

Molly was indignant. "Lucy wouldn't come here at night. The children will be in bed, but she wouldn't expect the weather to stop Caleb coming home. He would have to be snowed in or something like that, and even then it's not the first time he's had to dig the Land Rover out."

Everyone chipped in, trying to suggest something that Molly could tell Lucy. Then James said, "Look, Molly, why don't you try what Jonah suggests and tell her there's a power cut? Tell her the generator has packed in. Say he can't leave us without power. Say he's working on it, but the weather is so bad it would be better if he stayed the night."

"I don't know. I'll try, but she might insist on speaking to him herself. I can only try."

Jonah questioned Caleb over and over again about the man he had seen in the kitchen. Caleb tried to remember the sequence of events from his leaving home that morning, but there was a blank between turning off the Slug Road toward Lanshoud and coming to in the kitchen. Jonah kept up the questioning. "Try, Caleb. Anything you can remember might help. Was his face close to you?"

Caleb was agitated. "He was a young guy." Gradually I could see memory flooding over Caleb's features. "He was in his twenties, I think. I can't remember anything else."

"Keep trying," Jonah said.

"It's all right, son. Don't upset yourself now." Molly patted Caleb's arm, concern etched on her face. Then she glowered at Jonah.

Jonah repeated, "You said he was a young man?"

"Mid-twenties, I would say, and he had dark hair." Caleb was relieved that it was coming back to him.

"Twenties?"

"Yes, I'm sure."

Great. Oh well, then we were back to square one. He couldn't be my father; he was too young.

"Caleb, did he speak to you at all? Did he say anything?" Jonah kept the questions coming.

"Yes. He just told me I would be all right, but that's all I can remember."

"Did you see him leave?"

"No, I must have passed out."

"OK, Caleb you've done well," Jonah said, clapping his shoulder. "I don't think he can tell us any more, not just now anyway," he said to James.

It was nine o'clock, and I was falling asleep on my feet. We were all emotionally drained; fear, tension, and lack of sleep had taken their toll. Looking around the room, I could see the exhaustion etched on strained, pale faces; everyone needed to rest. Jonah took command. He organised us into shifts so that those less tired would take the first watch. We would stay together, sleep in the same room, and split the watch between two groups. We all agreed that Molly, Alice, and Caleb should be exempt from taking a turn on the monitors, but Katie and I were adamant that we would take our turn. Jonah, Tosh, and Nathan took the first watch. James offered too, but Jonah said it would be better if he stayed with me.

We brought duvets, pillows, and rugs from the bedrooms, enough for everyone, and spread them out on the morning room floor, moving

Luke

furniture so that we all lay in the glow of the firelight. We switched off the lights and used only the firelight to fight off the darkness. It was warm, and I felt safe. I lay with my head on the pillow watching James, who lay on his back with one arm behind his head staring at the ceiling. He turned and caught me watching him. "Are you OK?" he mouthed. I nodded yes, and for a breathtaking moment, he held my gaze, looking deep into my eyes. I felt butterflies in my stomach, but the spell was broken when Molly let out a snore that sounded like a cow bellowing. I had to bury my head in the pillow to stifle laughter. It went on like that for a while with Jess, Alice, and Molly in bellowing competition.

Paddy, tired and irritated, punched his pillow and complained. "How are we supposed to sleep with that racket going on? It's like pigs in a trough."

James and I were buried in our pillows snorting with laughter. Oddly, I did feel OK, but I found it difficult to sleep. I was acutely aware of James being close, of him watching me. The truth was I had an aching desire to crawl over beside him, to feel the comfort of his arms around me. I tossed and turned for ages before I finally fell asleep.

I heard movement and woke to find James, Paddy, and Emilio on their feet and Nathan, Jonah, and Tosh settling down. I groaned. I was still tired and painfully stiff from sleeping on the floor. I pushed the duvet back and made to get up, but James came over and stopped me.

"Stay where you are. You don't have to get up; just go back to sleep," he whispered.

"What time is it?" I whispered back.

"Three a.m. There has been no activity; it's all very quiet. There's no need for you to get up."

"No, I'm awake now," I said, stretching. "I want to take my turn." I looked around for my fleece. It was cold, and the fire was almost out. James tossed me the fleece and shoveled more coal on the fire. Katie was still sound asleep, so we left her. Paddy and Emilio went to the dining room to watch the monitors. I wanted to make tea but was reluctant to go alone, and because James insisted on no one being alone, he came with me.

The lights were on in the kitchen. We had left nearly every light in the house on except for the morning room, where we slept. I had just put my hand on the brass knob of the kitchen door when something in the kitchen crashed like glass breaking. James stepped ahead of me and swung open the door. Inside, the door of the large double fridge lay open, and a box of eggs and a glass bottle of fresh juice lay smashed on the floor, with the juice splattered everywhere. A young man stood with his hand on the fridge door.

"Forgive me; I had intended a more civilized introduction," he said. Then to James, who pulled a carving knife from the block on the worktop, "You can put that down. I am friend, not foe."

James scanned the kitchen. "Go get Emilio and Paddy."

"No, I'm not leaving you."

"Go," he said, pushing me back. I ran.

I presumed this was the man Caleb had seen, a young man casually dressed in a blue sweatshirt and jeans. He grinned as Emilio and Paddy came crashing through the door with me at their back. "Ah, the troops to the rescue." Unperturbed by our dramatic entrance, he knelt down and mopped up the spilled juice. "There is no need, really. I am quite harmless."

"Who are you?" James asked.

Composed and collected, the man leisurely carried the broken glass in a shovel and dropped it into the bin, and then he rinsed the cloth in the sink and wrung it out. "Well, I had planned to break it to you in my own time, but it seems it is out of my hands, and now is as good a time as any. I think we should all sit down." Perfectly relaxed, he strolled over to the table and drew out a chair, inviting me to sit. No one sat.

"I would like to make us some coffee; would you mind? I make very good coffee," he said, opening the door of a top cupboard and putting his hand straight onto a bag of coffee, just as though he was perfectly at home. "Really?" He looked at the kitchen knife in James's hand. "You can put the knife down. I am not dangerous."

He lifted out a jar, opened it, and shook the beans out into a grinder. "I keep these special Turkish beans here at the back of this cupboard. I lived there once, in Turkey, a long, long time ago." He busied himself preparing the coffee, grinding the beans, which left a rich aroma in the kitchen, normally a comforting smell, but it was out of place, out of sync with the situation and definitely not comforting. He poured cold water into the pot and added a spoonful of the ground coffee. "One for each person and one for the pot is best. Now I'll start by answering your question, Camille."

Luke

I decided I was not going to be intimidated. "If you are talking to me, my name is Erica."

"Of course it is. I did not intend to offend you." He hesitated. "I think of you as Camille because that is what I have always called you."

"Why is that, since I don't know you?"

"Ah, but I know you, and it is the name your mother and I chose for you—your biological mother, that is." He looked at me pointedly, hoping, I think, for some kind of realisation on my part. He waited for a response, and when I made none, he said in a deliberate and emphatic way, "Your real mother, Marianne Belliere. I know you have discovered this truth already."

"And why would you be involved in choosing a name for Marianne's baby?" James asked.

The man turned back to the work surface and continued preparing the coffee. "I like to add sugar at this point. Tell me if this is a problem. You all take sugar?" He placed the pot on the gas to heat before he answered James, then still with his back to us, he said, "Because of course, I was her husband. I am Camille's, or as you prefer, Erica's, father." There was a pregnant pause during which he studied our faces. "At that time I was called Pierre Belliere. The name has a certain ring to it, don't you think?" He raised his eyebrows.

There was, of course, no way this young man could be my father. He was insane to think we would believe him; yet, on some subliminal level I had the strangest feeling he was telling the truth. In spite of that feeling, I said, "Don't be ridiculous. How could you be my father? How old are you?"

"It will take time to explain, but you are right, of course. I am younger than you, but inversely, I am also very much older." The water reached boiling, and he poured the coffee, filling about three quarters of each cup. As we stood wary and anxious, he said, "The foam on the top you see is the delicious part. After that it loses its taste." He boiled the pot again and then filled the cups to the top.

As he carried the cups to the table, Paddy said, "How did you get in here?"

The man put the cups down carefully. "Let it settle. It is not filtered, so you must let the coffee grounds settle at the bottom of the cup before you drink it. Would you like cream?"

"You were asked a question," James said angrily.

"Yes." He sat down at the table and thought for a moment. "I use the tunnels that lie behind the walls of Lanshoud."

"Tunnels!" James and I exclaimed in stereo. No one had mentioned them to me, and James had seen nothing on the floor plans he had been given.

"Yes, they have been in use for centuries. They were built by the Knights Templar, who fled here to Scotland in 1307 to escape Philip IV's massacre of their order. You are aware, I hope, of this part of your history." Then bizarrely, he said, "We had help, of course."

"We...had help?" James asked. "Who are the 'we'?"

"My fellow Templars and I were given help to build Lanshoud by the Scottish stonemasons, and in return we taught them how to live by chivalry and honour and duty. You may be interested to know that that is how Freemasonry originated in this part of the world." He was totally relaxed, as though we were some kind of guests being given a guided tour instead of confused, scared, and sleep deprived, wary of him and prepared to defend ourselves against him.

"Are you trying to tell us you are a Knight Templar? I didn't realise the order had survived into this century," said James in a slightly acidic tone that suggested he was dealing with someone mentally unstable and possibly dangerous.

"Actually yes, there are some secret branches still around. But no, it's a few hundred years since I was a member of that order." He stopped and looked at us to see the effect his last comments had made. "The tunnels run everywhere behind the walls of this house. They suit my purpose; I have been able to live in Lanshoud when it was necessary and had somewhere to hide if I had to."

"Whom were you hiding from?" James asked.

"From the same entities that have been terrorising you, from the Wild Hunt."

CHAPTER TWENTY-THREE

Abigor

He held the chair for me. "Look, please sit down. I will answer all your questions. Please, sit."

This was my father? He was not much more than a boy with a slight, wiry frame. He had soft, light-brown hair that flopped over hazel eyes, long on the top and shaved at the back. He was dressed casually, as you would expect for any young man in his twenties, yet his language and his manner were just a little too formal for a young guy, and his English was beautifully enunciated as though it was a second language. He indicated the chair opposite. "You are tired. This coffee will help wake you up. It is very strong and very good." I looked at James, and he nodded slightly. I sat down.

"You cannot imagine how many times I have rehearsed how I would tell you my story. It will be difficult for you to understand, difficult for you to believe." He studied my face. "You look like Marianne, you know. You have her colouring. Your beautiful auburn hair and the green eyes are Marianne's. Even the tone of your skin is the same as hers. She was a great beauty, your mother."

"Was?"

"She died when you were still a baby."

"How did she die?"

"Does that matter?"

"It matters to me."

"She was killed..." he hesitated, "by the hunt. Camille—Marianne chose that name for you; you were born Camille Belliere. My name, my real name—and believe me, I have had more than a few—is unpronounceable in your language. For now I am English and known as Luke Treadstone. I work for a company in Geneva as a research physicist. When you were born, I lived in France, and I called myself Pierre Belliere. It's the name I used when I married your mother. Her name was Marianne Picard. I have never married any other woman, nor have I fathered another child. You were quite unique."

"Unpronounceable in our language? So what are you trying to say? That you are some kind of alien?" James asked.

He held up his hand in a stopping gesture. "Look, I realise that you must see me as some kind of lunatic, but please hear me out. For you to understand, it is better that I explain it my own way; just try to have an open mind." He sat back in the chair and took a deep breath. "I am a scientist, a physicist. In my own world, I was hailed as a prodigy, a genius; my work, my interests, lay in the study of space and time. Consider that more than one hundred years ago, Albert Einstein proposed that nothing could travel faster than the speed of light. He was wrong. In my world, in another existence, I experimented, and just like Einstein, I, too, searched for an explanation for the universe. But unlike Einstein I discovered the speed of light was not absolute, and I perfected the ability to travel faster than light, faster than time. I manufactured a machine I thought would propel me through time, and it did, though not in the way I expected. The result of my last experiment was that I smashed though multiple dimensional membranes, travelling not just back in time but sideways, and ended up here in your world in the past of a parallel universe: The planet Earth, the year 44 BC, in Italy in the Rome of Julius Caesar and Mark Antony."

Profound silence again. Picture it: there we sat, my companions and I, like something out of Alice in Wonderland. It was around four o'clock in the morning, and we were sitting around a kitchen table—a lawyer, a former seminarian now turned student psychologist, a clairvoyant, and my father, who was younger than I was and who thought he had been a Knight Templar. It was surreal, and I couldn't have made this story up if

I had tried. They say there are people in asylums who genuinely believe that they are Napoleon or Cleopatra or even the Messiah and who live their lives unsuccessfully trying to convince other people of what they genuinely believe is their true identity. Perhaps you are reading this thinking we should have run screaming out of the room away from this madman, but we were inclined to listen with less incredulity to this fantastic tale of time travel and a parallel universe, given our recent experience and the tragic death of Gill and Jack at the hands of specters. So no one laughed, and no one expressed scepticism, our grip on reality was already challenged, and now completely bemused, we were lost for words, so affected were we by the horror of the last few days.

"There are other planes of being, of existence that you are not aware of." He shoved back his chair and walked back to the dishwasher, opened it, and took out the Quantamatic dishwasher container. He unscrewed the lid and removed the packet with the long detergent tablets lying side by side suspended in plastic. He placed them in a standing circle on the table. "Look, imagine you stand in the center of this curved packet, and each of these tablets is a mirror, and you see yourself over and over again, farther and farther away, till the distance becomes infinite and blurred. Each of the realities you glimpse is different from the one in which you exist, but the difference may be only the position of this cup I am holding. However, the farther you travel the greater the difference. Go far enough through these mirrors and there are other strange, alien, dangerous places that can be entered through portals, such as the Bermuda Triangle. I passed through one of these portals and through one of the dangerous places. My flight halted, and I was suspended for a period of time, and in a diaphanous haze I saw things living people should not see. Not only did I see, but I was seen, and so I was marked by the master of that world. He claimed me, and I could have been lost, but I was pulled away by an unknown force and so escaped a terrible fate. In his fury, the master of darkness sent his minions to bring me back, and so they have hunted me since, following me through your world and your time to bring me back to theirs."

Oh God, I thought, maybe Lewis Carroll knew me. Maybe I was his model for Alice, and this was the Mad Hatter's tea party, except it was a coffee party.

Paddy cleared his throat. "Am I right in thinking that you are saying the demons are actually from another world and not hell?"

"Another world, another dimension, another universe, hell, Hades, the Pit, call it anything you like. I don't know the answer to that question. I only know it is a place of evil and darkness and pain. It is home of the Wild Hunt, and they have a master, the Lord of Darkness."

Paddy asked, "I don't understand. Are you saying you passed through hell, and this master of darkness is who we call Satan?"

"He has many names. Look, you don't have to understand. No one really can, and unless you have studied quantum physics, I can't explain even the question to you. I don't understand, and I have been studying the universe through many lifetimes. The more I discover, the more I am awed by its complexity. Human life is no more than a speck of dust in the grand scale of things. Consider the size of earth compared to the sun and the sun compared to Antares. At the other end of the scale just now at CERN, we are working with neutrinos, subatomic particles that are so small they pass through our bodies at faster than the speed of light. Scientists believe they are on the verge of discovering great things, yet the finest minds cannot agree what these things might be. The great geneticist Haldane said, 'The universe is not only stranger than we imagine, it's stranger than we CAN imagine.'

"I can only tell you what I have experienced, what I know to be true, and that is that there is no one reality. I don't know if the hell I passed through is the hell of Christianity. I don't know if heaven is another dimension or universe or something stranger. I only know that I ripped through the world I lived in and have not been able to find my way back and that I have not aged since the day I arrived in Rome over two thousand years ago. I have been in danger of death many times, but I don't die, and if I am injured, I heal instantly."

We listened intently. No one questioned any of this.

"My arrival on earth and my subsequent adoption by a merchant at that time is a long story that I will tell you at another time; I was adopted by that merchant and traveled with his caravans over the East. I was with him for almost fifteen years before it was noticed that I wasn't ageing. I had to leave when he became an old man, whereas I still had the body of a twenty-five-year-old. He arranged for me to leave in one of his caravans, and I ended up in Palestine. That is how I came to be in Palestine at the time of Christ."

"Oh, so you met Jesus Christ?" Paddy was sceptical.

"No, I never had that honour, but I heard him preach, and I was there when he was crucified."

"The relics in the cellar—the spear and the crown. You put them there?" Paddy asked.

"Souvenirs, I thought at the time I collected them. I was helped years later by the Knights Templar to bring them here to Scotland." He paused for a moment, refilling the coffee cup. "My situation now is that I been through hell—literally, if you like. If you find your way to the world of darkness, you are not permitted to leave. Its master is jealous and cunning. My energy stream took me through hell, and he sent his hunt to bring me back. The Wild Hunt, it is sometimes called. If you don't believe me, read the legends and folk history of Europe."

"We already have," I said.

"Then you know that most of the world tells tales of the Wild Hunt. Well, the hunt has followed me through time, and this has been witnessed by many people in many countries, who incidentally have mostly been ridiculed for telling what they saw, in spite of the fact that the Wild Hunt has sometimes left death and destruction in its wake.

"Through all the centuries of your world, I have fled the Hunt, across countries, across oceans. They follow me to collect me to take me back to hell. I know you are incredulous, but I have been wandering this planet for thousands of years with no way back to my own world and in fear of being dragged back to a nightmare. You say you have read of the hunt. Then you know that I am telling you the truth. The Wild Hunt has been roaming the world for centuries, killing and maiming all in their path."

"Jack told us about the hunt," I said, and a sudden pang of heartache hit me when I remembered Jack and Gill's death. I said, "and the harlequins. Jack told us about the harlequins."

"Yes, I left you clues. I wanted you to know the danger you were in."

I suddenly felt bitter. "A bit late and a bit too cryptic, or Jack and Gill might still have been alive today," I spat at him.

Of all he had said, nothing had a greater impact on my sanity than his next few words.

"But they are not *dead*, Erica." He shook his head.

I stared at him in disbelief. "What? What do you mean they are not dead? Their heads were lying on the doorstep," I yelled at him, horrified.

"No, no, no, they were rescued; they are in a hotel in Aberdeen. I swear to you. They are being brought back today because they have insisted on coming back here. They could not be persuaded for their own safety to stay away. You have good friends."

I shook my head, unable to take in the enormity of what he was saying. I reached for James, who put his arm around me, supporting me.

"I am telling you the truth. What you saw was staged, designed to make you believe it was the mutilated body parts of your friends, to strike terror into your heart. Yes, those were human heads, but not of your friends. The demons were thwarted and probably killed two random strangers or robbed graves. You were expecting Jack and Gill to return; you already feared for their safety. You had seen their car outside, even though Emilio told you at the time the things that came to the door were not Jack and Gill. You still fell for Abigor's tricks. You saw what you expected to see. The bloodied heads were unrecognisable but because you were in shock, no one looked closely, no one examined them. You saw what Abigor wanted you to see."

"Who is Abigor?" James asked.

"Who or what, Abigor is a grand duke of hell, commander of hell's legions. The leader of the hunt has failed to bring me back, so his master has sent Abigor. You may have heard him called Eligor or Eligos. He is a demon of the highest order."

"I have heard the name Abigor, the mythological general of hell's armies," Paddy said.

"Yes, well, that piece of mythology left two human heads on your doorstep," Luke said with a tone of exasperation that suggested we just weren't getting it.

"Molly and Alice were outside. Why did they not kill Molly and Alice?" Emilio asked.

"Because they were leaving you a message, and they chose Molly and Alice as messengers. If they had not arrived, you may not have opened the door. Look I'm guessing; I don't really know why."

"If they are after you, why did you come here? Why did you bring Erica here? Why did you put her in danger?" James's tone was hostile.

"Every person I became close to they killed, including Marianne. That is why I had Erica's identity changed, and that is why I have hidden her and stayed away from her even when she was a child, which was probably the only time I could have built a relationship without drawing suspicion.

Until a few months ago, they only hunted me. I thought you were safe, but a few months ago the riders were seen near your home. That is why you had to come here, and thank God you did because now Abigor is leading them. You were due to inherit Lanshoud. I set that up years ago. Only the codicil forcing you to stay was added to the will at the last minute. Inside Lanshoud you were safe. That is why I forced you to come here."

"Were safe?" James asked "Past tense?"

"There are barriers the demons cannot cross."

"These psychic barriers around the house, did you set them up? Did you perform exorcism on Caleb?" Emilio asked.

"No, I don't have that power, but I have acquaintances who do, whom I have always been able to call on for help. They're the same ones who saved Jack and Gill and who will bring them here today. However, though they have been able to the hold the hunt at bay, Abigor is a different kettle of fish." He paused, looking into the cup, swirling the coffee around. "In essence, I moved you here, Erica, to protect and provide for you and because I hope soon I will be able to go home. The scientific advances of this century will soon make that possible; technology is moving at breakneck speed. I have provided you with only a fraction of the fortune I have accumulated over thousands of years. I have left you treasures like the relics in the cellar. I have secreted more all over the world." He smiled. "By the way, that priceless little harlequin—let me solve the mystery for you; you can tell the Inspector." He waggled his fingers in the air. "I have no fingerprints." He leaned over the table, looking directly at me. "So is there anything else you want to know just now?"

There were so many questions swirling around in my head that I didn't know where to start. "I need some explanations." I bit my lip while I tried to keep my voice steady. "Did you set up Paul Cameron to marry me?"

"Yes and no. I couldn't watch over you alone. I could not travel through the world alone. I had help from many loyal friends, employees if you like; specifically a family that I first met in France in the seventeenth century; the family Picard, and through generations they have kept my secret. The woman who brought you up, whom you thought was your real mother, the woman who cared for you and loved you, was Marianne's sister. She was your aunt. She was not a Scot, she was French; her name was Brigitte Picard. When Marianne was killed by the hunt, Brigitte and her husband fled with you to Scotland, and for love of you and your mother they cut all ties with their families.

"The man you called your father, who brought you up, was Dutch, but his name was Andries De Vries, not Aalbert Vansterdam. He and Brigitte were already married and working for me actually. They met here at Lanshoud, and they were married in Scotland in a little town near here; they told you something near the truth. They were married in a little church in Laurencekirk, not the great cathedral of Rotterdam, Saint Laurenskerk. The rest, the background of names, a Scottish family, was pure fabrication. Paul Cameron was Andries's young brother Frederik De Vries. When Brigitte and Andries were killed in the car accident, Paul stepped in to look after you. Marriage was not on the agenda. That was not something we had arranged; you simply fell in love."

"And Paul's death. Was that truly an accident?" I asked.

"Yes, but Paul was not at sea that day. He was with me in Paris. He flew there for a meeting because the hunt had been seen by farmers in the countryside there, and he came to help me. Do you remember at the time Paul died, an aircraft, a commercial airliner, went down at sea, a flight from Paris to Heathrow?"

"Strange as it may seem to you, I wasn't reading newspapers or watching TV when Paul died." I could hear the bitter edge in my own voice.

"Paul was a passenger, and it was his return flight home," he said softly.

"How did you manage to cover that up?" James asked.

"He was traveling as Stephen Roberts; all his documents were in the name of Stephen Roberts."

"And Gwen and George Cameron. Who were they really?" I asked.

"They worked for me."

"Then the body they identified wasn't Paul's?" I had a sudden memory of the pain and grief of that funeral. "You mean to say you let me bury a stranger whom some other family are still searching for. You let me grieve over a stranger's grave." I cried, anger and frustration oozing out of me.

"No, Erica, you buried your husband Paul. Gwen and George claimed Stephen's body. It was brought back to Scotland and placed in the sea near the shore on an incoming tide, so that it would easily be found. His boat, *The Dutch Lady*, was taken out and destroyed. It was your husband you buried, Frederik De Vries."

Around six a.m. I excused myself. I couldn't wait any longer. I passed Jonah in the hall heading for the bathroom. In the morning room, I stepped past the still-sleeping Molly, Alice, and Caleb. Nathan and Tosh were up and piling duvets and pillows on the sofas. Jess was awake and whispering to Katie, who was lying propped on an elbow listening intently. I knelt down beside them, smiling.

"What is it?" Katie asked, confused that I had anything to smile about.

"Katie," I said breathlessly, feeling hot tears pricking my eyes, "Katie, its Gill. She's alive. Jack and Gill are not dead."

She sat up quickly, pulling back the duvet, her tousled black curls making her look younger than she was. She stared at me, confused. "What are you talking about? Have you lost your mind? I saw them, for God's sake. I saw them."

"No, you didn't. It wasn't them, just some other poor souls made to look like them."

Tosh and Jess gathered round. Jess held both hands over her mouth.

"How can that be?" Tosh asked.

"Remember, think about it. How long did we actually see the heads? Everyone was too distraught. We slammed shut the door, covered them up, threw a blanket over them. Even Jonah didn't examine them. Then they disappeared."

"What are you saying, Erica? How do you know this?" Nathan pushed his spectacles up the bridge of his nose to get a better look at me, as though he could read what I was saying on my face.

"Come with me, all of you. There is someone in the kitchen you have to meet."

The door opened, and Jonah came into the kitchen. "Are we having a party or something? Who are you?" he asked Luke. Luke waited for me to answer Jonah.

It was too much. I started to giggle, and my ability to pull myself together was lost by the reaction of the people standing around me. In hindsight, I suppose stress, lack of sleep, and the overwhelming relief that Jack and Gill were alive were all contributing factors. I tried to answer Jonah, but laughter engulfed me. I was helpless at the absurdity of any explanation I could give for this bizarre situation I had found myself in. Finally, through guffaws, I managed to spit out, almost choking, "He's my father."

CHAPTER TWENTY-FOUR

Rafe and Uri

Luke told us he had received instructions from the people he had asked for help and that for our own safety, everyone except he and I should leave as soon as it was light. There was no question about Molly, Alice, and Caleb leaving; they went gladly. In fact Molly couldn't get home fast enough. Jess, on the other hand, hemmed and hawed, but it was obvious she was desperate to go home. With tears in her eyes, she said she felt like a coward deserting me. I pointed out to her that there was nothing to worry about, we would be safe, there were people coming to help, and we could have a catch-up when it was all over. Nathan and Tosh had other commitments, and they left reluctantly with the promise to keep in touch and return anytime they could be of any help. The rest were adamant they were not leaving.

Around noon—I know that was the time because I had just asked Paddy; recently we all seemed to regularly ask one another the time—a car crunched onto the broad sweep of gravel at the front of the house. It was raining heavily; cold and miserable with dark clouds making it seem more like evening than the middle of the day. Coupled with the weather and broken sleep, we had begun not only to lose track of the time but even the day of the week, and we were so isolated from the outside world that I had forgotten it was supposed to be summer. Though the East Coast was usually drier with less rainfall than the west, there had been few dry days and little sunshine since we had come to Lanshoud. Scottish weather is never predictable at the best of times; even weather forecasters regularly get it wrong. It is not unheard of to have all four seasons in one week, and I have known many summers that were a complete washout. The high latitude of Scotland means that although winter days are very short, summer days are long, but this summer, here in the woods, it was different. The days seemed short like winter, and the chill was constant. It felt more like November or February than July.

Katie opened the front door as Gill came bounding up the stairs, her cream raincoat billowing behind her; she was not the usual glowing Gill; she looked stressed, tired, and a little disheveled. She was pale, free of the impeccable makeup she always wore, she looked older. She closed and shook a dripping umbrella and dropped it in the bronze brolly holder at the door.

"Hi, guys. Did you miss me?" she said, throwing her arms open for a group hug. "I have never been so glad to see you. Is everyone OK?" She held my shoulders and examined my face in detail. "I've been worried sick." Then she spread her arms and enveloped Katie and I in a cloud of silk scarf and perfume.

"Miss you? We thought you were dead." Katie cried. "Why didn't you call us, you moron? I've still got swollen eyes."

"I know, I know. I'm sorry. We did try, but with no landline, no mobiles, we couldn't contact you, and they wouldn't let us leave." She folded her arms. "But I am very touched that you cared."

Katie thumped her, then hugged her again.

"Is that them? Those men over there, are they the ones who wouldn't let you leave?" I asked, looking out to where two men were lifting bags and boxes from the car.

"Yes, we were on our way back on Thursday when they stopped us. They stopped us on the Slug Road *at gunpoint*." Her voice rose. "I mean, and can you believe it? Here in Aberdeen, gunpoint? It was straight out of a James Bond movie. We had just turned off the Slug Road when they blocked our car with theirs and stuck a gun in Jack's face. They insisted we get out and into their car. They said it for our own safety, and we would put all of you here in danger if we didn't go with them. It was bloody terrifying. They were really threatening and not taking no for an answer."

"We saw your car, Jack's car. It was outside," Katie said. "In fact, it's still out there."

"No, it couldn't be." Gill shook her head. "Unless someone moved it, Jack's car was abandoned on the Slug Road."

I realised what must have happened.

"What is it? Gill asked. "What are you thinking?"

"The riders must have brought it back. The car has been part of the tableau, the scene set so we would see what they wanted us to see." I turned to Katie. "Luke was telling the truth. Think about it. The heads, how closely did we look at them? Nobody examined them, we were all so shocked."

Gill frowned. "Who's Luke? What heads?"

"It's a long story," I said. "Katie, would you mind making some tea, please?"

"Sure. Never mind, Gillian," Katie said, linking her arm through Gill's and leading her away from the door. "C'mon, I'll make you a cuppa."

"Wait, wait, wait," Gill rattled out, holding Katie back. "Take a look out there. Look, I actually brought you something nice." She turned back towards the open door and pointed, eyes shining. "Have you actually looked at my escorts? Come on, Katie, you're slipping. Check out those two guys. They're a bit strange. I mean they're not great conversationalists; in fact they hardly string two words together, but wow! The taller one is Rafe. He could give Brad Pitt a run for his money, and the other is Uri. Now you wouldn't say no to him on a cold night, would you, huh?"

"Guess you're not in love anymore then?" Katie asked acerbically.

"Oh no, you've got that wrong. I am still besotted," Gill protested. She shrugged her shoulders. "I was merely giving a heads-up to my less fortunate friends."

I really had to laugh. There we all were, in Cloud Cuckoo land. I felt like Alice wandering about, clueless, down the bottom of the rabbit hole, so stressed that I was having palpitations, and there was Gill, fresh out of her James Bond kidnap story, her upbeat take on love and life undaunted by the experience. I thought that maybe I should be taking a leaf out of her book.

James and Jonah were in the hall when Jack came in carrying the bags; Katie and I hugged him. James took one of the bags off Jack and asked him about the two men.

"I don't know," Jack said quietly, looking back at the strangers still standing at the car. "They kept us in that house, no explanation, just that it was for our safety and yours; refused to let us come here, hardly spoke two words. I'm not sure who they are. They might be police or government or something, and they're heavily armed."

At this point Luke walked past us out the door to the car, so focused on the two strangers he didn't even glance at Gill or Jack.

"Who's that?" Gill asked. "Another one of them?"

I sighed. "That my dear, is my father, and as Katie said, it's a long story."

"Your what!" Jack asked, half laughing.

"Your father?" Gill asked. They both looked out, incredulous, to where Luke stood by the car talking to the two men.

"That boy is your father? Are you serious?" Jack asked, watching Luke.

"Yes, and I am, and before you ask, I think it might be true."

Both strangers were dressed in long, almost identical, ankle-length, soft split leather coats that flapped behind them as they climbed the stairs into the house. Belts around their waists with a variety of weapons attached were clearly visible under the coats. We stood in the hall for a moment or two while Luke introduced Rafe and Uri. I welcomed them and thanked them for coming and told them how grateful we were that Gill and Jack were safe. Making conversation was difficult, very one sided, a bit like pulling teeth. They were as silent as Gill had suggested, and their faces were expressionless. Luke enthused about how capable they were and how they had helped him in the past, but he still didn't actually say who they were, and he sidestepped my attempts at asking.

Out of the corner of my eye, I saw Emilio standing back at the foot of the stairs. He didn't come forward to be introduced as Paddy had. Initially I thought it was just the touching thing, but he had been watching for some time. There was something strange about him; he looked odd, almost mesmerised by the strangers. For some inexplicable reason, I felt a chill, the kind that freezes the pulse and sends goose bumps down the legs. I knew Emilio was seeing something I couldn't see; something wasn't right. I walked over to him, and in hushed tones I asked him, "Emilio, what is it? What's wrong? Do you know them?" I glanced back at the men; the one called Rafe was openly staring at us as though he could hear us even though he was well out of earshot.

Emilio shook his head, and his breath left him in a sort of laugh. "No, but I believe you have no need to worry. I think your help has well and truly arrived."

Paddy was in the kitchen, exercising his culinary skills learned in Rome by preparing an Italian dish for dinner. Gill, Katie, and I were making sandwiches and exchanging blow-by-blow accounts of the ordeals faced over the last few days.

Gill held up a knife full of butter and waved it at Paddy. "They drove us towards Stonehaven and then turned up a farm track leading to a little cottage; it was a tiny place, just one bedroom, a small living room, and a little kitchen. Jack tried to find out what was going on. Jack was so brave; he really wasn't intimidated by them." She continued buttering. "But they made it quite clear that conversation wasn't on the agenda, and that we were there until they decided it was time to go. We eventually slept, but they didn't, and I don't know where they ate but it wasn't with us; they were totally weird. Then this morning, out of the blue, they told us to get in the car; we were going. I told them we were going back to Lanshoud, and if that wasn't where they were taking us, then their only option was to leave us there." She slapped the butter on the bread. "They didn't even argue. The one called Uri laughed and said my loyalty was admirable, and you know what? It didn't even sound like sarcasm."

Paddy leaned with his back against the sink, wiping his hands on a tea towel. "There is no doubt they are a strange pair, but then, so is Luke."

"I think Emilio knows or suspects something, but he's not saying. He was really strange. He didn't even acknowledge them," I said.

Paddy laughed. "Oh, c'mon. Emilio knows something about everybody. He just picks up vibes."

"No, it was more than that." I chewed my lip, trying to remember what it was that had struck me as odd. "The one called Rafe...the way he looked at Emilio, not smiling, just a cold stare, and Emilio seemed, oh, I don't know..." I struggled to explain. "He was transfixed almost. They were standing at the front door, and Emilio and I were outside the study, and even though I was whispering, I know Rafe was listening, and I am absolutely sure he could hear us."

"Did Emilio seem afraid of them?" Paddy asked.

"No, not afraid. At least I don't think so. He seemed more in awe than afraid."

Gill got up and refilled the kettle. "Jack thinks they are some kind of police or government agency, or something like that. I think their names, Rafe and Uri, sound Russian or Eastern European."

Paddy nodded. "Rafe is very…Nordic looking—the long, pale hair and skin, the high cheekbones. Give him a helmet, and he would make a good Viking."

Gill nodded. "I know what you mean, but the thing is, they don't have Scandinavian or Eastern European accents. In fact, they don't have any accent at all. Their English is perfect."

The kitchen door opened, and Jonah asked us to come to the drawing room because, he said, raising his eyebrows and rolling the R's when he said the names, Rafe and Uri wanted to speak to us. He turned to go, and Paddy called him back. "Hang on a minute, Jonah. Come in and close the door." Jonah came in and leaned on the back of a kitchen chair. "Do you know anything about them yet?" Paddy asked.

"Nope. According to Luke, they are part of some kind of elite fighting force that has dealt with the hunt in the past. I tried to question Luke, but he was vague, evasive even. I couldn't pin him down to a straight answer. Look, I'm sorry, Erica." He shook his head. "I know he is supposed to be your flesh and blood, and I reserve judgment on that one, but for God's sake, he's as weird as the other two. Anyway, all I could get out of Luke was that he has always been able to call on them for help in dealing with the hunt. As to who they are, well, your guess is as good as mine." Jonah put on a silly singsong voice. "If there's something dead in the neighborhood, who you gonna call? Ghostbusters?" He laughed at his little joke. "Now as for Luke, he thinks he has been fighting these so-called demons for centuries. Which leaves me to think what? Hem, let me think." He slapped his head with the flat of his hand, eyes wide laced with drama. "I know! Maybe they are time travelers, or another family like the Picard's, fiercely loyal." He put his hand on his heart. "Serving Luke generation upon generation." Sarcasm dripped from his tongue. Hand still on the doorknob, he shook his head. "Oh, give me strength. Look at you, have you people lost the plot completely? Are you really swallowing all of this claptrap? For God's sake, wake up," he almost shouted. "Something is going on here, but it's not ghosties and ghoulies. What a load of bloody nonsense. Look, Erica, there is one hell of an amount of money tied to you and in this house, and it's got to be something to do with that. Please tell me you don't really believe in all the demon nonsense."

"I don't know, Jonah. I am keeping an open mind."

"Unlike yours, Jonah. Yours has been bolted shut for a long time, eh?" Paddy laughed.

"Oh, I give up." Jonah held the door. "C'mon, shift yourselves. Let's go hear what the weirdo's have to say."

I got up to follow Jonah. As I did, I looked out of the kitchen windows. "Just look at that mist." The rain had stopped, and now a thick, white mist was gathering.

Jonah let the door close and came to look out the window. "It's the Haar," he said wonderingly, "but it shouldn't be this far inland."

"What's the Haar?" Gill asked.

"It's one of the traits of East Coast weather, thick white mist, sea fog. When the cold sea air meets the warmer air from the coast, it turns into clouds and blows along the edge of the land and billows, like clouds on a mountain. It can be so thick you can hardly see your hand in front of your face. It's dank and dark sometimes and so cold it can penetrate through to your very bones, but this isn't right. In Stonehaven, you see it all the time, but here we're too far inland. And anyway we are in the middle of the woods, and it had been raining all morning." Jonah went closer to the window and put his hand on the glass. "It's freezing out there." He took his hand away, and the print was etched in ice on the inside of the window. "That's not right either."

I shivered again, and not just because there was a chill in the house.

The drawing room, which was usually cold, being the largest room in the house, with a really high ceiling and large floor-to-ceiling windows, gave an overall impression of cold, which was increased by the décor, which was pale blue and creamy white, with the same colours carried over onto the upholstery. The fireplace was also white, some kind unpolished marble. Now however, it was at least warm because someone had taken the trouble to light a huge fire.

Luke was standing at the fireplace in a stance that suggested he had been making a speech, or maybe he was feeling the cold. Though there were plenty of chairs and sofas around, James stood and offered me his chair nearest Luke and then sat on the arm of it beside me. They were all looking at the windows and talking about the strange, swirling mist.

A moment or two later, Rafe and Uri came in; they had ditched the leather coats. Uri wore jeans and a polo-neck woolen jacket with a full zip; the stretch of the jumper bulged at his waist and did nothing to hide the gun. He closed the door behind him, folded his arms, and leaned back against it. Rafe joined Luke in front; he also wore jeans but with a hooded zipped jacket. The jacket was lying open, and I could see the gun at his belt.

Rafe surveyed the room, looking at each of us in turn. He had the most intense blue eyes I have ever seen, and the firelight glowing behind him gave his shoulder-length, blond hair a kind of aura. Paddy was right; he did look Scandinavian, blond but not like a Viking. If I imagine a Viking, I think of a muscular, bearded type. Rafe was not a muscle man; he simply implied strength. Power was implicit in the way he walked and in his tone when he spoke. It was unstated but quickly understood by all of us that he was in charge. There was a contradiction in the way he carried himself and the impression I got. Though he was tall with broad shoulders and spoke like some kind of CIA agent, somehow the impression I got was of someone soft and gentle but strong, like the strength a child sees in its father. Just like the first time I had seen Emilio, it struck me that here was someone else with presence. It wasn't that he was what you would call handsome. I know Gill had suggested that when she said he could give Brad Pitt a run for his money. He was good looking, but not in a Brad Pitt kind of way. There was no ruggedness in Rafe; his command lay in the air of authority that clothed him like a cloak. Just as I had recognised it in Emilio, I could see it in Rafe, but that poise, that charisma, whatever it was that made him stand out in a crowd, was way beyond anything Emilio had. Uri, on the other hand, was dark. He had short, black hair and a bit of a five o' clock shadow. He too was tall and striking, and he had the same deep-blue eyes as Rafe, almost too bright to be real. It occurred to me that they might both have been wearing coloured contact lenses.

Rafe strolled around the room. He looked at each of us in turn, saying nothing. He seemed to be looking for something, and I had the feeling he had found something he didn't like, something unpleasant, but he seemed to change his mind. He stopped in front of me. "You know that we are here because Luke has asked for help, and you should be very grateful that he did; otherwise, all of you," he turned on his heel to look at the others, "would have paid a terrible price for your loyalty to your friend. Mark my words," he said forcefully, "you may still pay that price, for nothing is certain. For now there is an option, and you still have time to leave. Consider your position carefully. If you stay, you may have to fight. If you don't fight, then maybe you will be dragged off by the hunt and delivered to their master, who waits impatiently." He paused. "I know what you have experienced. I know that you, Erica, saw a spectre, a helmeted face through a window, and the severed heads on the doorstep, the noise, the drumming of lances and spears on doors and windows." He turned to the others. "But that was all just window dressing, physically harmless, intended to, and successfully did, I believe, create an atmosphere of terror and despair." He stopped in front of Katie, who was sitting, clutching her arms, and looking like a scared rabbit. "The architects of this prevailing emotional blanket of horror are just malevolent half breeds, soldier demons, half spirit, half imp, nuisance makers, charged with creating fear. If you felt afraid then, it is nothing to the dread you will feel when confronted with Abigor."

He moved forward to Jonah. "The Lord of Darkness has sent his most terrible warrior Abigor for all of you. Abigor, a grand duke of hell, commander of sixty legions. Abigor with his lieutenants will attempt to collect you, and collect you he will unless you obey me without question."

Jonah ran true to form. "Oh pleeeease gimme a break, a *grand duke of hell*? What a load of piffle. The whole thing sounds totally ridiculous." He stared into Rafe's face. "I don't believe any of this crap." Jonah was angry. "What organisation do you belong to anyway? Where are you from? Have you a license for these firearms you're carrying?" He fired off questions, one after the other.

Rafe was unfazed by Jonah's outburst. "I really don't care what you believe, and those things out there don't care either, but your refusal to believe in their power could make you careless and could cause your death or the death of your friends or worse." He looked deeply at him then bent down and spoke softly, almost whispering. "Wake up, Jonah. Believe, it is not too late for you." Jonah looked up at Rafe, and it was the first and only time I have seen Jonah lost for words. He looked surprised, disturbed, but he didn't challenge Rafe again.

Rafe lifted his face from Jonah. "In answer to your question, I suppose you could say we are mercenaries of a sort. Tonight we work for Luke, and so we are sent here to protect all of you; an armed force was required, and so that is what we are."

"Who sent you? If you are mercenaries, do you have a chain of command? I mean, who's in charge? And these weapons you're carrying—are they legal? Do you have permits?" Jonah had recovered and continued his interrogating.

Rafe turned his head slowly and considered Jonah. "If you are unfortunate enough to face Abigor tonight, I doubt very much that you will care if the weapons are legal or not. There are many of us, Inspector, and we answer to a higher authority than yours. The weapons carry live ammunition but not of the usual kind. The ammunition is made of a substance that is deadly to demonic entities. However, please take note: if you are careless and aim at a human being, the impact will cause wounding and could be fatal, so you must be careful with your aim."

"Which of us are you expecting to use the weapons?" Jack asked.

"Everyone will be armed," Rafe answered.

"I doubt if anyone here has ever used a gun," James said.

"Do not worry; you will have no difficulty using them. You point the pistols and squeeze the trigger. The same with the machine gun; you point and squeeze the trigger." Rafe reached for the gun at his waist. He held it up and released the magazine. "These are the pistols. They are magazine fed, delivering thirty-three rounds before you have to reload, which means after you have depleted your stock of bullets, you can quickly change it and get back to the fight." He slammed the magazine back into place with the heel of his hand. "You will each be given a supply of magazines preloaded with the ammunition. The machine guns are best used to provide suppressive fire. They are also magazine fed; just keep your finger on the trigger. It will force them to take cover, and it will also reduce their ability to attack. Uri and I will teach you how to use them. Please try to understand, a terrible adversary is coming, but you will have ability to protect yourself."

Rafe walked back to the centre of the room. "This night you will all be tested and must not be found wanting. This night will be a measure of your willingness to work together for the safety of all. Learn from us; we will teach you hard-and-fast rules to keep you safe. The demon is ingenious and cunning. Abigor will try to find a way in. Though the lesser spirits of the hunt need to be invited before they can enter, he is stronger. He and his lieutenants do not need an invitation. They *will* find a way in, and you must be ready to stop them by using the weapons we will give you."

"There are only two things the creatures fear: the eye of God and the wrath of their master. Hell is at constant war with the Creator, the supreme, all-seeing, all-hearing Being. The demons fear only that his eyes may turn toward them. He answers calls for aid, and it is by his will that they can be sent back to the darkness. Ask him to help in your hour of need; pray to God. Ask and you shall receive." He hesitated, then added, "What help you need." He smiled gently at Katie. Her face relaxed, and a hint of a smile passed her lips. "You will carry a gun at all times; you will carry a gun, and you will use it if you have to. You must follow any instructions Uri and I give you without question."

He lifted his head and studied the ceiling for a moment, then looked down at Katie. "You are all…" He stressed the word *all,* "marked by the hunt. By choosing to stay here with Luke and Erica, you have shown loyalty and friendship to an exceptional degree. You have been told what is coming. You are aware of the danger, yet you don't flee as the others did. That makes you either very brave or very stupid." He pondered for a moment. "I suspect a little of both. They no longer come just for Luke. They will take you too. So tonight you must become an army with Uri and I in command. Do you understand?" he said again, looking at each of us in turn, eyebrows raised askance. We each said yes or nodded like little dogs on a car's rear window. "They are not here to kill Luke. He did something no one has ever done. He found his way back out of hell. He humiliated Satan; he demeaned him by escaping and continuing to outwit the hunt. Satan wants him back and all of you with him." Rafe walked towards the door, and Uri opened it. "After you have eaten, we will prepare together. Be brave. All is not lost. We will have help. Mike and Gabe are coming; we just have to keep you safe till they get here."

CHAPTER TWENTY-FIVE

Waiting

They left us sitting in the drawing room, and as Luke made to follow them, I called him back. "Luke, stay for a moment." He turned to face me. "We need to know who these people are. We have a right to know, surely?"

"Yes, of course." He hesitated, and then shook his head; he shrugged his shoulders as if he was not sure what to say. "Only I cannot tell you more than you already know. You will all find out soon enough."

Jonah stood up abruptly, stepping between Luke and the door. "I'd call this soon enough. I think we should find out right now." His attitude was aggressive.

Luke wasn't shocked. He was more surprised, I think. He made to sidestep, but Jonah blocked his exit. "What's your problem? Answer her question."

"Please get out of my way. I cannot explain to you," Luke said heatedly. "And anyway, you..." he stressed the *you*, "would not listen to the truth even if I was willing to stand here debating it."

Jonah stood firm. "Try me," he said.

There was a moment of tension, then Luke thought better of it. He sighed and stepped backward. Waving his hand to suggest limitless possibilities, he said, "They are part of..." He stopped, considering his reply as though he was struggling to find the right words. "An order." I thought it was a bit odd. Surely he must have realised we were going to ask questions about these strangers coming out of the blue to help us.

"An order." Jonah nodded, pursed his lips, and looked at the floor. "Oh, well, that explains everything." He raised his head and almost spat, "What kind of order?"

"Rafe has already told you. They are mercenaries, hired to do a job."

"An order of mercenaries, a fighting force for hire, ready to tackle supernatural forces? Now that is impressive. What's the name of this order?"

"They don't call themselves anything."

"Not listed in the phone book then?" Jonah ended on a high note. "You know, you're doing it again. You get a kick out of keeping secrets, don't you? How about you try answering the question."

"OK," Luke said, raising his hands, palms toward Jonah. "Let's just say they are an organisation whose name you would not recognise."

"Again, try me."

"I told you I can't. Not yet."

"OK, then what about this Mike and Gabe?"

Luke sighed heavily. His voice developed a patronising tone that I just knew was going to irritate Jonah. I felt tense and not just a little worried. "They are just two people more experienced at dealing with demons of Abigor's calibre. Look, my friend…" He clapped Jonah on the shoulder. Bad move, I thought. "I am not a threat to you. I am grateful to all of you for your loyalty to my daughter. I would tell you more if I could, but it is the wrong time. You will understand when you are ready to listen. Now I must go; I have work to do." He made to step past Jonah again.

Without moving, Jonah stretched his arm out to stop him and repeated slowly and loudly what Luke had just said. "I'll understand when I am ready to listen. Do you never give a straight answer?" His tone was hostile. "If, as you are suggesting—and I stress the *if*—Erica is your daughter. You've scared the life out of her. You might actually have put her in danger. You appear in this house uninvited, come up with a cock-and-bull story about time traveling, and bring in these gun-toting weirdos, all of which, I might add, will put you nicely away behind bars, for a very long time." Jonah's tone was searing. "Now I'm going to ask you again, and this time try being a little less cryptic." I had the feeling he was going to explode.

Luke was tense. "Get out of my way."

Jonah's gaze darkened. "When you have answered my question in a rational manner."

Paddy and James shot out of their chairs. James stepped between them. "Let him go, Jonah."

Luke's eyes were burning with fury. He faced up to Jonah, his voice raised, angry. "You chose to be here. You have no more time than I have to stand around while I think up a neat little package of words that you will be comfortable with. I have told you the truth. Your inability to accept it is your problem. You can stand here all night. I am not at liberty to tell you more." He pushed past Jonah and went out the door. Jonah let him go, and there was a collective sigh of relief.

I tried to placate Jonah. "I believe him. I think there really is some reason why he can't tell us more."

Jonah was sharp. "Forgive me, Erica, but you must admit there are good reasons why you, more than most, may be more inclined to believe him."

"Fancy a whisky, Jonah?" Jack asked.

"You're reading my mind." Jonah smiled, relaxing a little. He liked Jack.

From somewhere in the corner, in the shadow, a silky-smooth Spanish voice said, "Do you mind if I suggest that tonight is not a good night to take alcohol?" Emilio had been sitting quietly watching the altercation; I had forgotten he was there.

"Yes I do mind, unless you have a very good reason," Jonah answered, his tone still a little sharp.

"Tonight you will need your wits about you," Emilio said. "Alcohol dampens your perceptions."

"Well, don't you worry about me. Mine have always been sharpened by a good malt," Jonah said. "Pour it, Jack."

"May I, Erica?" Jack pointed to the drinks trolley.

"Yes, of course," I said.

Jack lifted an unopened bottle of sixteen-year-old Lagavulin. He twisted the cap, cracking it open, and poured the amber liquid into a whisky glass. Jonah took the glass from Jack and added a drop of mineral water from a bottle sitting on a tray on the coffee table.

"Anyone else?" Jack asked, holding up another glass. Paddy nodded.

"I'll have some," Gill said.

Paddy took the glass from Jack. "Maybe they are some kind of Knights Templar. Didn't Luke say they still exist today?"

"He did, and he was telling the truth. They do." Jack settled back in a chair, savouring the whisky.

Paddy paced the floor as though it was helping him think. "The Templars were a religious order. They were monks as well as knights, so it would fit with some of Luke's story. Luke said that he had been a Templar, and he spoke of these mercenaries always being around to help him escape the hunt. So if you have mercenaries who are called on to fight spirits or demons, you have soldiers with a spiritual slant. Look at the way Rafe was speaking tonight. Did you notice the way he said to Katie, 'Ask and you shall receive'? It's a well-known prayer: 'Ask and you shall receive, seek and you shall find, knock and it shall be opened to you.' Not the kind of conversation you would expect from an ex-soldier type mercenary."

"I know for a fact there are various organisations around claiming to be Templars. I had had dealings with one branch, and they were downright lunatics, well known to the police," Jonah said. "I am not saying that there are not genuine descendants from Templars, but most of them are just eccentrics, somewhere in line with Jedi Knights and Trekkers. They are mostly overweight businessmen by day and Templars by night and on high days and holidays. They are not gun-toting muscle men like these blokes, but I do get where you are coming from, Paddy. You could be right. There might be some connection there."

"I think you could be right because if not, then what else could they be?" James said. "By process of elimination, they're not police, not secret service. They are mercenaries who specialise in demons, so if they are not some order of warrior monks, what else could they be?"

Emilio, still sitting in the corner at James's back, muttered something in Spanish. James turned on him. "What did you say?" He realised he had been sharp and corrected himself. "Sorry, Emilio. I didn't catch that."

Emilio sighed heavily. "Like Luke, I prefer to keep my own councel." He glowered at Jonah. "At least until my companions are likely to be more receptive to my opinion." He eased himself up from the chair. "Now I for one would like to eat."

For the next few hours, with consummate patience, Rafe, Uri, and Luke spent time with each of us in turn until they were sure we were proficient at loading and handling both hand and machine guns. I didn't realize what an impact it would have on me. The idea of holding—never mind using—a gun troubled me, but strangely, the weight of it in my hand and the understanding that I could protect myself from anything that came in the night gave me a feeling of confidence. I felt instantly safer when I knew I had something that could kill the demons—or rather, as Luke had taken pains to correct us and explain—not actually kill them because they couldn't technically be killed, but with a direct hit I could dispatch them back to where they came from.

James asked Luke about the ammunition, which after all looked just like standard ammunition. Luke said it was made of, among other things, sea salt, garlic, dragon's blood, brass, and silver.

"Dragon's blood!" I interrupted him. "You are not serious?"

Luke smiled. "Yes, dragon's blood, though not literally the blood of a dragon. Dragon's blood is a bright red resin secreted by the bark of a tree when it is damaged, the dragon tree, which is native to the Canary Islands and Morocco. The resin hardens into garnet red drops, like little drops of blood. It has been used for centuries to repel demons. That's all I know, but even without the ammunition, our friends have ways of sending them back to hell, and anyway, Gabe and Mike will be here soon."

"Gabe and Mike? Who are Gabe and Mike exactly?" I asked.

He remained vague. "The big guns," he said, walking over to help Gill load her handgun.

I wondered why we weren't barricading ourselves in, but James said he had spoken to Luke about it, and it seemed there was no point. If they wanted in, they would get in. One got in already in Caleb. Luke had also said we could use anything as weapons if we had to. Any weapon could be used to stop them in their tracks; however, if we could manage to even wound one with our newly acquired weaponry, we could do some serious damage.

We ate in the kitchen, the meal that Paddy had prepared earlier. Luke declined to join us, saying he would eat later, and we had no idea where Rafe and Uri had vanished to.

The fog hung around the house all day, and by seven o'clock, far too early for a summer evening, darkness came. Outside everything was black and still; all afternoon the house had bustled with nervous energy, and now the air of tension was palpable. Fires had been lit in the drawing room, morning room, and study. I had no idea who lit them. Candles were put into every candle-holder in the house and torches distributed, and Luke had lit a few oil lamps he had brought up from the cellar. Now we were just waiting.

The landline that had been working all morning was down, and by nine o'clock, the electricity was also off. The generator in the cellar had packed in again and since it only ran a couple of lights anyway it was not worth the trouble. Uri told us to stay together in the study because it had only one window to watch and two exits, one of which was the conservatory, which was locked and secured with dead bolts. Uri advised us to rest if we could. He said the most likely time for the riders to come was between three and four in the morning. When I asked why then, he said that the veil between their world and ours was at its thinnest during those hours. He then said, and I quote, "Rest and do not be afraid. We will watch over you while you sleep." James remarked it was a strange turn of phrase, almost like an adult speaking to children. Jonah added everything about them was strange.

We took the duvets we had used the night before through to the study from where they had been piled in the morning room. We lay close together near the fire. Though everyone was tired, no one slept. Even so, there was none of the usual banter going on, the badgering that had become the norm. We were drawn together by a need to trust and rely on one another, and so we had developed the type of friendship that was secure enough to tease and torment, all the time knowing that there was no offense intended and none taken. But this was not like sitting around the fire with a glass of wine telling ghost stories. There was no thrill. As the night wore on, there was just fear, fear I could almost taste.

We lay still listening. The house was grimly silent, as though even the house itself, the stone walls were waiting. Try to get some sleep, Uri had said. I thought there was little chance of that. I lay feeling so tense my muscles were beginning to ache, yet at some point I must have dropped off. It wasn't a deep sleep; I tossed and turned, trying to sleep, worrying that

I would be too tired to be of any use to man or beast when the time came. When I awoke, I would have said I hadn't slept at all, but time had passed.

I woke to the sound of Jack and Jonah whispering and James putting more coal on the fire. Paddy was still asleep, but Gill was stirring. Katie was up, sitting silently on a sofa beside Emilio. She was vacantly watching James build up the fire. She didn't see me move, and I startled her when I sat beside her.

"You slept well," she said quietly, smiling.

"What time is it now?" I asked.

"Quarter past two," she answered, looking at her watch.

"Good morning," Emilio said quietly. Gill was still sleeping.

"Morning? This isn't morning," I said, groaning. "It's still the middle of the night."

"Do you feel better after some sleep?" he asked.

"Yes, although I think if I had to choose between them for comfort, the morning room floor has a definite edge on this one."

"I think then, that floor must be...I think the phrase is *better sprung*," he said, smiling.

"Emilio, how can you smile? This is such a mess, and I feel responsible for you all being here." My throat was burning, and my eyes were filling up. I so did not want to cry.

Emilio leaned past Katie and whispered, "You are not responsible. I chose to stay here. You may not agree with me, but there are paths presented to all of us throughout our lives. We choose to take them or to ignore them. It may not be obvious to you, but there is a reason, different for each one of us, why our paths have brought us here. For me..." He sat back looking around the room. "I feel needed; my gift, or curse, as I have often thought of it, has been of use to you, and it gives me a sense of worth instead of the usual sense of being a freak. For this I thank you." He smiled.

Gill was awake. She lifted her head off the pillow, peered at us through her tousled black hair, half shut eyes, and whimpered. She lay back down again and pulled the duvet over her head. A few minutes later she threw it off and said, "It's no use. I'm aching all over, and it's freezing in here." She pouted at Jack.

Jack fixed her with his gentle, reassuring eyes. "C'mon, me darlin'," he said, exaggerating his Irish accent. He pulled her up and wrapped a rug around her, giving her a hug and rubbing her arms to create heat. "Sit here near the fire." He pushed a red-and-gold oriental overstuffed pouffee with his foot over to the edge of the hearth. "Sit down there and get some heat into you."

"Heat? You must be joking. That fire just looks warm. There is actually no heat coming from it," she said grumpily, putting her head on Jack's shoulder.

"Give it time. James has just put fresh coal on, and anyway, it's because you're tired," Katie said.

Paddy sat up as though he had heard something. "No it's because the temperature in the house is dropping."

It was dropping; I could feel it, that chill, that creeping ice crawling slowly up my back. Within a few moments it seemed as though the cold was seeping through the walls of the house into my bones. I asked Katie if she had slept, and she said she thought everyone had had some sleep, but there had been some noises.

"What kind of noises?"

"The tapping," she said, "on the window, on and off for the last hour, and muffled cries, shrieking."

"Shrieking? It's started then." I shivered, feeling another tingle in my spine.

"The cries are at a distance, but they are getting louder, closer." Jack said.

"Jonah went to speak to Luke and the others, but he couldn't find them." Katie shrugged her shoulders. "James and Jack tried too. They are nowhere to be seen."

Jonah shook his head. "There is not a sign of them anywhere. The three of us searched the house top to toe; it's empty. There are candles lit all over the place, the outside doors are all locked, and the deadbolts are in place, but there is not a living soul anywhere. We wondered if they might have gone through the tunnels that Luke uses."

"What, you think they might have left us here?" I said, my stomach knotting at the idea that they might have abandoned us. "You really think they would leave us to face this alone?"

"Who knows?" James stood up from his kneeling position at the fire. "We don't even know who they are. How could we know what they are capable of?"

"No." I shook my head. "I don't believe that," I said emphatically.

Emilio sighed loudly. "And you are right not to believe it, Erica. They would not leave us. They would not abandon us in our hour of need." Emilio was ardent in his defense of the strangers.

"Oh no? And why is that? What makes you so all-fired sure they haven't bailed out?" Jonah asked. "Do you know something we don't?"

"I know because I feel their essence, the power of their being. I see their aura, and it is pure." Emilio was nonchalant. "I do not believe they would abandon us. I believe they are tasked with protecting us. They are not like anyone you have dealt with before, Inspector."

"Oh, believe me; I have dealt with plenty of nutters in my time, and as for your sensing their essence? Well, you know what I think about that, and by the way, if you want to try for first place in the weirdness contest, you are outclassed by them. The competition for first place is pretty stiff around here. Luke and company are way out of your league when it comes to eccentricity and sidetracking. And while I am on the subject, I am sick to the teeth of no one giving a straight answer. How can you be so convinced these men wouldn't abandon us? The truth is pal, you don't know anymore about them than we do."

Emilio looked Jonah straight in the eye. "I am not your pal, and they…" he hesitated. "Are not men."

CHAPTER TWENTY-SIX

The Healer

"What do you mean they are not men?" I asked Emilio.

He shrugged. "It is my perception."

"So what do you think they are, huh? Aliens that Luke's brought back with him from his distant world?" Jonah chuckled, shaking his head.

"What I think is that time will tell."

"Oh, that's a copout, Emilio," James said.

"Not a copout, James. As Luke said, you will find out when you are ready. There is no point in pressing me. This is one time I am truly sure of what my senses tell me, and the time is not right."

Though there had been concentrated listening for the better part of an hour, no one had heard a sound. The night had gone deathly quiet. Jonah parted the heavy drapes and peered out of the window into the gloom.

"What can you see?" I whispered to him.

"Nothing. It's pitch black out there." He drew the curtains wider for a better look.

Katie got up, more to stretch her legs than anything else. "I ache all over," she said, stretching. "It's going to be a long night at this rate.

What I mean is that all that preparation, all the anxiety, and all they can conjure up is half-hearted tapping on windows and a screaming match outside.

You know I'm slowly getting past the stage of being permanently scared. Do you think there is the slightest possibility they've gone?"

"I hope so. If that's all they've got, I for one am happy," Gill said, pulling the rug more tightly around her shoulders. "I would be quite happy to crawl into that big, soft bed upstairs. Mind you, even this floor is better than that creaky, lumpy, smelly excuse for a bed we slept in last night in that pokey old cottage. God, it's been a long weekend."

"I don't think we should presume they have gone. I don't imagine they would give up so easily." Emilio, still sitting on the sofa, turned his head toward the window. "No, they are still out there."

"Really? Is that a wild guess, or is it your magic antenna working?" There was no nastiness this time in Jonah's tone. He was just teasing.

Emilio, however, didn't take the bait. He was staring at the window, but his eyes seemed focused on something in the distance beyond the glass. "There is something here, something foul."

Jonah moved closer to the window. He tensed. "Wait. There is something strange out there. I can see it." We all turned quickly to the window.

"Oh no, sorry Emilio, it's just your reflection." Jonah grinned.

"Cut it out, Jonah," Jack said.

Emilio was cool. His face serious, he was still staring out the window. He didn't even respond to Jonah. "There is something, something powerful."

"What time is it?" Gill asked. "I feel jet lagged, and I haven't even had the benefit of sun, sea, and sand to make me feel good about it."

"Time? I don't even know what day it is," Katie said, sounding thoroughly disgusted.

"Sunday," Jack said.

Sunday. Just a year ago, Sunday meant a long lie, bacon and eggs for breakfast, newspapers for Paul, magazines for me, and then, weather permitting, taking *The Dutch Lady* for a sail. Life had been so simple, so safe. None of us know really what's round the corner. We all think we know what we will be doing next day, next week, next month, but the truth is we don't because life is fickle and fate is capricious. There are no certainties in life, and no one should be complacent. I didn't appreciate enough what I had; I had to lose it to do that.

No amount of happiness with Paul should have made me give up my life, my friends. If Gill and Katie had been different people, less loyal, less willing to put up with me saying I couldn't meet them because Paul and I had plans over and over again, I could have been alone when my husband died, but they had not allowed his indifference and sometimes downright hostility to their intrusion in our lives to alienate them. They were always there in the background, at the end of a phone line.

"Don't you think it's strange that no one has tried to make contact? Shouldn't someone be looking for you?" I asked James. "Or you Jonah?" I asked.

"I hope not," Jonah said. "Look what happened when Jack and Gill tried to come back. No, I live alone. I have an ex-wife in Wales, but trust me, she won't be looking for me, and anyway, I took some leave. Molly and Caleb had too much of a scare, and they were told to stay away until we contact them, so they're not likely to try. I was a bit concerned about the local postie, but there's not much we can do about it."

Always the joker. I wondered if it was just a cover-up for the fact he was as nervous as the rest of us.

"What about you, James?" I asked.

"My father knows where I am, and my boss sent me here, remember?"

"Jack?"

"No, there's just my mother, but she is used to me just visiting every other month or so. She won't be surprised if she hasn't heard from me."

Katie wandered over to the window. Not able to see anything, she peered out, almost putting her nose against the glass. "Hey, look at this. The window is freezing over, just like the kitchen window earlier."

The window had a haze over it, like hot breath on cold glass, and it appeared to be icing on the inside. Katie put her hand on the glass to wipe it and then laid her hand flat, feeling the extent of the cold. Suddenly there was an almighty crack. Something had struck the glass so hard it should have shattered but the glass hadn't broken. Shocked, Katie made to take her hand away, but she couldn't move it.

"My hand is stuck," she said, puzzled, straining to pull her hand off the glass. We didn't take her seriously at first. Then Jonah tried to help her, but the hand was stuck solidly to the window.

They were both concentrating on her hand and didn't see it, but there was a face in the window. The face was clearly etched, grey seen through the haze on the glass and against the inky blackness of the night, illuminated by the oil lamps, coal fire, and candles in the room. Suddenly the chill I had felt earlier crawled up my spine at breakneck speed, crashing into my skull.

Katie looked up, saw it, screamed, and panicked. Trying to pull away, she grabbed at Jonah with her free hand, almost falling over a side table as she backed away from the window. Jonah, who had been focused on trying to separate her fingers, looked up and cried out, startled. I was right behind them. I could see it clearly. It had an oval-shaped face; high, tattooed cheekbones; and large, almond-shaped, glowing red eyes with vertical yellow pupils like a reptile. A forked black tongue shot back and forth from its mouth, and it was licking its way down the glass toward Katie's hand.

I shuddered in horror. Backing away from the window, I crashed into James, knocking him over. We landed on the carpet in a heap. I pushed him trying to get up. I couldn't tear my face away from the obscenity in the window, but then Katie's cry for help broke the mesmeric hold the scene had on me, and I scrabbled at James trying to get to her. Only his grip on my arms stopped me from fleeing to her in sheer panic. James pushed me out of the way. Swiftly and calmly he caught Katie, who was about to faint, and held her while Jonah and Jack tried to free her hand from the window. It was stuck solidly; the skin looked as though it had melted, fused to the glass.

"Gill, get some hot water," Paddy cried.

James, still supporting Katie, got between her and the window. He hid her face on his shoulder, her arm twisted at an awkward angle.

Emilio appeared with Gill and some lukewarm water in a jug. There was no hot water and no way of heating it. They poured it over the glass above her hand to no avail; it remained as fixed as ever.

"Break the glass," I cried. "Get her away from them."

"No," Emilio shouted. "It's too dangerous. They could pull her out."

The thing backed away from the window till we couldn't see it, and a child took its place, a little boy with floppy hair almost in his eyes, except he didn't have any. No eyes, no mouth, just a gaping hole. It opened its mouth-like hole and shrieked, then, howling like a dog, it raised its thin, spindly arms with grey flesh peeling off, and using its huge hands, it tapped the window with its claws, rhythmic tapping, louder and louder. It scuttled up the glass like a spider, to the top, then started crawling down again toward Katie's hand. Katie was hysterical, and then, just as suddenly, she went silent.

"Keep her awake. Don't let her faint, James," Jonah cried.

James lifted her head from his shoulder. "Katie, Katie, don't sleep."

She was deathly pale, her eyes almost closed.

The attack started, just a soft pulsing sound different from the rhythmic tapping of before, then throb, throb, like a heartbeat, beating, then pounding, growing louder and louder until it reached a deafening crescendo. Doors, windows, even the very walls seemed ready to cave in. Screams pieced the night, howling, shrieking like tortured animals in the agony of death throes. It struck such a terror into me, so intense that I felt it as an actual pain in my throat.

It quieted down again. There was a soft, wet slap as something hit the widow. It was such a muted sound that we didn't realise at first that it had penetrated and cracked the glass above Katie's hand. Grey flesh and gore began to slide down the window, and black, foul-smelling fluid dripped through the crack. The smell was overpowering. It was a smell of decay, of putrefaction so rank that it made us all retch. The slime slid down the inside of the window, slowly creeping toward Katie's hand. Jonah pulled harder but stopped when he realised her skin was tearing.

It had almost reached Katie's hand when Jack called out, "Do it, Jonah. Do it...DO IT."

With an almighty wrench, Jonah tore Katie's hand off the glass. She screamed and collapsed onto James. What looked like a perfect red imprint of her hand was left on the window. It was actually bloodied skin.

James swept up her legs and with Jonah's help laid her on the sofa. I tore the slip from a pillow and wrapped it around her raw, bleeding hand. She had fainted, which was a blessing. Gill brought the first aid box, and I dressed and bandaged the hand as best I could.

Jonah and Jack stood in front of the window, guns pointed and ready for the thing when it finally broke through. Suddenly there was a flash of lightning; the night sky blazed with flares of brightly coloured lights and bursts of gunfire, the intensity illuminating untold numbers of stooped, deformed shapes on horseback. With a spectrum of colours something was attacking the hunt. From inside it looked as though someone had set off fireworks.

The frenzied caterwauling was epic. Pieces of flesh flew past the window, and horses and dogs screamed and howled amid a hail of bullets. Then, just as quickly, there was silence.

We stood frozen, afraid to move, afraid to breathe; you could have heard a pin drop in the room. Eventually Jonah went closer to the window, gun raised cautiously, wary of any sound or movement. The lights had gone; outside it was pitch black again.

Katie came round. I gave her some Ibuprofen and Paracetamol, which were the only pain-killers in the first aid box. There was no skin left on the palm or under the fingers of her right hand, just raw flesh. The wounds, so superficial, were excruciatingly painful, and the pain-killers totally inadequate. After half an hour, they had done no more than take the edge off the pain. Katie lay on the sofa deathly white, with a sheen of cold perspiration covering her face. Her eyes were hot and full of anguish.

"This is ridiculous. We will have to get help. Where is Luke? Did you tell him?" I asked Emilio.

"There was no one there to tell," Gill said. "There is no one in the house except us."

We all jumped when the door of the study opened and Luke came in. He didn't speak but opened the door wider and stepped back to admit the man standing there. The man wore the same long leather coat that Rafe and Uri had worn, and like Rafe he was tall, broad-shouldered, and slim. Where Rafe was blond, this man had rich, copper-toned, curly hair, though he had those same intense blue eyes, so bright they reminded me of the flame on a gas cooker.

The man scanned the room, and his eyes rested on Katie, who was lying on the sofa, restless. He watched her for a moment, then turned his head towards the hall and called, "Raphael."

His voice was deep, melodious, and commanding. In the blink of an eye, Rafe appeared at his back. He turned and looked at Rafe, expressionless, and then he looked back at Katie. Rafe followed his gaze to the sofa where she lay.

Kneeling beside her, Rafe lifted her bandaged hand. Katie cried out, her face contorted with pain. He turned the injured hand to examine it; she struggled and tried to stop him touching it. Jonah intervened, asking what the hell he thought he was doing, but Rafe simply looked up at Jonah, and Jonah stepped back. Rafe unwound the bandage, and Katie moaned but didn't resist. Carefully he lifted the edge of the dressing, which was stuck to the wound; she whimpered again, trying to pull her hand away.

"Katie," Rafe said her name softly, gently. She tossed her head from side to side. "Katie, look at me," he commanded.

Katie looked up into Rafe's eyes. Her breathing was frantic. He held her gaze.

"Now close your eyes and let me hold your hand. I will not hurt you."

Katie looked into Rafe's eyes as he held her hand in both of his. Gradually her breathing slowed, and she did as he asked. When she closed her eyes, he covered her hand with one of his and placed his other hand on her forehead. Still kneeling on one knee, he closed his eyes and bent his head.

In no more than a heartbeat later, Katie's laboured breath had returned to normal. She sighed deeply, and a flush of pink came back to her cheeks. "Sleep now; your pain has gone," Rafe whispered to her. He stood up and turned.

Rafe gave me a ghost of a smile and nodded. "Leave her to rest." He left, stopping for a moment in front of the man. They didn't speak, and Rafe just left the room. They were men of few words.

The man turned to follow him. "Thank you," I called out.

He stopped and turned back. "I did nothing," he said, still no expression on his face. "Rafe is the healer." I knew he had instigated Rafe's intervention, but there seemed no point in saying so.

"Then for what you did outside, for coming to help."

"I did nothing. The others have dispatched them." his voice was flat. He turned on his heel and left.

Luke closed the door. "The gunfire you heard was Mike and Uri. Mike, they tell me, is their most experienced fighter. Rafe told me few, if any, can stand against Mike. At any rate they have dispersed the hunt for now, but they say they it won't be long till they will return. If you need anything, you should get it now, while it's safe," Luke said. "I am going to make some tea and coffee. I will bring it through. It's safer if you stay here together."

"Well, he seems a chatty type. He's about as talkative as the other two. Mind you, he seems a little less friendly," Jonah said. He rubbed his hands over his head and face. "I could do with another drink."

"Yes, idle chatter is not their forte; they don't speak unless they have something worth saying," Luke agreed. "That was Gabe. I had never met him before, but I get the impression he doesn't want to be here."

"I noticed," Jack said. "He looked at us as if he had a bad smell under his nose. I have to say, Jonah, the other two didn't seem that friendly either."

"He doesn't want to be here, and let's face it, who would? None of us, if we had a choice," Gill said.

"Ah, but you did have a choice, and you chose to stay," Emilio reminded her.

I covered Katie with a rug. Shock and exhaustion had taken their toll, and she was asleep. Carefully, so as not to waken her, I tried to re-bandage her hand. The dressing that been stuck had fallen off. When I lifted the blood-soaked gauze underneath, Katie's hand was completely healed.

"Oh my God," I cried in shock. "Look at her hand, look." I leaned back, holding her palm upward for the others to see. "How?..." I trailed off, bewildered. "I don't understand. How is this possible?" I couldn't believe the evidence of my own eyes. I turned Katie's hand for them to see. The soft, pink skin was unbroken, healthy. I looked up at the window where the bloodied, perfectly shaped hand-print was still on the glass. "He healed it. How could he heal it like this?"

Everyone came over for a closer look. Paddy knelt down. He gently took Katie's hand from me, turning it this way and that, carefully so as not to wake the near-unconscious Katie. Then he put her hand down and covered her with the rug. He sat back on his heels, chewing his lip, looking lost in thought. Then, as though thinking out loud, he said slowly, quietly, "Rafe is the Healer." He turned to Jonah, looking at him as though he was trying to remember something. He pointed to the door. "That guy said it, you all heard him." He looked strained trying to remember something that was just out of memory's reach. Then it hit, and he looked as though he had been struck by lightning. He spun round on Emilio. "You know, don't you? You have known all along. I heard you earlier when Jonah was going off on one. I heard you mutter in Spanish. It has been preying on my mind. James asked you. Why didn't you say something? Why didn't you warn us?"

"What could I say? Who would believe me? " Emilio answered, shrugging. "I could feel the power emanating from them. They have auras of such intense light. What could I have told you? Who would have listened to me?"

"About what?" Jonah asked.

"Listened to what? Paddy, what are you talking about?" Jack raised his voice.

Paddy's eyes were wide, glazed over. "Talking about?" he whispered. He shook his head. "I can hardly believe I'm even thinking it. I have just realised what it was Emilio said earlier. He said, 'Ellos son los angeles.'" He spun round on Luke. "These men aren't warrior monks or mercenaries, are they?" He raised his voice. "Who is there truly capable of standing against a demon army?"

Paddy and Luke stared at each other for a moment, then Luke said, "You're right, Paddy. As I said earlier, you would find out when you were ready. Tell them, Emilio, in English. Tell them what Paddy heard you say. They are ready to know. "

Emilio licked his lips. "I said, 'Ellos son los Angeles.' He hesitated. "In English, THEY ARE ANGELS."

CHAPTER TWENTY-SEVEN

The Messengers

"Don't you get it? Raphael, Uriel, Michael..." Paddy was almost shouting when abruptly he was cut short by the man who again stood in the doorway.

"And Gabriel," the man added.

Paddy was too dumbstruck at the thought that he might be right to say anymore.

Nevertheless, there it was—or rather, there he was, Gabriel. Suddenly I was batting with Jonah. I never imagined I would take sides with Jonah, but this latest revelation...well, that was stretching the imagination just too far. Paddy and Emilio couldn't be right. Up until that point, I had believed everything, or at least I had tried to trust that people were telling me the truth. My time-traveling father, younger than me, demons riding on phantom horses outside the house. I couldn't explain these things, but I had seen the riders and had heard their inhuman screams. This, on the other hand...angels coming to the rescue? Could there honestly be the slightest, tiniest, minuscule possibility that it was true? My head was spinning. No this craziness had to stop somewhere.

Before taking time to put my brain into gear, I asked him loudly, "Excuse me. Who are you exactly?"

He waited a second before he answered me, unsmiling, in that flat even tone, as though I hadn't heard him tell us five seconds earlier. He said, "I am Gabriel."

That was all, just that. Not "I am the angel Gabriel" because after all, that would have been just ludicrous. "I am Gabriel," he said, in the manner of someone who is not a Gabriel Smith or Gabriel Brown, but in the manner of someone saying, "I am Napoleon" or "I am Socrates." No need for first names.

Bravely or stupidly or both, I said as sternly and with as much authority as I could muster, "Gabriel who?"

Now that stunned everyone; they all turned to look at me as though I was stupid. It was as though they knew who he was and couldn't believe I didn't.

With complete disdain, he said, "I have never been asked that before. I am just Gabriel."

There are times in most people's lives when for some inexplicable reason, something incredible that they hear for the first time has such a ring of truth about it that they instantly believe it: This was my moment. Every instinct I possessed told me this tall, good-looking, stern, unsmiling man, dressed in boots, jeans, and a leather coat, with curly copper hair in need of a trim, who looked critical, whose tone was sharp, who looked as though he would rather be anywhere else other than in the room in which he was standing, was really who Paddy thought he was. Was actually real, was an angel. I could hardly believe my overwrought brain was even considering it because if I really was considering it, that would mean that I believed I was standing in the presence an angel, in which case, surely then, I would have to be insane.

I had been through the stage of growing up when I rebelled against my church upbringing, when I questioned my belief in God. Therefore, how could I now believe this was an angel? If I was talking to an angel, and one called Gabriel at that, then was he The Angel Gabriel? The Archangel? The one who told the Virgin Mary she was with child? It was incomprehensible, but I believed him. Unfortunately, while my heart was telling me he was real, my head was telling me that if I believed that he was here, in front of me, talking to me, then I was indisputably back down the rabbit hole again. It was at that point it occurred to me that I might have lost my mind. What if after Paul died, grief had unhinged me? What if I was delusional and Lanshoud was actually a mental hospital, an asylum, and we were all patients? Maybe the people I thought were my friends were actually lunatics, and as for Dr. Luke and his angel buddies, maybe their leather coats were actually white coats. That possibility was almost more credible than the situation I was facing just then.

Gabe, as it turned out his friends called him, wanted a word, Luke said, in the kitchen. Just me, he insisted. Fighting off protestations from James and Jonah, I followed him through to find all four of the men, angels, whatever they were, lounging about. Uri sat with a mug of something hot at the table. Not actually sitting, he was more sprawled, lying back in a chair, legs akimbo, mud caked on his boots and splashed on his coat. I guess my preconception of what angels should look like—to be exact, long, white dress; fluffy, white wings; and a halo—was just a little off kilter because this one was wingless, drinking coffee, and in need of a shave.

Gabriel sat at the end of the table, picking something out of his teeth, not very angel-like either. Rafe leaned against a counter, arms folded, his leather coat open, exposing the guns at his belt. The one who must be Michael stood beside Luke, towering above him. By virtue of the fact they were all very tall, broad-shouldered, big, powerful-looking men, their sheer size was intimidating, and when the long leather coats and boots were added, it simply enhanced the overall perception, and as a result they made the very large kitchen seem very small.

"This is Michael." Luke introduced him. Michael had blond hair, lighter than Rafe's, almost white. He had a strong chin and looked more rugged. Now unlike Rafe, he could pass for a Viking, and of course he had the prerequisite gas-flame-blue eyes.

The Viking look-alike made no attempt to move or to shake hands, so I quickly stopped my impulse to just that. I just smiled and nodded a greeting while he seemed to be sizing me up. Luke handed me a mug. "Tea?" he asked. "I have made a pot, and I'll take some through to the others." I took the tea from him and sat down at the table, mostly because the table stopped the mug from shaking, and the mug stopped my hands from shaking. "I'll just take this through." Luke lifted a tray full of mugs and biscuits, and Uri got up and followed him.

No one spoke. It had just got to the point of being an uncomfortable silence when I tried to break the ice by saying something lame. I thanked them for coming, for helping us, for healing Katie. I rattled on, telling them how terrified we had been, how we had no idea where to turn to for help. I was in the full flow of verbal diarrhoea when Michael spoke, halting me in mid-sentence.

"Luke is very proud of you, Erica. You have borne the last few days with remarkable fortitude. Now we must test your strength further. Luke has told you that we have sent the hunt back to its master. That much is true. We met the full force of the hunt outside, and Uri and I dispersed them, interestingly without needing help from Gabe or Rafe. They left just like that." He slapped his hand hard on the counter, making me jump. "In a flash, they were gone, in minutes. It was easy—too easy. You must understand that that is not what we have come to expect of them. They fled from us eagerly, and that is unheard of; for though they have reason to fear us, they fear their master more and would not resist his will, which of course is to collect souls and bring them back, especially you and Luke. That left us asking ourselves why they would flee so readily. The answer was simple: they left because Abigor is already here."

He was waiting for me to say something. I nodded. "Yes, we knew he was coming. Rafe told us."

"You misunderstand. He was not outside with the rabble. Abigor was in the room with you."

"No, he wasn't," I said. "They didn't get in. The window cracked, but nothing got in."

"Gabriel," Michael said without taking his eyes off me. Gabriel moved chairs and sat on the one opposite me. When they first arrived, I thought Rafe was in charge, for want of a better term. Then I thought Gabriel was the boss, but apparently it was Michael because they all jumped when he spoke.

Gabriel leaned forward over the table and looked me straight in the eye. "He was in the room with you. I could smell him."

I had just told him he wasn't in the room. Why was he insisting he was? "What are you saying? Do you mean he was there but we couldn't see him, that he was invisible?"

Gabriel took a deep breath and sighed. He had an air of exasperation, as if he were dealing with an imbecile and the imbecile was wasting his time.

He glanced up at Michael, who told him to carry on. Gabriel turned back to me but still took his time to speak, looking at my face, giving me time to reach my own conclusion. He was waiting for me to catch up, work it out for myself; I had a bad feeling about this. And then it hit me with a sickening, spiraling sense of inevitability, when for a moment everything was in slow motion, as it is when you lose your balance, can't regain it, and begin to fall, and each second turns into a minute as you wait to smash into the ground. With a rising sense of horror, I knew what he was going to say, and I did not want to hear it. I did not want to hear it, but it came anyway, crashing into my ears and my mind.

"Abigor was in the room with you. Abigor is one those people you call your friends."

The now familiar ice gripped my spine. I shook my head slowly. "That can't be, unless..." They waited patiently for my brain to process the information. I found my voice again. "Are you saying one of the others is possessed, as Caleb was?"

"No," Michael said emphatically. "Caleb was possessed by an unclean spirit. Caleb's soul was still there, still in that body sharing it with the entity. Someone you call your friend is just Abigor; no soul could share a body with him and survive. He is the deceiver. You see him as he wants you to see him; you know him as he wants to be known. You have never known the real person."

"No," I shook my head. I felt nauseous. Not again, the old scenario where people I loved or trusted were not who they said they were, another one to add to the list of my mother, my father, my husband, the Camerons. Only this was even worse. They were telling me that I had put my trust in someone not even human. I was shaking my head from side to side, not wanting to even consider what they were suggesting. I thought, how flawed must my psyche be when I cannot tell if people I am close to are genuine, when I am totally incapable of recognizing deceit, and now to crown it all, I have made friends with some creature from the Pit.

Michael's voice was deep and gentle. "Abigor is cunning. He is a master of disguise and deception, and his ingenuity is greater than you could possibly comprehend. He is adept at impersonation, pretense, and subterfuge. Suffice to say even Rafe and Uri did not recognise him, and Gabe couldn't pick him out from among the people in the room, though he knew without doubt he was there."

I felt sick. James, Jonah, Paddy, Emilio, Jack, it couldn't be true. The very idea was unthinkable.

"He takes the form of man or woman when it suits his purpose," Gabriel said, reading my thoughts.

I was still silently shaking my head from side to side, the idea too horrible to contemplate. My throat had dried up, and when I tried to speak, I croaked. "Are you telling me that Abigor has been here with us all along? Are you saying he was already here when Rafe and Uri came? Even before? I don't understand. If he was with us before you came, before we had anyone to protect us, why did he not take Luke then?"

Michael answered, "Games, just games. He relishes the chase. He is like a cat playing with mice. He enjoys the game, he amuses himself. In the beginning, he would have been waiting for Luke to show, just passing the time. He is arrogantly confident. He would be lapping up the anxiety and fear around him. He feeds off it."

"No, it can't be any of those people in the study. Gill and Katie have been my friends for years. The others I have come to know. They have stayed to help me. They have willingly put themselves into danger."

Michael dismissed my protestations. "Yes, and that is admirable. Nevertheless it's true that among them is one of Satan's elite, and the problem is once he realises we are on to him, the game will end. We need to find him. You can help us do that, Erica."

"How? What can I do?"

"Look at each one of the others, narrow it down to who it is unlikely to be. Eliminate those you believe are genuine. Think, Erica. You know these people. Work on what you know."

"You want me to judge their character? Me? Based on experience, I am the wrong person to judge personality or character. In fact, I am probably the last person in the world to find him and without doubt the easiest for him to deceive. Would you like a list of the people who have managed to deceive me very successfully up till now?"

"This is not the time for self-pity. Just tell us what you know," Michael said and waited as I sat with my head in my hands. I wanted to run away. I wanted to be anywhere but there in this kitchen of this madhouse with a bunch of gun-toting angels.

"Katie and Gill have been my friends for years. It is not Katie or Gill."

I sat clutching the coffee cup, taking comfort from its heat as the faces of people I thought I knew well swam into my mind. Suddenly from out of nowhere, a wave of anger washed over me. I shouldn't be here; this shouldn't be happening. I shouldn't be sitting in this old house in the middle of nowhere discussing the possibility that Katie or Gill might be trying to kill me. I should be sitting in my home with Paul. We should have had a child. I should have stopped him going away days at a time, made him change his job. All the things we should have, could have done, now gone forever. All I had left in the world was the people in the study. It was unfair. I needed to have someone I could trust, someone on my side.

The force of their gaze pulled me out of my reverie. "Jonah is a police inspector. He came when we called the police. At first it seemed he didn't believe us. He suggested that we were just skittish women in a large house, not used to isolation. Then one night he turned up. He wanted to help; he said he believed that there was something strange going on." I tried to remember what little I knew about Jonah. "All along, Jonah has firmly refused to believe in supernatural forces. He doesn't understand Emilio, and I have felt he is threatened by Emilio's ability to see and hear things that he can't. Sometimes I think the idea of anything supernatural scares him, and his way of dealing with it is to constantly challenge Emilio. He comes over as loud and bossy and is suspicious of everyone, but still, in spite of the way he behaves, there is something wholesome about Jonah."

"Then there's Paddy. Paddy came with the parapsychology team from Edinburgh. He is a psychology student. He had been in a seminary; he studied for the priesthood. He had been witness to several exorcisms when he was in Rome. Paddy believes in the supernatural, and he believes he has seen demon activity. He studied with a famous exorcist appointed by the Vatican, but Paddy believes he is not good enough for the priesthood. His faith, he feels, is not strong enough. When we thought there was no choice and we had to attempt an exorcism, Paddy was reluctant to try." I thought about Paddy. His long-lashed, brown eyes were gentle, kind. That night I had sat with him on the stairs when he talked about his time in Rome, Paddy had seemed vulnerable, lost almost. "Paddy carries things. He has a crucifix, holy water, a Bible, a Roman missal. Surely these things would repel Abigor?"

Gabriel answered, "Yes, if they are genuine, Abigor would not like them. They would not necessarily repel him, but he would not choose to be around them. Anyway, how do you know they are real?"

"When Caleb was possessed, the entity inside him singled out Paddy and hurled abuse at him. Paddy threw salt to protect us from it."

"That could have been all part of a pantomime, staged so as not to arouse your suspicions," Michael said, reminding me again to question my seriously flawed ability to judge character. He needn't have bothered. The chances of my ever trusting anyone again were slim—in fact, probably nonexistent.

I cleared my throat and started again. "Emilio is a gifted psychic. He was invited by the parapsychology team from Edinburgh. Nathan, who led the team, knew Emilio; he had worked with him in the past. We were trying to make sense of what was happening, and Nathan suggested Emilio might be able to help, to find out why the hunt was here. He came willingly to help us." I shook my head. "Not Emilio." But even as I was saying this, I remembered Emilio sitting back, not really getting involved when Jonah challenged Luke or when Katie was injured. "Emilio is very private. He doesn't engage a lot in conversation. He left his native Spain because he was hounded by people looking for help to contact family who had died. He bonded with Alice, who is our housekeeper's daughter. Alice has learning disabilities, and it turned out she too was clairvoyant. Alice adores Emilio. I think if he was foul in any way, Alice would have known."

"You are not listening," Gabriel said, leaning across the table with a kind of smug look. "Alice would be easy meat in Abigor's hands. Her clairvoyance would make her easy to lead. She would see only what he wanted her to see."

I moved on. "Jack is a lecturer in history at Glasgow University. Gill, who is my close friend and has been for many years, met Jack before I even knew about the will, before the letter arrived. Jack came to help because he was at a loose end during the summer holidays. He came because Gill asked him to. This is the first time I have seen Gill besotted with a man. She has trust issues and can be quite callous, but this is a serious relationship. That's a big thing for Gill. Although Gill appears flighty and shallow at times, it's a pretense. It's a persona she chooses. She is clever and honest and loyal to her friends. Where men are concerned Gill is vulnerable.

Experience has taught her that they are not to be trusted, but when I see her with Jack, she is happy and secure. She loves Jack, she trusts Jack."

"Of course she does. Abigor would make sure she trusted him. What better way to get close to you?" Michael said.

"And then there is James. He is from the firm of solicitors that Luke hired to manage the estate."

I thought about James. James seemed a lovely, uncomplicated man. He was not darkly handsome as Paul had been, but his boy-next-door looks were appealing, and he gave the impression of being reliable and dependable. He had a calming influence on those around him. I felt close to James. I felt secure when he was near. I trusted him. "He is here because he was to oversee the transfer of Lanshoud and the money attached to Luke's will. It was his job. James has become a friend; he has helped me a lot over the past weeks. There is so much I could say about James that I don't know where start." I was adamant. "It's definitely not James. And that's everyone. There is nothing else I can tell you. Could there be a mistake?"

"There is no mistake." Michael came closer, towering over me at the table. "Accept what we tell you. Abigor has been eating with you, talking to you, sharing the room in which you slept. He has played you like a puppet, whispered to you in your sleep. You are in grave danger from one of the people in whom you have placed your trust."

Luke and Uri came back. "They are concerned about you," Luke said. "James is agitated. He wants to know that you are OK. If she doesn't go back soon," he said to Michael, "Jonah and James will come looking for her."

"You have been warned, Erica. Now you must be strong and take great care. He will not dare to return to Satan empty handed. Play along until he betrays himself, and he *will* do that. Look and listen to everyone carefully. You know these people. Trust no one. It is only a matter of time before he will give himself away. He will be getting tired and bored with his game."

I leaned on the table and closed my eyes. I couldn't bear it. I felt sick with a different kind of fear and with a strange sense of loss. I raised my head, and in the seconds that had passed since I had closed my eyes, the men had gone. "Where did they go?" I looked around.

"Who knows?" Luke said, shrugging his shoulders. "They move very quickly and silently. One minute they are there, the next they are not."

"Tell me the truth, Luke. Who are they?" I felt stupid actually saying the words. Even after all that had happened, I was prepared for him to laugh. "They are not really angels, are they?"

"Yes, of course you doubt it. I would be more surprised if you accepted it without question."

"They don't look like I would imagine an angel would look like. Even the personalities, I mean Gabriel, he seems irritated all the time, not very happy to help."

"No, but that is probably because they have been sent. They are not here by choice. At any rate, Gabriel has nothing but contempt for the human race; he doesn't understand why God loves mankind. He believes we are not worthy. He despises the wars and famine and destruction of the planet, and let's face it, he is right."

"He told you that?"

"No, Uri did." Luke stood up and pushed his chair in. "Listen, Erica, you should go back. The others will want to know what we discussed. Just tell them we discussed the fact that after this is all over, I am going home."

"Is it true?"

"Yes. They will take me back to my own planet, to my own time."

"Why now?"

"I have no idea, and they don't know either. They simply follow orders."

"What do you mean? How could they not know?"

"I mean they have absolutely no idea why suddenly they have been told to take me back to my own world. They are the messengers and soldiers of God; they do what they are asked to do, when they are asked to do it, and without question."

"I just don't understand why through all the ages of time that you have spent in this world, with the hunt chasing you, suddenly they are here to protect you now."

"They have always been there to protect me, though I managed many times to elude the hunt by myself. Think of it like this: the demons exist outside your concept of space and time. They leave hell and come here in whatever time they choose. They go back and forward in time with ease, today, tomorrow, a hundred years is all minutes, hours to them. They have never stopped chasing me. What appears to us as an hour, a day, a week, a thousand years may be just moments apart to a time traveler. The hunt does not live in the same time frame as we do. Chased back to hell by the angels, it may be only moments before they leave hell again, but the time they return to on earth, maybe a hundred years in earth time. Do you understand?"

"Yes, but I still don't understand why God casts them into hell and then lets them leave whenever they please. I grew up with the story of the beautiful angel called Lucifer and his followers, who turned against God and were cast out of heaven into a pit called hell. So tell me, why would God then allow them to leave hell at will? Why does he allow them to be here, roaming outside this house?"

"You are asking me questions I don't yet know the answers to. Perhaps it is because God has given man a choice, and many have chosen to turn away from the light. Chosen to use black arts to conjure demons and encourage them to manifest here on earth. It would not be free will if our choice did not include the evil path. As for me, well, I had no help to send them back initially because I didn't ask for help. That is how it is, that is how it works. Anyway, I didn't believe in God. In the world I came from, there are religious beliefs that divide it, but they all share a common belief in a Creator. The major religions are like many of the major religions in this world. Their holy books are like the Jewish Torah, the Qur'an of Islam, and the Christian Bible in that they contain many references to angels, and in all they are simply the messengers of God, sent to do his work. All these holy books teach the same thing. We make our own choices, our own decisions; and we often make the wrong ones. When we need help, we have to ask for it, and when we do, the angels are sent. Remember what Rafe said: 'Ask and you shall receive.' Well, I didn't ask. Not at first, anyway. Even so, there were times when something helped me, and in hindsight I guess it may have been angels. I didn't believe in anything I didn't have concrete evidence for. I was young and a scientist; I thought I knew it all. I thought everything could be explained away by numbers. Asking God, asking any 'imaginary friend' or anything else for help didn't come into the equation. I had nothing but contempt for people who believed in gods. I saw it as no more than the beliefs of primitive man. I was above that, far too clever for anything spiritual, anything I couldn't see or explain. I was arrogant. I believed that reliance in anything that could not be explained, could not be proven, was a pastime for idiots.

"Your mother Marianne said just because we cannot explain God does not mean we should dismiss him out of hand. I asked her how she could believe so strongly in something without evidence. Her answer was that she had faith. I laughed and asked her to explain faith, and she said, 'How can I explain it to you? How could I describe sight to a man born blind, or sound to a man born deaf?' Her faith was strong, and so because I loved her, I tried to see things from her point of view. But how could I when I saw faith as the realm of ignorant men? Belief without proof was unacceptable in my eyes.

"Then one day I sat at a conference listening to major scientists on both sides of a debate, all fervently arguing their point of view. The subject was the existence of a single universe versus the existence of many universes; universe or multiverse, each speaker zealously defending what he or she believed. These brilliant minds had faith in their own conclusions because in truth, the scientific evidence was ambivalent. Neither theory could be proven. I listened, and I thought, in reality, how was this any different from Marianne's faith? Perhaps in time she had as much chance as these scientists of being proven right.

"As for having passed through hell, to me that was just another dimension. I didn't know what the hunt was at that point. I soon learned, and as time passed, I lived in fear of the hunt finding me. It was Marianne, my lovely, beautiful Marianne, who opened my eyes, who taught me to ask for help. Marianne was devoutly Christian. I had never met anyone like her; I used to tease her about her beliefs. Who knows, maybe if I had opened my mind and asked for help, she would not have died. Maybe I left it too late.

"The person I was then was headstrong, with an inflated ego born of believing I was intellectually superior to those around me. I did not believe in God. God was a story for children to make them behave or for those who did not understand science. I considered myself above those kinds of fairy stories. Like the ancients of old who believed the world was flat because they had not sailed far enough to discover there was no edge. If mathematics or physics could not explain it, then as far as I was concerned, it didn't exist. I, who believed I had the most open of minds, had it tight shut against anything I could not explain on paper. Therefore when I came in contact with angels, I reacted to their presence exactly as you have done." Luke clasped his hands and looked at the table for a moment. "Now they will take me home, to a time when my parents will not realise I had ever left."

"They are taking you home? And to the past? If they take you back to the past, then you won't meet my mother. So where does that leave me?"

"It is another reality. Nothing will be changed in this one. Nothing will change for you. Come, you must go back to the others, and don't be sad. You may have my genes, but Aalbert Vansterdam was the man who became your father, so do not miss me for a second. I am far too young and handsome for you to even think of me as your father." He smiled.

CHAPTER TWENTY-EIGHT

The Cellar

I had no sooner put my hand on the door of the study when thunder crashed so loud it shook the window frames.

"They're *back*," Emilio said in a sing-song voice.

It wasn't thunder, but a pulse, a beat, boom, boom, boom, louder and louder like the thudding of a gigantic drum. It pulsated like a heartbeat, and that made it infinitely more terrifying. Then abruptly, silence. Gill came over and put her arm round my waist, and as we stood together, I could feel her trembling.

"What the hell was that?" Jonah whispered.

"That is an army marching," Emilio said, his eyes with that unfocused look he often had that made me wonder if he could see through walls.

Something cried right outside the window. Like the sound of a crow, it squawked and fluttered, battering its wings against the glass. Then it tapped the glass, very gently, like someone just trying to catch our attention. Jonah, machine gun in hand, placed himself in front of the window, freezing into position, getting ready to fire at anything that moved. Jack had just followed him when without warning the window burst and the huge panes of glass shattered into a thousand shards, showering Jonah with lethal daggers of broken glass. Jonah and Jack started firing randomly into the darkness, and the resultant caterwauling gave the impression they had scored direct hits.

Blood trickled from Jonah's cheek, but he had amazingly escaped with not much more than a scratch. Outside the sky lit up as the angels attacked the demon army. Screams rent the air, and weird shapes flew past the window. There were more sounds of breaking glass, and it seemed that every window in the house was being smashed. Paddy, Jonah, and Jack had begun firing randomly at anything that came close to the gap in the wall that had once been the window. I saw Katie out the corner of my eye. She stood still—too still, I thought. She wasn't trembling or showing any indication that she was afraid, she was simply petrified like a statue, emotionless, looking vacantly in the direction of the gunfire. James took her arm and pulled her over to where we stood. Thunder boomed overhead and Lightening or gunfire flashed I'm not sure which.

"I think you should get out of here. Get out of here now. Go." He ushered us towards the door. "Into the cellar quickly; you will be safer there, where there are no doors or windows."

Gill grabbed her gun and the one I had left behind, and we ran, pulling Katie with us out into the hall. The huge oak front doors were heaving in and out as though they were going to burst. James shouted, "Gill, grab those lanterns." He pointed to the console table as he ran ahead of us, torch in one hand, gun in the other, wrenching open the cellar door.

I half pulled, half carried Katie down the dark, damp stairs while Gill, her gun and mine sticking out of her fleece jacket pockets, held one of the lanterns aloft to prevent us breaking our necks on the smooth, slippery stone. James pulled over some crates and helped me to sit Katie down, "Stay here. I have to help. I'll come back as soon as I can."

"Take this, Gill." James slipped the key into Gill's pocket. "Lock the door behind me. Don't come out for anything until we tell you it's safe." He ran back up the stairs.

The cellar was freezing and terrifyingly dark, with only the light of the lanterns to keep out the darkness. They provided only an uneven circle of dim light around the two crates. Katie was shivering violently. I looked for something to cover her and found a box full of none-too-clean dust sheets. I pulled them out and wrapped them around her, hugging her and rubbing her arms to create warmth. I was really worried; it was obvious she was suffering from shock. I locked the door. Gill rooted around and found more

The Cellar

dust sheets, and we made shawls out of what was left of the sheets and then we sat together with Katie between us.

"She looks awful," Gill said.

"Katie, honey, can you hear me?" I asked her, trying to get her to focus on me. But she was distant, her eyes lifeless.

"The lights are on, but nobody's home," Gill said, putting her arm round Katie. Though she was making light of it, I knew Gill was worried too. "I don't think we should worry. I am sure Rafe will be able to help her."

"I hope so. I am sure he will," I said as much to reassure myself as her. The truth was I was not sure. If, as we supposed, that was the angels out there fighting, they could just disappear as fast as they had come. Katie needed medical help. "She's shocked. We need to keep her warm. There's not much else we can do right now."

With nothing to do but wait, we just sat there listening, straining to make sense of the faint sounds coming through the solid granite walls. We could hear gunfire upstairs, and then it seemed to go quiet. There was no way of knowing if the silence was a good or bad sign.

Gill said, "Help me here, I am trying hard to remember there are Archangels up there, and they cannot be overcome, can they? They're the ultimate superpower, right? So the men will be safe." It was a statement, not a question.

"Right," I said, not convinced of anything.

It was piercingly cold. My hands and feet felt like two blocks of ice, and as we became more and more chilled, we huddled close together for warmth. Every so often there was a noise that seemed to be close by us, in the cellar, and we were occasionally freaked by the shadows cast by the flickering oil lanterns that seemed to have found currents of air where none existed. Light conversation wasn't on the agenda. Gill hadn't even asked me what had happened in the kitchen. We were incapable of conversation, too scared to do anything other than just listen.

We stayed like that for a long time, until we could no longer hear anything from outside. The only sound was an occasional unnerving rustle, which I found myself hoping fervently was a rat because now I knew there were worse things capable of rustling paper than just rats. Relief flooded over me when at last the cellar door opened. Someone came in and closed the door.

Gill stood up. "Who's there? We can't see you," she called, lifting the lantern. But the light didn't reach the top of the stairs. No one answered. We heard the sound of footsteps very slowly descending. "Who's there?" Gill called again. I held my breath, conscious that Gill still had my gun. We both jumped, startled, when suddenly Emilio stepped into the circle of light. "Why didn't you answer me? You scared the hell out of us," Gill said, partly relieved, partly annoyed.

"Is everyone OK? Have they gone?" I asked. "What's happening?"

Emilio didn't answer at first and then he said, "What's happening? Let me see." He screwed up his eyes and put a hand to his ear as though he was listening for something. "No, nothing to worry about," His behavior was odd. "Yes it has gone quiet; there's not a lot happening just now, just a bit of noise, a bit of a mess," he said. Gill was already heading past him on her way up the stairs. "Eh, excuse me, where do think you are going?" he asked, waving the key.

"I have a key." Gill stopped. "James already gave me one. Did you lock it behind you?" She looked in her pockets, confused for a moment. "No I can't find it. Just give me that one." She held out her hand. Emilio held the key out of her reach. Taken aback, Gill asked, "What are you playing at, Emilio? Give me the key." She tried to grab it.

"Ah, ah, no, I do not think so. You are much safer in here." He lifted it higher.

"What's wrong with you? Give...me...the...key." Gill raised her voice; she was becoming increasingly annoyed. "This is not time for games Emilio."

I watched them, my by now pet butterflies starting to crawl again in my stomach. There was something wrong with Emilio, something not quite right in his tone, in his manner. It was out of character. Suddenly with his free hand, Emilio grabbed Gill round the wrist; he pulled her forward until her face was inches from his, and he spat out, "I said NO."

Gill stopped, astounded by his aggression, then she cried out, and he let her go. She staggered back, clutching her hand, looking at her wrist with an expression of pain and disbelief. "Look what you've done; look at my wrist. I want out of here. I have to see Jack," she yelled at him.

On her wrist, Emilio's finger marks had left inflamed, angry-looking rings that looked like a fiery-red bracelet. He was totally unconcerned. "No, you cannot see Jack." He turned away from her and developed a placatory tone. "You see, it is not safe. You must stay here, for your own good."

Alarm bells were ringing, loudly, very loudly in my head and obviously in Gill's too because she backed off and didn't challenge him again. At that moment, the cellar door banged. "Erica, it's me, open the door."

"It's James," Gill sighed with relief.

"Open it, Emilio," I said, hoping beyond hope that he would and that my gut instinct was wrong. But it wasn't because Emilio didn't move.

Gill called out, "James, Emilio's got the key, and he won't let us out."

"What? It's all right, Emilio. They can come out. It's gone quiet again. Luke says they are gone for good," James shouted back. We could hear him wrestling with the door handle. And then it opened, and the beam of light from his torch pierced the darkness, searching out the stairs.

"Do come in, James," Emilio called out, his voice was different somehow, deeper with a harshness to it.

Gill noticed it too. She looked at him, puzzled, then turned quickly and headed for the stairs. She had climbed three when she suddenly lost her balance and fell forward onto the stone steps. Her face whacked off the stone. She cried out and slipped back down onto the floor.

"Oh my God, Gill." I ran at the same time as James started down the stairs. The cellar door immediately slammed shut behind him. Blood from her mouth and forehead poured down the front of Gill's fleece, turning patches of navy into black. James helped her to sit while I used the scarf from her neck to mop up the blood. She had split her lip and had a gash on her forehead about an inch long; it looked deep enough to need stitched.

"Are you OK? What happened? Did you trip or something?" I asked her, scanning her face for damage. The crack had been so loud, I was afraid she might have broken something.

"I'm all right," she said, taking the scarf from my hand and turning to face Emilio. "I didn't trip. Someone pushed me."

I was about to say no one had pushed her because no one had moved, when a whimper from Katie distracted me. I went to her, but she simply pulled her dust cover tighter and started crying quietly.

James put his arm around Gill, "C'mon, I'll take you up to Jack. He's asking for you."

"The door is locked." Emilio shrugged.

James ignored him. "Jack's been injured. His shoulder is torn, and he has lost quite a lot of blood."

Gill immediately forgot her own injuries. "What?" She tried to get up.

"Wait." James eased her back down. "He will be fine. You need to take a minute." He turned to Emilio. "Why did you not tell her?"

Emilio laughed. "Because it suited me, but that is not important because now, no one is going anywhere. We are all going to wait here for Luke." Such was the bizarre tone of his voice and attitude that James and Gill stopped in their tracks, and I had a sinking feeling again. Emilio's expression was pained, his eyes full of pretend sorrow "Oh, the mind-numbing boredom of it all. I think I have had quite enough of playing games."

At those words I felt ice pricking at my spine again. It wasn't so much what he said, though the reference to games might have triggered warning signals. No, I felt the adrenaline rush because his voice had completely changed. He didn't look any different. He was as immaculate as always, not a hair out of place, not a crease in his clothing, a veritable tailor's dummy, not for him the disheveled look that was the new style adopted by the rest of us. It was not what I could see but rather what I felt wasn't right, actually, in hindsight. It was what I could hear; Emilio had lost his Spanish accent.

He spoke pointedly at James. "This is how it will be. We will stay here and all wait for Luke. Is that clear, or which bit of that do you not understand?" Emilio held up the key, considering it, and that was the cue for James to lunge at it. With one almighty sweep of his arm, Emilio lifted James clean off his feet and threw him against the far wall. James grunted, the breath taken out of him, but he was stunned for only a few seconds. Then he was back on his feet and heading toward Emilio again. I knew, I knew then…I had no doubt.

"DON'T!" I shouted, diving forward to stop James. We crashed into each other; I staggered, falling backward and sideways. He grabbed my arm and just stopped me landing on an old wrought iron wringer. I thought we were both going to land in a heap, but he managed to steady us both. I looked up into James's startled face. "He is Abigor. He is the demon." He looked at me, confused. I screamed at him. "EMILIO IS ABIGOR."

CHAPTER TWENTY-NINE

The Angels

For a moment we stood frozen in time, shell shocked, as though there had been some cataclysmic event and all the air had been sucked out of the room and now there was none left to breathe. James and Gill were looking at me as though I had just spoken in Swahili, but at the same time, they didn't argue. It was as though they both knew on some subliminal level that I was telling the truth. Still holding onto James, whose grip on me was so tight it was almost painful, I turned to face Emilio. But he was gone. In a flash he had moved and now stood behind Katie. He had one hand on her shoulder, and Katie, her face the colour of cheese, sat on the crate looking blissfully unaware of the danger, looking as though she had lost her mind.

Gill pulled out her gun and pointed it at Emilio, both hands shaking. I tensed, doubting her ability to hit him without hitting Katie; she obviously doubted it too. When Emilio with his smooth, deep Spanish accent now gone, said "Don't be stupid put both guns on the floor and kick them over here. NOW!" he screamed at her. Her hands shaking she did as he asked. Before Gill had time to step back, he had picked up the guns. "And you." He spun round on James, who had been reaching behind for the handgun in his belt. "Don't even think about it unless you want her to die now." He pointed at the floor, and James put the gun down. He hooked his finger, and James kicked the gun over to him.

Emilio turned his attention to Katie. He cooed at her "Now, Katie, there is no need for you to be afraid," he said, turning her head and tilting her chin. Katie looked up at him, her eyes vacant. "They are going to do exactly as I tell them, and no harm will come to you." He patted the now-doll-like Katie on both arms. "Now you," he looked at James, "will go and find Luke and tell him anything you like to get him here. Only Luke, no one else, and James, do not think for one second that you can trick me. It is completely beyond your capability, and this one…" he stroked Katie's hair, "will reap the consequences if you even try." He smiled a smile that chilled me, that didn't reach his eyes.

James, who had been holding my arm, hesitated for only a moment, then let go. He looked into my eyes. "I have to do this, but I swear I'll be back." To Emilio he warned, "You hurt one hair of their heads and I'll—"

Emilio laughed his face contorted and ugly. "You'll what? Do you know who I am? Spawn of man; I am a prince of hell? You WILL obey me." He screamed at James, his face again transformed by anger. He lifted Katie's hair, exposing her neck, and to my horror, flicking his tongue back and forth, he licked her skin. He spat, "We four could have so such fun and might still, if you make a mistake."

This time the cellar door, not surprisingly, opened at James's touch and in no more than five minutes, he had returned with Luke. The door of the cellar again opened easily and shut quietly of its own accord. Luke hurried down the stairs, looking around.

"What is this?" he asked, looking at me and then Gill. "I thought you said it was Erica who had been hurt."

"Luke do come and join our little party." Emilio said smooth and cajoling again.

I stepped forward to Luke not taking my eyes of Emilio. "Luke he is Abigor, Emilio is the demon."

Luke faced Emilio and automatically pulled his gun.

Emilio had grabbed Katie again by the hair and was now bending her head back. He sighed heavily. "Put the gun on the floor and kick it over here."

No one moved.

"NOW!" he thundered. "And do not make the mistake of thinking you can fool me."

There he had said it again, it seemed he had a need to warn us that we could not fool him and it was making me consider we might have a choice. He took one finger and ran his nail down Katie's face. Still trancelike, she barely moaned and didn't even struggle. A thin red line ran from her temple to her chin, oozing blood. He held her, pinning her to the packing case with one hand. Not once had he taken his eyes off James and Luke.

Gill and I cried out and James started forward. "You bastard," James said. Luke held him back.

"The gun," Emilio said.

Luke placed his handgun on the floor.

"That's better. Now we can all relax."

Luke stepped forward, "I know it's me you want. Why don't you just let them go?"

Emilio caught his breath and gave Luke a brief sarcastic glance. "Let them go! Bravo! Chivalry is not dead after all." He shook his head, laughing. "You imbecile, do you honestly believe that I, a prince of darkness, would deign to waste his time collecting your scrawny little soul? I feel contaminated by just being in your presence for so long." He grabbed Katie by the hair and wrenched her head back. With the movement, fresh blood ran down her face and pooled in the soft concave indent of her throat. His voice softened. "You know, strangely, there is a little something about this one that tickles my fancy." He bent his head, and to my disgust, he lapped the blood, like a cat lapping milk. "Hmm, she has that certain sourness about her. I like that. It has notes of disappointment, undertones of low self-esteem; yes, I sense she thinks the world has been bad to her. She doesn't like people so much. Let me think…hmm… there are a man and woman she would like to have killed. Oh yes, that is so tasty." He licked Katie's blood from his lips as he feigned ecstasy.

"If it isn't me you have come for, then who?" Luke asked.

"Who? No, no, no, not who, but what?" Emilio corrected.

Luke stood confused.

"Isn't it obvious?" Emilio grinned. "Oh well, let me help you. It is very simple. We have use for the spear. You are just incidental, and the collection of these souls is all…well, just in a normal day's work, so to speak. What is termed the Spear of Destiny, however, is of great use because it is covered in the blood of the Christ and so is a great bargaining tool for my negotiations, with the less wholesome individuals in this world. Ah, I see you understand.

So now you and you..." he pointed to James and I. "Will go and get it and quickly, for my patience is running thin." He pulled Katie's hair tighter. "Go bring it here to me, or I will feast on this meat tonight."

James looked to Luke for guidance. Luke nodded. "Do as he says. He will kill her if you don't."

The room below the wine cellar had been creepy the first time, when Alice took us there. Now it was more so, given that the only light we had was one torch. James shone the torch around the room, stopping at the chest in the middle. The spear lay as we had left it; in the ancient cloth, inside the box made of the wood that Emilio had said was the wood of the cross. James carefully lifted it from the box and stood it upright; it reached way above his head. He unwrapped the cloth, exposing the iron head, still sharp, still with the dark stain of old blood. We stood silent for a moment and I felt tears pricking my eyes. It had been many years since I had considered the existence of God, but now instinctively I asked God for help, in an unspoken prayer.

"Do you know something? I don't get it. Why did Emilio not just take the spear if he wanted it so badly? He had plenty of opportunity."

"Because he can't go near it, can he?" James answered. "Remember, he fled from the cellar when we first found it. Maybe he wants it for its power, but he can't touch it.."

"Well if there's the slightest chance it could harm him, maybe you should just launch it at him," I wondered out loud. "And another thing: Where are the angels? I thought they were here to protect us?" I felt tears sting my eyes. "Where are they now, when he is torturing Katie upstairs?"

"I am here." A voice said from the darkness, causing my heart to almost leap out of my body. I grabbed onto James just as he swung the torch round, causing it to bypass the target and shine on the wall. But caught in the beam of light as it flashed past, I saw Michael. James swung the torch back and around in a circle, but he was gone. James frantically flashed the torch into the four corners of the room, but there was nothing, no one.

"Did see you him?" I whispered, my heart thumping in my chest. "It was Michael. I saw him, he's here." I clung to James, who scanned the room with a beam of light, but there was no more sign of Michael. James carried the spear back upstairs. It wasn't heavy but it was awkward. I led the way with the torch, unnerved by the shadows that leaped in and out of its beam.

They had remained exactly as we had left them. Emilio stood with his hand on Katie's neck. Her face had stopped bleeding, but she remained in her trancelike state.

James stopped in front of Luke and held out the spear to Emilio. Luke reached out and took the spear from James, swung it forward, the iron head pointing at Emilio. I wondered what he intended to do, charge forward. There was no room to heft and launch a spear of that length. It was all academic anyway because Emilio hesitated for no more than the blink of an eye.

"Put it down, or with one slip of my nail I will slit her throat." Again he had bunched Katie's hair and pulled her hair back, exposing her white throat. Katie made no response. Her eyes still glazed over, she allowed Emilio to pull her head back and forth like a puppet.

Luke stood the spear upright again. "What is it, Emilio? What are you afraid of?"

There was a flicker of uncertainty on Emilio's face. "Not of you or of that. Because it amuses me, I will tell you. I simply do not want to be sullied by contact with the blood on that thing." He gave a flourish in the air. "I would have left it where it was, but so many of the leaders of your world set such store by its power—and I use the word power reservedly because it has none in its own right. You see, its power lies in their belief that it will help them to win wars, control nations. Like the leaders of old—Constantine, Barbarossa, Charlemagne, Napoleon, Hitler—they search for it tirelessly and will pay any price to get it, including selling their souls because to this day they believe a piece of old wood and metal controls the destiny of the world. They believe carrying it will make them supreme king, emperor, lord of the world." He laughed again almost hysterically, an ugly, guttural sound, and as he shook with laughter and rocked the doll-like Katie's head back and forth.

There he is again, I thought, telling us the spear has no power over him. So if it is just and piece of wood and metal why go to all this bother to get it, I wondered.

"So, with most of the artifacts believed to be the Spear of Destiny scattered throughout the world's museums, hidden in vaults, buried in secret locations, most of them already carbon dated, etcetera, etcetera, and proven not to be the real one—just think what will happen when I put the real one into circulation. Unscrupulous, greedy men will kill to own it, causing wars, murder, mayhem, and destruction greater than earth has ever known." His eyes flashed with delight. "And no doubt," he laughed, "all in the name of Christ. Ah how ironic is that, don't you think? What's the matter? You are all so quiet. Don't you find this is amusing?"

I didn't believe him; I just didn't believe he was unafraid of the spear. He was obviously wary. I saw his uncertainty, I saw the tension when Luke had pointed the spear at him; he was lying. The jokes and the banter were just another ploy to distract us from the truth. I did not believe fear of contamination from relics alone had stopped him; he could after all have sent one of his minions to collect them. At any rate my speculation was all academic, for at that point, Luke took a calculated risk and simply tossed the spear at Emilio. The spear struck without force and clattered to the ground, yet the effect was extraordinary. Emilio cried out, howling like an animal, he seemed to shrink and staggered backwards pulling Katie with him. He recovered quickly dragging Katie to her feet and rose as though he had grown taller. Then he turned on Luke."

"Fool, this night you will meet my master."

Immediately a voice spoke from the darkness. "Not this night Abigor."

Emilio spun round, letting go of Katie, a transient moment of fear washed over his face. So fleeting was his panic that if I had blinked, I would have missed it.

"Michael! Well now, I wondered when you would show up. Poor show it took you this long to find me."

Michael appeared; light glowed around him piercing the darkness of the cellar. "He told you he wants the spear. Why don't you pick it up for him."

Luke stepped forward to reach the spear and Abigor started to shrink away from him.

"What? You don't want it now? Look how he cowers, how he trembles. He has been weakened by the power he denies." Michael's voice rose to an almost deafening level "The truth is he fears it, for it can send him back sniveling to his unforgiving master, shattered and defeated."

Luke picked up the spear, Emilio seemed to rise in stature; he flung Katie away like a ragdoll and turned to face Luke. At first I thought it was a trick of the light, for from where I stood, it seemed as though Emilio had a cloak on his back, bunched at his shoulders and coming to a point at his feet. I watched, mesmerised by the incredible scene, as then slowly they unfurled, wings, stretching up, towering over his shoulders, rising above his head and spreading out. Densely black, darker than night, the smooth silk-like feathers of gigantic wings reflecting the light of the lanterns. Emilio's clothes gone, revealed as he truly was, not the suave sophisticated Emilio, not a half-breed imp, not twisted and ugly and foul like the denizens of hell that had haunted us for the last few days, but the body of a young man of immense beauty, long limbed and broad shouldered, with smooth flawless skin. He stood before us, the fallen angel Abigor, the servant of Lucifer, his huge wings revealed in all their glory.

He pointed his finger at Luke and a stream of darkness started from the tip, but a beam of intense light shot from Michael, striking Abigor, who screamed an unearthly terrible sound and bent almost double his wings curled around him.

Sometimes when you are truly terrified the mind closes down. I think that's what happened to me, because for the next few hours all I could remember was Michael's voice booming.

"DEMON in the name of the Lord God, I ORDER you back to the Pit."

CHAPTER THIRTY

Memory

I'm uncertain how to describe or what to tell you happened next because we all had slightly different memories of our experience of that night in the cellar, in Lanshoud. Everything happened so fast, and when we talked about it later, none of us were sure how much of what we remembered was real.

Katie to this day can't remember anything before suddenly waking up from a deep sleep, wondering what she was doing in the cellar wrapped in a dust sheet. Which, when all things were considered, was probably a blessing? If you were to ask her, she would tell you that she felt afraid because she had a pain in her cheek and when she touched it there was blood on her fingers. She was confused and disorientated; even more so because Gill, James, and I stood before her, pale, dusty, and disheveled.

Gill remembers a fleeting sense of something she describes as dark and beautiful and terrifying and Michael's voice coming out of the darkness and then light, blazing, and bright, white light that dazzled and temporarily blinded her. She felt a wind and smelled a scent so wonderful it overwhelmed her. By the time her eyes cleared, there were just the three of us. Luke and Emilio had vanished, and the only light remaining was that of the lanterns and torches. She remembers Katie standing up and the dust sheet falling from her shoulders. She remembers that no longer doll-like, Katie's eyes were focussed, and she looked confused and frightened.

James remembers seeing the dark angel, he remembers the powerful black wings, and he remembers Michael's voice. He too was dazzled by the light, but he does remember seeing enormous white wings and a flash of Michael's face. He remembers the wind and the perfumed air. He thinks he saw the mouth of a gigantic tunnel that seemed to be made of cloud,

gray-white, turning and whirling; he thinks, he is not sure, the whirling mist and the bright lights, in the way strobe lights can, had left him disorientated.

I have told you all that I remember—that is, up to the point of Emilio's turning into Abigor. I have not embroidered it in any way. Fact or fantasy, it was real to me. This is the rest of what happened, in as much detail as I can remember.

Abigor was beautiful, that much is true, but then he had been an angel before he was cast out of heaven with Lucifer. His enormous wings were black as night, and the feathers shone like silk. Almost as soon as Emilio materialised into his real form, the light appeared from the direction of Michael's voice and at my back and at each side, growing brighter and brighter until from its depth shapes appeared that formed into the archangels Michael, Gabriel, Rafael, and Uriel. Their gigantic, seven-or-eight-feet-tall, snowy-white wings moved, gently undulating, creating a breeze and giving off a strange, alluring, indescribable scent as though all the lovely flowers and exotic perfumes of the world had come together to assault my senses.

Abigor cowered in on himself. He started to vanish, his form becoming almost transparent. I could still see his face contorted in fear and rage. Michael assaulted him with his voice. He commanded him to return to the pit from whence he had come and his army with him. He told him he was at the mercy of God, and he was not permitted on this earthly plane. Then angels surrounded him, the topmost point of their wings touching, and they began to turn slowly. They spun faster until beneath their feet a tunnel appeared, a grey-white mist turning and twisting. It looked like I imagine a wormhole would look an ever-turning passageway through space and time. Abigor's form grew stronger, then faded again. He fluctuated in and out of being, like the Cheshire Cat. I heard Michael's voice say, "As always, your arrogance and your need to amuse yourself, your predilection for games has been your undoing." Then Abigor was gone, sucked down the tunnel in a flurry of feather and flailing limbs, and then the tunnel itself was gone.

In front of me stood Luke, and at his back stood Rafael, his beautiful white wings gently undulating. Luke was smiling. "It is time now for me to say goodbye. I am going home. Remember me and be happy for me." He kissed my cheek, and then they vanished, leaving us alone in the dark, dim light in the cellar.

For a long time, no one moved until Katie broke the spell by asking where she was, and then Gill cried out "Jack" and ran toward the stairs.

Jonah and Paddy were fine, as was Jack; Rafe had, of course, healed him. We opened the door front door and stepped outside into the fresh morning air. The sun was shining, and the birds were singing as though it had been no more than a bad dream. Jonah slammed the door shut. We didn't bother locking it; there was no glass in the windows anyway. We hardly spoke. Still in the same clothes, we climbed into one of the seven-seater four-wheel drives that Katie and I had bought that faraway Sunday in Aberdeen and never used since and which still sat, amazingly unscathed, outside the garage, keys still in the ignitions since the day they were delivered. We drove to Stonehaven and sat on the harbor wall, eating bread rolls and bacon from the café. We drank coffee from paper cups, our legs dangling over the wall, watching people going to work and fishing boats heading out to sea. We watched the men in the lifeboats inspect their gear and the café owners put tables and chairs outside, responding to a favorable weather forecast. The world was going about its business.

We told no one what had happened to us, for who would believe it anyway? The danger we had faced together and the secret we now kept bound us as friends forever. We met again, all of us, at Jack and Gill's wedding. Gillian was a stunning bride. Katie and I dressed in champagne silk, were her bridesmaids, and James was best man. Paddy had returned to the seminary in Rome but came for the wedding and served at the altar. Jonah taught me to tango at the wedding; he was full of surprises. Tosh brought his new fiancé Aiko, a beautiful, petite Japanese girl. They were to be married in the spring in Okinawa, Japan, and we were all invited to the wedding.

Nathan and Jess came too. Jess, unable to put the experience behind her, had given up her interest in parapsychology. Some things, she said, you do better not to know, for your sanity's sake. Nathan had found his funding and his department was flourishing. He had celebrated by buying new spectacles, but the new ones continued to slide down his nose, just like the old ones. Molly, Caleb, Lucy, and the children were all there too. Molly and Caleb no longer worked at Lanshoud. Molly retired with a good pension from the estate, and Caleb was generously rewarded for his services.

James employed a company to repair the damage at Lanshoud, and they restored it to its former glory. He also arranged for a firm to take over cleaning and maintenance. The Spear of Destiny lay still in the cellar where we had left it; when they felt they were ready to return and before the repairs were carried out, James and Jonah went back to Lanshoud and replaced the spear in its box. It rests now, with the crown and nails in a place that only a handful of people know of, in the vaults of the Vatican in Rome, away from a world where man would use them to gain power over his fellow man.

Someday I will return to Lanshoud. I love James, I know that now, but it is less than a year since Paul died. Perhaps in time James and I will be together. Who knows, for now we are just taking it slowly.

THE END

Printed in Great Britain
by Amazon